"My fee isn't the issue."

"Then what is?"

"I asked for the *real* reason you want that painting."

Amelia's chin trembled. She tightened her lips.

"You can't honestly expect me to believe you would be willing to throw away the money you do have on a piece of worthless, not very good art that doesn't even belong to you. What are you holding back, Amelia?"

She remained silent.

Hank used to have more patience than she had. It was a good bet he still did. He waited her out.

It took less than a minute. When she finally did speak, her voice shook. "During the past year and a half, I've lost my business, my reputation, my husband...." She cleared her throat. "You name it, I lost it. I lost so much, it got to the point that I stopped believing I could win." I want to start living again. I want the right to be happy again."

"And you believe that finding this painting will do all that?"

She surged to her feet. "Yes!"

Dear Reader,

I'm not much of a gambler, unless you count organic gardening, which between the weather and the bugs is pretty chancy. I suppose you could count computer card games as a form of gambling, too, since they're definitely risky with respect to how much of my time they end up consuming. Come to think of it, strolling down the cookie aisle in the grocery store is a huge and rather dangerous gamble, depending on how hungry I happen to be. So I can relate to my heroine's decision to buy a lottery ticket, in spite of the astronomical odds against winning.

Every aspect of writing *Winning Amelia* was a pleasure for me. For one thing, it's set in the picturesque small town of Port Hope, which lies halfway between our farm and Toronto and thus is my favorite spot to meet my city friends for lunch. Though there isn't actually a Mae B's, the restaurant where my heroine worked was inspired by some of the places I've visited. The house where she lived was based on the one where I grew up—the simple, story-and-a-half design was used in Port Hope as well as in neighborhoods throughout southern Ontario. As for the oddball characters that crop up in the book, let's just say the countryside provides plenty of fodder for a writer's imagination.

Above all, I enjoyed creating a story for the Heartwarming program, because it's one that can be read by anyone. It celebrates not just romance but real, lasting love. That's the kind of love that survives the big, dramatic issues like kids and finances as well as the everyday stuff of an ordinary life. And love like that is well worth any gamble!

Warm wishes, and happy reading!

Ingrid

HARLEQUIN HEARTWARMING

USA TODAY Bestselling Author

Ingrid Weaver

Winning Amelia

Recycling programs
for this product may
not exist in your area.

ISBN-13: 978-0-373-36630-9

WINNING AMELIA

Copyright © 2013 by Ingrid Caris

Printed in U.S.A.

INGRID WEAVER

began her writing career by propping an old manual typewriter on her children's play table. Twenty years later she is a *USA TODAY* bestselling author of thirty books and the recipient of a Romance Writers of America RITA® Award. She currently resides on a farm near Frankford, Ontario, with her family and a varying collection of critters.

This book is dedicated to everyone in my family whose birthdays wound up on Amelia's lottery ticket. Those are truly lucky numbers.

CHAPTER ONE

By THEMSELVES, NUMBERS were meaningless squiggles. It was what they represented that mattered. This particular string of six—1, 3, 4, 17, 23, 29—happened to represent the birthdays of Amelia Goodfellow's family: her own, plus those of her brother, her sister-in-law and all three nephews.

The sequence also appeared to be the winning numbers in yesterday's Lotto 6/49 draw.

Crockery rattled against crockery. The *chinka-chink* sounded oddly like…the clink of coins. Amelia set the dishes back on the table and reached for the newspaper. The previous customer had left no tip, only a discarded *Toronto Star,* so maybe Amelia was too annoyed to be seeing straight. The sun was glaring off the moisture remaining from where she'd wiped the table, so it could have been a trick of the light. Or fatigue. Or simply a bad case of wishful thinking. Sure. No reason for her hands to be shaking like this because she'd probably made a mistake, right?

She squinted at the paper.

The lottery results were in bold print in a box on the lower right-hand corner of the front page, along with the weather forecast and the horoscope for anyone whose birthday was today. There had been only one winning ticket. 1, 3, 4, 17, 23, 29. Her lips moved silently as she read the numbers again. No matter how many times she repeated them, they remained the same.

The jackpot had been over fifty-two million, not a record but close to it. To be exact, it had been fifty-two million, four hundred and eighty-five thousand, seven hundred and twenty. More numbers. They were too mind-boggling to grasp, even for someone who had once made her living by dealing with figures.

"Excuse me, miss?"

Yet these were more than simply figures on a page. This was a new house for Will and Jenny. It was redemption for Spencer's crimes. It was the ability to think of tomorrow without feeling her stomach curl into a knot. It was the future. A brand-new, shiny, fire-engine-red, fresh-off-the-showroom-floor life in which she could stop apologizing and start living again.

"We'd like to order, please."

Bubbles worked their way into her throat, stealing her breath and making speech impossible. The sensation was so unfamiliar, and it had been so long since she'd experienced it, Amelia didn't recognize the joy immediately. Yet that's what it was. Pure joy.

"Hello?"

She looked at the paper again, just to be sure. There they were, in all their multmillion-dollar splendor: 1, 3, 4, 17, 23, 29, the numbers she always played, the numbers she could never forget. She pumped her fist in the air and whirled.

A pair of women was seated at the booth across from her. The older one raised a penciled eyebrow. "Well, it's nice to see someone so happy. Did you read good news?"

Amelia wouldn't have thought she could smile any wider but she did. Her cheeks ached from it. Those crazy joy bubbles were swirling through her blood now. Her knees shook as badly as her fingers. She stumbled backward and came up hard against one of the boxes that held fake philodendrons. Plastic greenery crackled against her palm as she steadied herself with one hand. In the other she still clutched the paper. "Good?" Her voice rasped. She had trouble getting the word past her lips because every facial muscle was locked into her grin. "Uh-huh. Oh, yeah."

The woman's amusement dimmed. Her gaze darted around the tiny restaurant, as if she were seeking help. The lunch rush at Mae B's was over. Apart from the ladies and an elderly man in the booth near the entrance, the place was deserted. "Are you all right, miss?"

Amelia nodded so hard, the pencil she'd tucked behind her ear slipped out and bounced on the floor. She left it there. She wouldn't need to write down any more orders, or depend on finding tips when she cleaned the tables, or wear this stupid, frilly, pea-green apron. She took off the apron and dropped it on the plastic plant, then tore off the corner of the page with the lottery results and put it in her skirt pocket.

The ticket. She had to get the ticket.

Mae Barton and her husband, Ronnie, regarded her sternly as she raced through the kitchen. Though Ronnie was tall and fair while Mae was dark and well-rounded, like many longtime married couples, they had begun to resemble each other. Their frowns were identical. "Where're you going?" Ronnie demanded. "It's not time for your break."

Amelia gasped through her grin. "Purse!" was all she managed. She yanked open the storeroom door and skidded to a stop beside the first shelf. Her purse lay where she'd left it when she'd come in this morning, right next to the big cans of ketchup. She unzipped the purse and pulled out her wallet.

"What on earth is going on?"

She glanced over her shoulder.

Mae stood in the doorway, her hands on her hips. "You had customers waiting, last I saw."

"Sorry, but…" Amelia's voice broke as she peered in her wallet. A ten, two fives and a handful of change. No ticket. She sucked air through her teeth.

Mae moved closer. "Amelia, are you okay? You don't look well."

She groped among the tissues, mints, sunglasses, keys and stray coins in the bottom of her purse for a few panicked moments until she remembered: little Timmy had emptied her purse onto the floor last month when he'd been looking for candy, and the dog had eaten her paycheck. Since then, she'd taken precautions. She hadn't stored the ticket in her wallet or her purse. She'd found a far better place. A good, *safe* place. She laughed.

Mae grasped her arm. "You're not high, are you? We told you up front we've got a zero tolerance policy for that sort of thing."

"I'm not sick or crazy or high, Mae." She retrieved the scrap of newsprint from her pocket and waved it in front of her. "I'm just rich."

"What?"

"I won Lotto 6/49."

"You *what?*"

Amelia's eyes misted as she looked at her boss. The Bartons weren't her friends, but they had hired her when no one else in town would, and for that she would always be grateful. They had taken a chance. Granted, they gave her receipts extra scrutiny, and they certainly hadn't let her anywhere near their books, but she didn't hold that against them. She would have done the same in their place, considering her reputation. She flung her arms around Mae and gave her a smacking kiss on the cheek. She felt her boss stiffen, but she didn't care—at this point she would kiss a ketchup can. "I won!"

"How much?"

"The whole enchilada."

"But—" Mae pulled back. "That's…"

"Fifty-two million, give or take a few hundred grand."

"Good heavens!"

"What's all the shrieking about?" Ronnie asked as he joined them. "It better not be another rat, after what I paid the exterminator."

"Amelia won the lottery."

"You're kidding!"

"The numbers were in the paper." Amelia returned the newsprint to her pocket and wiped her hands on her skirt. "I only found out a minute ago."

"Are you certain?"

Oh, yes, she was one hundred percent certain. She had bought the ticket at the corner store across from the high school on her way home from work on Thursday. She remembered that vividly. There had been a lineup at the cash and everyone was talking about the possibility of a record jackpot. Although the odds of winning were astronomical, she'd thought, why not take a chance? Her luck couldn't get much worse.

She couldn't wait to tell Will. And especially Jenny. She plunged her hand back into her purse for her phone before she remembered she'd cancelled her wireless plan in order to economize when she'd moved in with her brother. But even if she still had a phone, this was the kind of news she should deliver in person. The look on their faces would be priceless....

Actually, not priceless. The look would be worth fifty-two million.

She gave both Mae and Ronnie more hugs, along with a garbled apology about leaving early. She would make it up to them. Buy them a new freezer and some real plants. She believed in paying her debts, and now, finally, she could.

Luck seemed to be with her still, because Will's old Chevette started on the third try, and it only stalled once before she could put it into gear and pull out of the parking lot. She would buy her brother a new car, or better yet, one of those big, manly pickups she'd seen him ogling. She could get a new minivan for Jenny that had built-in TV screens to entertain the kids and would be large enough to hold their growing brood. She could provide cars for each of the boys when they were old enough to drive. While she was at it, she could get one for herself. Nothing sensible or conservative like the black Beemer that had been repossessed last fall. No, this time she would get something fun. Bright and shiny, maybe even red, like that future that was dangling in front of her.

A horn blared. Amelia had no idea how long she had been sitting at the green light, dreaming about new cars. With a jaunty wave to the driver behind her, she started forward. The summer tourist season was in full swing. There was more traffic than usual in Port Hope's historic downtown. Located an easy hour's drive along Lake Ontario from Toronto, it was a popular destination for day-trippers seeking a break from the city. Luckily—there was that word again—the congestion thinned quickly once she coaxed the Chevette into doing the climb up Walton Street. Within minutes, she had left the old brick and quaint shops of the heritage district behind.

Will and Jenny's neighborhood was a fair distance from the river and the lakeshore. It wasn't on the route of the self-guided tours that were marked on the town maps. By today's standards, the houses were small and plain. Most were one-and-a-half-story boxes that had been tossed up in a hurry more than sixty years ago during the post-war baby boom. Some had been customized with expanded porches, or extra rooms in the attic, but there was no disguising their humble pedigree. The properties that came up for sale didn't remain on the market for long, though. The area was close to schools, the streets were quiet enough for road hockey any season of the year, and the houses were within the budget of young families.

But her family wouldn't need to worry about budgets anymore, would they?

A sedan she didn't recognize was parked at the side of the road in front of her brother's house. A pair of strangers in sandals and matching turquoise, Hawaiian-style printed shirts moved among open cardboard boxes that were arrayed on the lawn. Closer to the front steps there stood a few chrome-and-vinyl chairs, an old brass plant stand and the exercise bike that had been stored in the basement. Amelia nosed into the driveway. Her way was blocked by a metal-legged card table displaying knickknacks and rows of paperback books.

She had forgotten about the yard sale. Jenny had started it yesterday. She'd claimed she wanted to clean out the basement this weekend, since Will was constructing an extra bedroom plus a playroom for the boys down there. Amelia suspected the primary reason for the yard sale was to raise extra cash. The closer Jenny got to her due date, the more nervous she became about their finances.

But she wouldn't need to worry anymore, would she? And Will wouldn't need to build any extra rooms, because Amelia would buy them a house big enough to hold everyone, no matter how many more babies they produced.

This just kept getting better and better, didn't it? Amelia got out of the car and practically skipped up the driveway. She was giddy with the possibilities that continued to pop into her mind.

Her sister-in-law sat on a lawn chair in the shade of the maple beside the driveway. Strands of dark hair had escaped from her ponytail and drooped against her cheeks. A faded Argos T-shirt that had once belonged to Will stretched over her pregnant belly. She bore little resemblance to the delicate woman with the sparkling brown eyes who had married Amelia's big brother fifteen years ago. Jenny was a nurturer, and like many women in her position, she tended to put her family's needs ahead of her own. Riding herd on three boys—four, if she counted Will—had taken their toll.

One of the first things Amelia was going to do once she cashed in the ticket would be to treat Jenny to a spa day. Or make it a week. Get her a new wardrobe, get Will one, too, then send them on a cruise as a second honeymoon.

Jenny's brow furrowed as Amelia approached. "What's wrong? Why aren't you at work?"

She rocked back and forth from her heels to her toes. There was so much she wanted to say, so many promises she was finally able to make, the words were getting dammed up behind her grin. She savored the moment. "I've got some news."

"You didn't quit, did you?"

Amelia laughed. She hadn't officially said the words. She'd been too stunned. But there was no reason to continue waiting tables now. "Not yet, but I will."

"How much do you want for this?"

The Hawaiian-shirt couple had moved to the edge of the driveway. The man pointed to the plant stand he held.

"Thirty dollars," Jenny replied.

"There's some corrosion on the leg here. I'll give you ten."

"It's an antique. Fifteen."

"Don't quibble, honey," his companion said. "It's already a bargain."

"All right, fifteen."

Jenny reached for the small plastic storage container beside her chair. It held a substantial layer of coins plus a surprising number of bills. She took the man's twenty, gave him a five for his change, and carefully snapped the lid closed.

Forget savoring the moment. Amelia couldn't contain herself. As soon as the couple loaded their purchase into the sedan at the curb and pulled away, she blurted it out. "I won the lottery."

"Why would you quit that job?" Jenny asked at the same time. "I realize it didn't pay much, but I thought you were happy that Mae..." She paused. "What did you say?"

"I won Lotto 6/49."

"Sure. Pull the other one."

"No, really, I did win. That's my news. I came home as soon as I found out." She waved her arm toward the items on the lawn. "You don't need to have this yard sale. With my winnings—"

"Seriously? You actually won something?"

"I won the jackpot. More than fifty-two million."

Instead of smiling, Jenny's lips trembled. "I don't find that funny, Amelia."

"I'm not joking."

"But..."

She tugged her sister-in-law to her feet and bent her knees to bring their faces level. "I'm not joking," she repeated. "I really did win."

It took a few seconds to sink in. Amelia understood the reaction, because she had trouble grasping this new reality herself. Repeated disappointments had a way of doing that to a person. After so much bad news, it became easier not to even hope for good.

Jenny's smile blossomed slowly, like a flower bud finally exposed to the sun. Her cheeks dimpled. The lines worry had etched on her face lifted into traces left by old laughter. And her eyes sparkled. "You won?" she whispered.

Oh, yes, this was definitely worth a few million. Amelia nodded.

Jenny screeched and threw her arms around Amelia, pulling her as close as her baby bump allowed.

"Hey! What's going on?"

At Will's voice, they both looked toward the house. He stood on the front stoop, clad in his typical carpentry clothes of blue jeans and a dark green shirt. He balanced eighteen-month-old Timothy on one hip while he held the screen door closed with the edge of a battered work boot. Toto, the paycheck-eating

Scotch Terrier, jumped against the other side of the door in a bid to get out.

Jenny broke off the hug. She got as far as saying Will's name before she started to sob.

He shifted Timothy under one arm and leaped down the stairs. "Baby, what's wrong? Why are you crying?"

Jenny wiped her eyes. "Amelia."

"Auntie Mia, Auntie Mia," Timmy chorused, squirming in his father's hold. He wore only a T-shirt and diaper, which was loosening with each wriggle. The dog slipped past the screen door and bounded toward them, adding his high-pitched yapping to the commotion.

Will glowered at Amelia. He was protective by nature, especially when it came to his wife. Although at five foot nine he was only an inch taller than his sister, his frame was packed with solid muscle earned from a lifetime of working with his hands. He could be an imposing figure to someone who didn't know what a marshmallow he was inside. He raised his voice over the din. "What did you do to her?"

Amelia laughed. "Down, boy. Those are happy tears."

"That's right." Jenny hiccupped. "Your sister won the lottery."

"What? Come on."

"It's true," Amelia said. "I played our birthdays like I always do. 1, 3, 4, 17, 23, 29. Those were last night's winning numbers." She withdrew the scrap of newspaper from her pocket and held it up to him, just as she had for Mae. "See for yourself."

Will caught her wrist to steady her hand. He looked at the paper, then at her, then back at the paper. His face paled beneath his freckles. "Is this for real?"

"As real as fifty-two million and change."

"You're rich."

She shook her head. Not for a second had she considered keeping the winnings for herself. Her family had stood by her through the bad times, and there was no way she wouldn't share the good ones. "*We're* rich, big brother," she corrected. "Stinking, filthy, ridiculously, never-worry-about-a-job-again loaded."

He released her wrist to pass his hand over his face. His fingers shook. Then he tipped back his head and whooped. So did Timmy. Laughing, Will swung the toddler over his head and spun in a circle. "We're rich, Timmy. There's a new word for you. Rich. What do you think of that?"

Timmy chortled and kicked, his entire

body expressing his glee. Will pulled him back down before the diaper fell off completely. Owen and Eric, drawn by the noise, ran around the house from the backyard. At ten, Owen was a miniature version of his father, right down to the thatch of red hair. A leather catcher's mitt engulfed his left hand—he was on a baseball kick this month. Six-year-old Eric had his mother's coloring as well as her nurturing instinct—instead of a baseball mitt, he held the neighbors' marmalade cat. Momentarily anyway. It streaked off as soon as it spotted Toto.

The boys needed no convincing to join the celebration. Seeing the adults happy for a change was reason enough.

It wasn't only cars she could buy the boys. She could get Owen season tickets to the Jays games and send him to a baseball camp. She could put Eric through veterinary school. There would be no limit to whatever dream they wanted to follow.

This continued to get better and better.

Amelia wiped her eyes as she led the way to the house. At first, she assumed the place looked different due to her excitement. Having a life-changing experience would give anyone a new perspective. Then she noticed the old sunburst-shaped clock was missing from the living room. So was the ugly wooden floor lamp with the lopsided base. The shelf above the computer held far fewer knickknacks than it had when she'd left for work this morning.

Apparently, Jenny had added more items to her yard sale that hadn't been limited to the junk in the basement. That was good, since the sunburst clock lost five minutes a week, and the lamp tended to fall over at the slightest bump. This also meant there would be less to move when Amelia bought their new house.

She wouldn't wait that long to move out of here herself, though. There was hardly enough space for her now.

In a fancier house, the room where she slept would be called a den, but here it was known simply as the back room. The door was ajar when she reached it. That wasn't unusual, so she wasn't alarmed. Everyone in the family was in and out of this room on a regular basis, since Jenny's sewing machine was set up in here, and the kids often played on the futon that served as Amelia's bed. She hadn't minded because she'd had no right to complain. There were no spare bedrooms, and as the saying went, beggars couldn't be choosers.

But now she allowed herself to think about it. Even though she adored her nephews, she was looking forward to the time when she could sleep on a real bed again and not need to check for toy cars and stray Lego blocks when she opened out the futon. She would enjoy regaining the little luxuries she used to take for granted, like privacy, and having a closet all to herself, and taking a long soak in the bathtub whenever she wanted without causing a lineup outside the door. Once she cashed in that ticket she could choose where and how she lived. She would never, ever, need to depend on anyone's charity again.

The sound of Jenny's voice came from the direction of the kitchen, along with Toto's yapping. "Timothy, put the bone down," she ordered. "It's Toto's."

"Mine."

"It's full of germs."

"Mom, I'm hungry," Owen whined.

"Me, too," said Eric. "Can I have a cookie?"

"How about an apple?" Jenny offered.

"Ugh!"

"Or some raisins—" Jenny groaned in exasperation. "Timmy, no! Get that bone out of your mouth!"

Amelia chuckled. Quiet was another luxury that was rare around here, although she was getting used to the daily circus and would probably miss it when she was gone. Once she cashed that ticket...

Uh-huh. The ticket. It was high time to actually hold it in her hand. She pushed the door of the back room completely open, then turned toward the wall at the end of the futon.

The space was empty. The painting that normally hung there was gone.

Her smile dissolved. The room spun. For the second time in an hour—could it only have been an hour?—she stumbled from shock. "No," she whispered.

There had to be a simple explanation. Maybe the wire that held the painting had broken. It could have bounced and ended up behind the futon. She grabbed one corner of the futon frame and slid it away from the wall, but nothing was there.

Heavy footsteps crossed the living room and approached the doorway. Will spoke as he drew near. "We'll use Jenny's van when we go to the lottery office. I wouldn't want to take that old Chevette on the highway all the way to Toronto."

Amelia dropped to her knees, then flattened herself on her stomach and pressed her cheek to the floor. Aside from a collection of dust bunnies, the space beneath the futon was as empty as the space behind it. She scrambled to her feet and clawed at the mattress to tip it away from the frame, but she found nothing other than a squished coloring book.

"Too bad we have to wait until tomorrow," Will continued. "But they wouldn't be open on a Sunday. What are you doing?"

Her gaze darted wildly around the room. She could see at a glance there was no place to conceal anything large. It wasn't here.

"Amelia?"

"Where's the painting?"

"What?"

She thumped the side of her fist against the empty wall. "The painting of the farm that was right here."

"I put it on the lawn with the other stuff."

"You *what?*"

"It was a piece of junk. I thought you'd be happy to see it go."

She pushed past him and ran for the front door. She didn't remember seeing the painting on the lawn, but then, she hadn't really looked. It had to be there, because no one would want something that ugly, would they? The painting itself was awful. Jenny had acquired it at someone else's yard sale with the intention of using the frame to dress up a mirror. The frame was old-fashioned, carved wood that was warped in places and gaped away from the canvas and had provided a perfect spot to tuck a folded slip of paper because it had been high up, out of sight and beyond the reach of little fingers and hungry dogs. It was a good, *safe* place that she'd felt so clever about finding. Please, oh, please let it still be there....

It wasn't. That much was clear from the instant she reached the front stoop. She pressed her fingers to her mouth but she couldn't feel them. Her entire body was going numb. That was a mercy. If only the numbness could reach her brain and her heart.

This couldn't be happening. She already knew what it was like to lose everything, but to lose it again? Before she'd even got it? Fate couldn't be *this* cruel, could it?

The door opened behind her. "Amelia?" Will asked. "You're scaring me. What's wrong?"

Her legs gave out. She sat down hard on the top step. "The lottery ticket."

"What about it?"

"I wedged it underneath the frame of that painting."

CHAPTER TWO

HANK JONES DID his best to concentrate on the conversation, because it definitely wouldn't be cool to be caught slack-jawed and staring. He'd heard that Amelia Goodfellow was back in town. Given the size of Port Hope, he'd known it was possible they would run into each other eventually, but not in his wildest dreams would he have imagined she would be waiting for him to open his office on a Monday morning.

Typically, the clients of Jones Investigative Services ranged from employers who wanted in-depth background checks on job applicants to estate lawyers tracking down missing heirs and people who wanted their spouses followed. Fairly routine stuff, which was okay with Hank, because it meant he hadn't yet taken on a case he couldn't solve. But he doubted this case would be routine. The last time he had seen Amelia, she had vowed never to speak to him again. She'd kept her word for almost fifteen years.

Nevertheless, here she was, sitting in the worn leather armchair across from his desk like any other potential client. For the first time since he'd started the business, he wished he'd put more effort into the office decor. He wondered what she thought of the wheezing air conditioner in the window behind him, or the five-year-old computer that hulked on his desk, or the prize pickerel that occupied the place of honor above the coffeemaker. He also wondered why her opinion should matter to him.

If she noticed the thrift-shop decorating scheme, she didn't let it show. She kept her face as politely neutral as her request. "Will you take the case?"

Her voice sounded the same. In his more fanciful moments, he used to compare it to syrup, but he was no good with words, and that wasn't right, anyway. Her voice wasn't sugary, and sweet wasn't an adjective people would use to describe Amelia. It was the way syrup flowed, rich and clear, that reminded him of her voice. It was also hard to stop the stream of her words once they got going. They tended to stick, too.

Her appearance hadn't changed much over the years. Her hair was a bit straighter and cut to chin length instead of corkscrewing over her shoulders, and it had darkened marginally, yet it was unmistakably the Goodfellow red. Did she still insist on calling it auburn? Beneath her flowered blouse and denim skirt, her figure appeared to be as slender as when she'd been a teenager, although she'd lost that coltish, all arms and legs look.

He suspected that even if he'd been blindfolded, he would have recognized her presence. The leather chair creaked as she shifted because she couldn't sit still. The air around her seemed to crackle with energy she couldn't quite contain. Amelia never did anything halfway. When she wanted something, she pursued it with her whole heart.

"Or would you have a problem working for me?" she asked.

The blunt question didn't surprise him. The Amelia he'd known wouldn't tiptoe around an issue. She'd been the most honest person he'd ever encountered. Well, except for her blind spot when it came to her hair color.

Would he have a problem taking her on as a client? As a rule, he didn't make spur-of-the-moment decisions. He preferred to inspect all sides of a topic first. That's what made him a good investigator. This situation was different, because he already knew the answer to her question. Of course, he wouldn't have a problem working for Amelia. He wasn't a kid anymore. He would never again be that idealistic fool, goofy with puppy love, laying his heart bare for her to trample with her size-eight feet. The pain had faded. They'd both moved on.

And the truth was, he was curious. Whatever had brought her here had caused her to swallow her pride and break one and a half decades of silence. Anyone, even if they weren't a professional snoop, would want to know what it was.

"This is what I do for a living, Amelia," he said. "The problems that happened between us were a long time ago."

"Distant past," she agreed.

"We were friends long before we made the mistake of trying to be more."

She exhaled. It was accompanied by a subtle lowering of her shoulders. "That's a good way to put it. Yes, we were friends once, weren't we?"

"And since you need help, I'm glad you came to me."

"I was hoping you would feel that way."

"Did you think I would kick you out?"

"After the way we parted, I wasn't sure. People can change."

"Not me. I'm the same old, dumb lug I always was."

"You were never dumb, Hank. Otherwise, I wouldn't want to hire you."

He smiled. "It's good to see you, Amelia. You haven't changed, either."

If he'd hoped to relax her, he'd been wrong. Instead of returning his smile, she shifted uncomfortably and glanced at her wrist. It likely was a reflex action, since she wore no watch. "Thanks," she said. "I apologize if this seems rude, but would you mind if we do the catching-up later? You weren't open yesterday, and I'm a little anxious to get things going."

The old Amelia used to charge straight ahead once she'd decided on her course of action, too. He could see for himself that she was anxious. The skin beneath her eyes appeared shadowed, as if she hadn't slept the night before. There were new lines at the outer corners, which added maturity to her gaze. The color was as striking as ever. He'd once compared it to the shimmering patches of blue-green his father's outboard used to leave on the surface of the water when they went trolling back when he was a kid. Not the smoothest compliment to use when trying to impress a girl, comparing her eyes to an oil slick.

"Hank?"

Her tone wasn't exactly cool, but it wasn't warm, either. It was cautious. Businesslike. Which he should have expected. As she'd just made clear, this wasn't a social call. He picked up a pen and readied a fresh page in his notepad. "You said that you want me to find a painting?"

"That's right."

"I'll need as many details as possible before I can plan how to proceed. You do have time to answer some questions, don't you?"

"Go ahead."

"How did the painting go missing?"

"My sister-in-law held a yard sale on the weekend. She sold the painting yesterday while I was at work. She remembers getting thirty dollars for the painting, but she doesn't remember anything about who bought it."

"So it was your sister-in-law who sold the painting."

"You remember Jenny? Will's wife?"

He and Amelia had been in their final year at high school when they'd gone to her brother's wedding together. They had laughed and danced and figured it was fate when she had caught the bouquet. They'd been sure they would always be as happy as they'd been then. That alone was proof they'd had a lot of growing up to do. Less than three months later, they had broken up.

"Yes," he replied. "I remember. How are she and Will doing?"

"Fine. They're expecting their fourth child next month."

"Is your brother still working at that custom furniture place north of town?"

"Lancaster Cabinets, yes."

"I heard business wasn't good last year. Are they doing okay now?"

"As far as I know."

"Why did Jenny have the yard sale?"

"She wanted to clean the excess junk out of the house."

"Can't blame her, with a fourth kid on the way. So this painting had been kept at their place?"

"Right. I've been staying with them since..." She hesitated.

He wouldn't pretend ignorance. "Since your legal troubles?"

"I see you've heard about it."

Anyone not living in a cave would have heard about it. The scandal and ensuing criminal trial that had bankrupted Amelia and her husband's investment business more than a year ago had been featured on the nightly news of every major network. It had been splashed across the national papers, too. There had been a mini business boom for local hotels and car rental agencies caused by the reporters who had come to her hometown looking for information to do background pieces. For a while, she had been Port Hope's most infamous native.

The scandal had also ended her marriage to Spencer Pryce. Feeling any satisfaction over that fact would have been mean and petty, so Hank had tried not to. Despite what she'd done to him, he would never want to see her hurt. "I'm sorry you had a hard time, Amelia."

She acknowledged his sympathy with a tight nod. "Thank you, but that's in the past, too. My only concern now is with the painting."

"I assume it was valuable?"

"Only to me."

"Could you explain that?"

"You know about my troubles, as you put it, so you must also know the courts seized Spencer's assets to make partial restitution for the money he stole. That included our joint property."

"I heard. It wasn't fair."

"Depends on your viewpoint. Our former clients thought it wasn't enough. They would have preferred a few pounds of flesh, too." She made an impatient motion with her hand. "That's beside the point. I'm telling you this because I want you to know how important that painting is to me. I have practically nothing left from my old life because I ended up liquidating my personal property in order to pay my lawyer's fees."

"Except for the painting?"

She hesitated. "No, it wasn't part of our art collection. Jenny found it at a yard sale last year. She bought it because she liked the frame."

"Are you saying this painting belonged to your sister-in-law, not you?"

"Technically, yes, but I thought of it as mine."

"I don't understand. Why?"

"It hung on the wall in their back room. That's where I've been sleeping. The painting was the last thing I saw at night and the first thing I looked at in the morning. I got to know every detail. It became very special to me. When I came home from work yesterday and discovered it was missing—" Her voice hitched. She swallowed, taking a moment to regain her composure. "All I've been able to think about since then is how to get it back."

Her emotion over the painting appeared genuine, but it seemed out of proportion. Her reaction didn't make sense. The Amelia he remembered had been impulsive at times, yet she'd also been practical. There must be something she wasn't telling him. "What was the painting like?"

"It was a landscape, a grassy hill with an old farmhouse and weathered barns. Oil on canvas. The scene looked a lot like the countryside around here."

"How big was it?"

"I couldn't give you exact measurements, but it was large. At least three feet wide and two feet high."

"Do you know who painted it?"

"The signature at the bottom corner was hard to decipher. It started with an *M* and could have been *Mather* or *Martin*. Possibly *Matthews*. The name's not important because I'm sure whoever painted it wasn't a professional artist."

"Why not?"

"It's not very good."

"But you liked it?"

"Yes."

"Then why did Jenny sell it? Did you two have a fight?"

"No. She wasn't being vindictive, if that's what you're getting at. She hadn't known how...precious it was to me. I hadn't told her."

"I see."

"And what difference does it make why she sold it? It's gone."

"I asked because if she'd gotten rid of it to hurt you, she might remember perfectly well who bought it but just doesn't feel like telling you."

Amelia lifted one eyebrow. "You've gotten cynical."

"No, I'm just being methodical. That's how I operate. I need to consider every angle."

"Jenny feels awful about selling it. She's almost as upset as I am."

"Was your brother at the yard sale?"

"On and off. Most of the time he was working on the rooms he's building in the basement and keeping track of Timmy. He's their youngest."

"Then he didn't see who bought the painting?"

"No. His other two boys had been at the park in the morning and played in the backyard after lunch. They didn't see anything. None of the neighbors did, either."

"You asked them?"

"I went to every house on the block. Not everyone was home. The people who were couldn't tell me anything."

It didn't surprise him that she'd already tried to solve her problem herself. That was typical of Amelia. The fact that she'd decided to seek anyone's assistance, particularly his, was an indication of how serious this was to her. "How had Jenny advertised the yard sale? Signs? An ad in the paper?"

"Both."

"That means her customers weren't limited to people in the neighborhood." Hank tapped his pen against his notepad. "With so many tourists in town, the buyer could have been visiting and just happened to see the signs or read the ad."

"I realize we don't have much to go on," she said, "but I really, really need to get that painting back."

"I agree, there's not much to go on. I don't know if I'll be able to help you."

"You can try, can't you?"

Hank had always admired Amelia's intelligence. Unlike him, she'd breezed through high school and aced every course. Her brilliance in mathematics in particular had earned her a full scholarship to the University of Toronto. He'd been thrilled when he'd learned about that scholarship, even though it had meant the beginning of the end for the two of them. She was certainly smart enough to grasp the fact that her painting could be a few hundred miles away by now. For all they knew, it could be out of the country. Tracking it down would be time-consuming and expensive, if not impossible. He was about to shake his head when he met her gaze.

There were tears in her eyes.

That threw him. So did the urge he felt to leap from his chair and take her into his arms.

Whoa, where had that come from? He gripped his pen harder and stayed where he was. "I'd like you to answer one more question."

"Okay, what?"

"What's the real reason you want this painting?"

"I already told you. I got very attached to it. It's important to me. Extremely important. I need to get that painting back, no matter how long it takes or how much it costs me."

"You just finished telling me you sold

most of your assets before you moved in with your brother."

"I can pay you, if that's what you're worried about. I might not have access to the kind of wealth I used to have, but I'm living rent-free and I make a decent wage plus tips at Mae B's. Name your price. Once you find that painting, I'll pay whatever you want."

Hank fought to keep his pity from showing. Amelia Goodfellow, their class valedictorian and girl voted unanimously the most likely to succeed, the brilliant financial advisor whose company had once been worth millions, was waiting tables at a hole-in-the-wall restaurant. The urge to hug her returned. "My fee isn't the issue."

"Then what is?"

"I asked for the *real* reason you want that painting."

Her chin trembled. She tightened her lips.

"You can't honestly expect me to believe you would be willing to throw away the money you do have on a piece of worthless, not very good art that doesn't even belong to you. What are you holding back, Amelia?"

She remained silent.

He used to have more patience than she had. It was a good bet he still did. He waited her out.

It took less than a minute. When she finally did speak, her voice shook. "During the past year and a half, I've lost my business, my reputation, my husband..." She cleared her throat. "You name it, I lost it. I lost so much, it got to the point that I stopped believing I could win."

"I'm sorry."

She clenched her hands in her lap. Her knuckles were white. "I don't want your pity, Hank. I'm only telling you this to make you understand."

"About the painting?"

"Yes. That's where I've drawn the line."

"How?"

"Losing that painting was the final straw. It woke me up. I'm through taking what Fate dishes out. This time, I'm fighting back."

"Okay, but—"

"I want to start living again. I want the right to be happy again."

"And you believe that finding this painting will do all that?"

She surged to her feet. *"Yes!"*

"Amelia..."

"I'm not asking for a guarantee because I realize it's a long shot, but it's possible to beat the odds. I *know* it's possible. The whole key is being willing to try."

This was the Amelia he had fallen in love with. Passionate, spontaneous, throwing herself one hundred percent into whatever she did. He hadn't realized how much he'd missed her.

"Will you try, Hank?"

"As you just said, it would be a long shot. I couldn't in good conscience take your money for—"

"Fine." She turned toward the door. "Then I'll find someone who will."

He shoved himself out of his chair and rounded the desk. "Amelia, wait. I didn't say I wouldn't help you. I just said I wouldn't take your money."

She faced him. "What does that mean?"

"I'll make a few inquiries, and I'll try poking around on the internet, but it will be on my own time. I won't charge you."

Relief appeared to be warring with pride. "Thank you."

"Don't thank me yet. I may come up empty."

"If anyone can find it, you will. But I don't need charity. I can pay you."

"It's not charity. Consider it a welcome-home present."

Her lips twitched. It was the first hint of a smile he'd seen. "Finding that painting would be a better gift than you could possibly imagine." She held out her right hand. "Thank you, Hank."

He clasped her hand without thinking. He concluded most of his meetings with a handshake. Often a handshake was the only contract he needed.

But the contact of his palm with Amelia's jarred him. Her energy tingled through his skin, just as it had when they'd been teenagers. His pulse sped up. So did his breathing. Her scent was something else that hadn't changed. It was earthy and inviting, like the tangy smell of new grass on a sunny spring day. Not that he'd ever said that aloud, because telling a girl she reminded him of a lawn was even less romantic than the oil slick thing.

Romantic?

Yeah, sure. There was as much chance of rekindling their romance as there was of finding her painting.

CHAPTER THREE

"I CAN'T BELIEVE you lied to him," Jenny said. "How can you expect him to do his job?"

Amelia finished paring a carrot and handed it to her sister-in-law. Timmy was down for his afternoon nap, so the house was unusually peaceful. Sporadic hammering came from the backyard, where Owen and Eric were attempting to construct a fort with the scrap lumber and drywall from Will's basement renovation project. Rather than relaxing, Jenny was taking advantage of the lull to get a head start on dinner...and to speak her mind. "I didn't actually lie," Amelia said. "I just omitted certain facts."

"Same thing."

"He doesn't need to know about the lottery ticket in order to find the painting."

"I'm surprised Hank agreed to work for you at all." Jenny placed the carrot on the cutting board and began chopping. "If I recall, you two didn't part on the best of terms."

"That was more than a decade ago. He's a professional. This is business."

"Didn't he think it was a little odd for you to make such a fuss over a worthless old painting?"

"I said it was important to me."

"You must have been very convincing."

"Well, it *is* important."

"At least you told him the truth about that much."

"I actually told him more truth than I'd meant to."

"How so?"

"He seemed as if he was about to refuse me, and I was feeling desperate. I got into how much I've lost lately."

"Ah."

"I didn't set out to play on his sympathy, but he probably feels sorry for me anyway."

"I'm not so sure. Is it possible he still cares about you? That would explain why he took your case."

"No, Jenny. What we had was only puppy love. It died a long time ago."

"Hmph."

Jenny's skepticism made her flinch. Hank had agreed the past was over and done. Their new relationship was purely business. Well, business between old friends.

But how businesslike was it to work for free? And what about that moment this morning in his office when their hands had touched?

The years had been more than good to Hank Jones. He'd reached his full height of six foot three by tenth grade, but he'd been lanky, to put it kindly. Now his frame had fleshed out into the classic, broad-shouldered, slim-hipped, male silhouette of underwear models and Hollywood hunks. He'd grown into his face, too. The angled jaw and sharp features that had seemed harsh on a boy looked good on a man. Okay, more than good—spectacular, particularly when he smiled. He likely did that a lot, since laugh lines crinkled the corners of his light brown eyes. His sand-colored hair was streaked blond by the sun and was as thick and straight as ever. It was too neatly trimmed to fall over his collar anymore, but he hadn't been able to tame it completely. The same stubborn, endearing lock that used to fall over his forehead still did.

But Hank's appearance was irrelevant. Amelia had other priorities here, namely fifty-two million and change worth of them. She wasn't interested in any man, and especially not one who had so thoroughly broken her heart. The bump in her pulse from their parting handshake was because she'd been in an emotional state over losing the ticket. That's why she'd opened up to him about her feelings, too. It couldn't have anything to do with her old crush on him. That would not only be absurd, it would be self-destructive and stupid. She rinsed off another carrot and applied her energy to the parer.

"Did I hear right?" Will asked as he moved into the kitchen doorway. Lancaster Cabinets was on summer hours, so it wasn't unusual for him to get home in the middle of the afternoon. "You really went to Hank Jones for help?"

Amelia nodded at her brother. "I went first thing this morning."

"That's too bad. I think you should have gone to someone else." He slipped his arm past Jenny to set his lunch pail on the counter and gave her a quick peck on the cheek. He patted her stomach. "How's our little football player? Is he still kicking field goals?"

"*She* decided to take up tap dancing," Jenny said.

Both Will and Jenny had resisted learning the sex of the baby she carried. They claimed it didn't matter and would prefer to be surprised. For Jenny's sake, Amelia hoped it would be a girl. "Why do you think I shouldn't have gone to Hank, Will?"

Her brother crossed his arms and leaned one shoulder against the doorframe. "Jones likes to play private eye. That business of his is a farce."

"What do you know about his business?" Amelia asked.

"Most of his work comes from his father, when he isn't out fishing. He checks out customers who want to buy a car from the old man's lot on credit. In my opinion, it was his daddy's way of putting him on the payroll, since he couldn't make it as a car salesman. It's not much different from getting an allowance."

That didn't sound like the Hank she'd known, but people could change. Had she made another mistake? "I hope that's not the case," Amelia said. "I went to Hank because I thought he would be a good detective."

"Are you sure that's the only reason you went to him?" Jenny asked. "Maybe you still have some of the old feelings left, too."

"Absolutely not. I told you, that's completely over," she said firmly. She returned her attention to Will. "Are you sure about Hank's business? From what I remember of his character, being a private investigator would suit him. He's observant, and he thinks everything through. He's thorough and methodical."

"You mean slow," Will said.

"He's tenacious," Amelia said.

"He's a stubborn idiot."

Jenny pointed her knife at Will. "That's too harsh. It wasn't Hank's fault that your truck loan fell through last year. It was because Mr. Lancaster had laid everyone off."

"Temporarily. We were hired back when he got more orders. I told Hank we would be."

"You're not being fair, Wilbur, and you know it."

Will muttered something under his breath. He hated being called Wilbur.

"If anyone was an idiot," Amelia said, "I was for losing that ticket. If I hadn't tried to be smart by sticking it in that frame, I could have bought you five new trucks by now."

There was an awkward silence. Will was the first to break it. "I've been wondering about that," he said. "Why did you store the ticket in the painting? I'm not criticizing you or anything, but it's not where most people would put a lottery ticket."

"I thought it was a safe place."

"Remember how Timmy emptied her

purse?" Jenny asked. "And Mae had to re-place her paycheck?"

"Oh, right. Sorry about that, sis."

"There was more to it than that, Will," Amelia said. "The main reason I thought of using the painting is because it reminded me of the wall safe Spencer had installed in our condo. It was behind the Kandinsky."

"The what?"

"The painting in our dining room."

"You mean the blue and yellow one with the weird zigzags?"

Amelia nodded. That was one way to de-scribe Wassily Kandinsky's Expressionist style. Spencer had bought the artwork pri-marily as an investment. It had turned out to be the most valuable piece in their collec-tion and worth almost as much as the condo. It had nothing in common with the ama-teurish landscape that had hung in Will and Jenny's back room, except for its function. "I used Jenny's painting because I regarded it as the poor woman's version of Spencer's wall safe."

Will snorted a laugh. "I get it now. That sounds like something you would do."

"I thought I was being clever," Amelia said. "It was a stupid idea."

"Water under the bridge. What's done is done."

She knew they were disappointed. Who wouldn't be, after the way she'd gotten everyone's hopes up? Because of her, the whole family had been on an emotional roller coaster. It had been a brief ride, one sudden climb followed by an equally sudden drop, yet Jenny and Will were taking the reversal of fortune in stride. Hiring someone to search for the ticket had been Amelia's idea, not theirs. They felt it was a lost cause. They preferred to accept what they couldn't control and get on with their lives.

They'd been the same way when she'd arrived on their doorstep six months ago, divorced, flat broke and unemployed. There had been no words of recrimination. They'd helped her carry the few possessions she'd saved inside, and then Jenny had fixed her a cup of herbal tea while Hank had dug out extra bedding for the futon.

Jenny patted her hand. "I think that carrot's done, too."

A quick glance showed her the carrot was turning into a matchstick. She passed it to her sister-in-law. "Sorry."

"That's okay. There's less to chop."

She had to admire Jenny's glass-half-full

attitude. Life probably would be simpler if she could master it herself. "Going back to the subject of paintings, I believe it's safest not to tell Hank about the ticket, so I'd appreciate it if neither of you mentioned it to him."

"Why?" Jenny asked. "You can't be thinking he'd steal it?"

"People have been tempted by far less."

"But you signed the back of the ticket, didn't you?"

She grimaced.

"Amelia?"

"There was a long lineup at the Min-A-Mart when I bought the ticket on Thursday. By the time I got here I was in a rush to put away the groceries I'd picked up on the way home, so I just tucked the ticket straight into the painting. Once it was out of sight, I forgot about signing it."

Will whistled. "That means anyone could cash it."

"I know. Stupid move number two."

"But Hank would be working for you," Jenny persisted. "It would be against the law if he tried to keep that ticket for himself, whether he could cash it or not. You could take him to court…" She stopped. "Oh."

"Right. Been there, done that, and couldn't afford to buy the T-shirt. The law doesn't stop anyone from taking what they want if they think they can get away with it. And the only people guaranteed to make a profit in court are the lawyers. I know mine certainly got rich off me."

"She's got a point," Will put in. "It might be best to keep Hank in the dark."

Jenny carried the cutting board to the stove and scraped the mound of diced carrots into the stew pot, then handed Amelia an onion. "You're not being fair, either. You're suspicious of Hank because of Spencer."

Well, duh, Amelia thought. She picked up a small knife and jabbed the tip into the base of the onion. "You know what they say about once burned."

"They're two entirely different people."

"So? They're both male."

"Hey," Will said. "What am I?"

"You're my brother, so you're an exception."

"Spencer Pryce was a lying crook," Jenny declared. "He took advantage of your innocence."

"You mean my gullibility."

"You've known Hank since you were kids," Jenny continued. "I think you should trust him."

"I can't. I used to think Spencer was a nice guy, too. We all did."

"But—"

"Being fooled once was bad enough." She pulled off a layer of onion peel. "I don't intend to trust a man around my money again. Ever. Except for Will, of course," she added.

Jenny pursed her lips. "Hmph."

Amelia flinched again. This time it was from guilt. She realized it might be unfair to tar Hank with the same brush as Spencer, yet she had little choice. It wasn't only men she couldn't trust, it was her own judgment. "Our mother used to make that sound a lot, too. Do you learn it during childbirth, or what?"

Will snorted another laugh.

"Well, I think you're making a mistake," Jenny said. "There's no excuse for lying."

"Depends on the circumstances," Will said. "Sometimes it's the best way to handle a situation."

"Don't listen to your brother," Jenny said. "He's a bad influence. You owe Hank the truth."

"She doesn't owe him anything," Will said. "Not after the way he treated her."

Amelia sighed. So this was what lay at the core of her brother's attitude toward Hank and his business. She should have expected it. Will could be as protective of his sister as he was of his wife. "That's ancient history," she said. "We were kids."

"He hurt you."

"Ancient history," she repeated.

"Maybe, but I haven't forgotten."

"Try, okay? The past is irrelevant. My only concern is the painting, and Hank's probably going to want to interview both of you."

Will opened his mouth to respond when he paused and tipped his head toward the hall. Timmy's voice drifted down the stairwell. It sounded as if he was rattling the sides of his crib. "Nap time's over," Will said. "I'll get him."

Jenny waited until they could hear Will's footsteps pound up the stairs. She put her head close to Amelia's and spoke quickly. "We made more than five hundred dollars from the yard sale."

"That's great."

"You can use it."

"What? Jenny, I can't take your money. You need it."

"It's to pay Hank. I meant to give it to you this morning but you left before I could."

Her eyes stung. She put down the onion.

"You're incredible. How can you be so generous?"

"I feel responsible because I sold that painting."

"Please, don't. You couldn't have known."

"I should have noticed the ticket!"

"No one would unless they knew where to look. It was folded up and tucked pretty deep inside the edge of the frame. And thank you for the wonderful offer, but I've got some money put aside in my first-and-last fund," she said. She was referring to the money she'd been accumulating in order to pay the deposit on an apartment rental when she moved out. It was only a little over three hundred and fifty dollars, which wasn't much—it would scarcely cover an hour of her former lawyer's time. "And I still have my job. Besides, I'll have plenty to give Hank as a reward once he finds the painting."

"Didn't he want a retainer?"

"No."

"What if he doesn't find it? How will you pay him then?"

"He, uh, said he doesn't want any money."

Jenny stepped back to study her. "He's working for free?"

She nodded.

"Then I was right! He's still got a thing for you."

"It's your pregnancy hormones talking, Jenny."

"Hmph."

Amelia covered her flinch by checking her wrist, then glanced at the clock on the stove. "And speaking of money, I'd better get going or I'll be late for my shift."

TWENTY MINUTES LATER, Amelia pulled open the back door of Mae B's. A haze of kitchen smells rolled out to greet her. It was a potent mix: onions from the soup of the day, which was always onion on Mondays, fat from the deep fryer, fresh rolls, stale coffee, plus a trace of mustiness that seeped from the brick walls of the old building in humid weather. Her empty stomach rolled. She braced one hand on the doorframe and turned her face to the breeze. She could have grabbed a sandwich before she'd left her brother's place, but one of the few perks of working for Mae was a free meal.

A petite woman jogged toward her along the alley from the parking lot. Shaggy, purple-streaked brown hair bounced against her neck and a small pink knapsack swung from her arm. She couldn't have been much past her teens. "Are you on your way in or out?" she asked breathlessly.

"In," Amelia said. "Can I help you?"

"Please, tell me it's not four-thirty yet."

Amelia shook her head. "My guess is it's not past four."

"Thank heavens," she said. She dug into her knapsack and pulled out a frilly, pea-green apron. She nodded toward the doorway Amelia was blocking. "Excuse me, I need to get past."

Evidently, Mae had hired a new waitress. Amelia's stomach did another lurch, but this time it had nothing to do with the kitchen smells. She stepped aside, then followed the woman along the back hallway. "My name's Amelia. I work here, too." At least, she hoped she did.

"I'm Brittany." She switched her pack from hand to hand as she shrugged into the apron, then fumbled to tie the apron strings behind her back.

"Hold still, I'll get that," Amelia said.

Brittany stopped so quickly her hair fell over her eyes. She flicked it back with a jerk of her head. A row of metal studs adorned the rim of her ear. "Thanks!"

"You can put your pack in the storeroom."

Amelia secured the apron with a neat bow. "It's the door on the right."

"Could you do it for me?" she asked, pushing the pack into Amelia's hands. "I can't be late on my first day." She laughed nervously and headed for the dining room. "I seriously need this job," she said over her shoulder.

Amelia ducked into the storeroom. The hook where her own apron usually hung was bare. She didn't need a detective to tell her the apron had been given to Brittany. She dropped the pink pack on the shelf beside the ketchup cans and went in search of her boss.

Ronnie was jabbing toothpicks into a BLT when she reached the kitchen. He greeted her without meeting her eyes. At her question, he nodded his head toward the corner beside the freezer where they had set up their computer. Mae was peering at the screen while she held a cell phone to her ear. From the sound of things, she was blasting someone about a late delivery.

Amelia waited until she had finished her call before she spoke. "Hello, Mae."

Mae swiveled on her chair to face her. She wouldn't meet her gaze, either. "I meant to call you earlier, Amelia, but things have been busy."

"Do I still have a job here?" she asked bluntly.

"That's what I wanted to call you about."

"I was wrong about winning the lottery. I told you that as soon as I found out." In fact, she had been too dazed to think of phoning Mae until Sunday evening. It was only after she'd had no luck going door-to-door questioning her neighbors that she'd remembered her dramatic exit from the restaurant and had attempted to do damage control. "You said it was okay."

"I reconsidered."

"You said you understood yesterday. You told me I could come back."

Mae gave her a tight smile. "I'm sorry, Amelia. We've already found someone else."

"How? It's only been a day. You wouldn't have had time to advertise."

"Ronnie called her. She's his niece, and he knew she needed the job. She's putting herself through college."

"I need the job, too."

Mae's expression hardened. She rose from her chair. "You don't need it as much as Brittany does. She's trying to better herself. You've already got a degree. You had your shot at a career."

"Sure, but—"

"You know as well as I do that you're overqualified for this job. You weren't happy being a waitress, Amelia. While I don't have any complaints about your work here, I realized it wouldn't last."

"Quitting was a mistake."

Mae shook her head. "The reason you quit might have been a mistake, but it was bound to happen sooner or later. We knew it was only a matter of time before you moved on to something better. I have to do what's right for my business, and I need waitresses I can count on."

Amelia took a deep breath, prepared to argue further, when she realized she had nothing to add.

Mae was right. This would have happened eventually, winning lottery ticket or not.

Unfortunately, her final financial safety net, flimsy though it might have been, was now gone. Worse, she was pinning her hopes for the future on a man she wasn't sure she should trust.

For someone who had vowed she wouldn't let history repeat itself, this was beginning to seem far too familiar.

CHAPTER FOUR

HANK HAD LEARNED that Tuesday evening was usually the best time to find people at home. It took into account anyone who might have gone away for a long weekend or might have needed an extra day to recover from a busy one. It was usually too early in the week for people to host dinner parties or pay social calls. There were variables like soccer games, or shift work, and with kids home from school for the summer, there were unforeseen, random events like emergency visits to the hospital to get a broken bone set or a split lip stitched, but on average, Tuesdays were good.

He left his car near the corner of the street where the Goodfellows lived and began with the house at the end of the block. Despite the pleasant breeze that had come up as the sun lowered, the front window was shut tight. The flowers in the bed beneath it had gone brown and the lawn was in bad need of a haircut. Even from the sidewalk he could see a raft of advertising flyers sticking out of the mailbox beside the front door.

Tuesday or not, the owners likely were away, and judging by the condition of the flowers and the lawn, they'd probably been away for more than a week. Still, Hank believed in being thorough. That's why he was canvassing the neighbors even though Amelia said she already had. He knocked on the door, waited a full three minutes, then moved to the next house. This set of homeowners was in, but they told him they had been at their cottage all weekend, as their sunburns and mosquito bites attested.

He had no better results as he worked his way along one side of the street. It wasn't until he reached a tidy bungalow in the middle of the other side that his luck changed. No one answered his knock at the front door, but the front window was open and lace curtains stirred in the breeze. A minivan with a Ducks Unlimited bumper sticker was parked in the driveway. Hank stepped around a bed of petunias and followed the smell of burning charcoal to the back of the house. A white picket fence enclosed the rear yard. He stopped at the gate.

A stocky, middle-aged man stood in front of a round-bottomed barbecue where a row of hamburger patties sizzled on the grill. He had a beer bottle in one hand and a spatula in the other. Close to the house there was a picnic table on a patio made up of square paving stones. A teenage boy with earphone wires trailing past his neck drummed the edge of the table with his index fingers. Seated across from him, a woman with startlingly blond hair waved flies away from a stack of plates and a bowl of what appeared to be potato salad. She was the first to spot Hank. She raised her eyebrows. "Hello?"

Hank put on his most affable smile. "Sorry to disturb you folks."

The man turned toward him. His round face was bisected by a sharp-beaked nose. "Whatever it is, we don't want any."

"I'm not selling anything." He pulled the folder with his ID from his jeans and flipped it open. "My name's Hank Jones, and I'm hoping you could answer a few questions for me. It won't take long."

The boy stopped drumming and regarded Hank warily. He had a younger version of the man's round face and prominent nose. "Are you a cop?"

"Policeman, Jacob," the woman said softly. "Mind your manners."

The boy shrugged. "Yeah, whatever."

The man hooked the spatula on the barbecue. He started to lift his hand, as if to take a swig of his beer, but awkwardly halted the motion. "What's this about, officer?"

Something else Hank had learned, like finding people at home on Tuesdays, was that allowing people to believe he was connected to the law wasn't a good idea. For one thing, it was illegal. For another, it didn't necessarily lead to better results. A lot of individuals tended to watch their words more carefully than they normally would if they thought they were talking to the police. Above all, it was a lot simpler to tell the truth, because lies could get hard to keep track of. "I'm not a policeman, sir," he said. "I'm a private investigator."

"A private investigator," the woman repeated. She surreptitiously fluffed her hair. "How interesting. I've never met a private eye before, Mr. Jones."

He returned his ID to his pocket. "It's not anywhere near as exciting as on TV, ma'am. I'm just helping out the Goodfellows. Do you know them?"

"Not real well," the man said, apparently speaking for his wife. "I know them to see them. They're in the white house with the black shutters down the block."

"Yes, that's right. Were any of you here on Sunday morning?"

"Sure, we all were."

"Hey, is this about that painting?" the boy asked, pulling out his earphones.

Hank rested his forearms on top of the gate, striving for a relaxed pose despite his prickle of excitement. "Painting?"

"Some red-haired chick asked me about it Sunday night."

"Jacob…" the woman admonished.

"Lady. Whatever. She caught up to me in the driveway. She was from that house where they had the yard sale and wanted to know if I saw who bought some big painting."

"Wait a minute," the man said. "What were you doing in the driveway Sunday night? You're grounded, remember?"

"Uh…I was fixing my bike. The handlebars were loose."

"That's not what it sounded like. You said she 'caught up' to you. You went out, after we specifically told you to stay here, didn't you?"

"We didn't say he had to stay inside the house, Les."

"You're too soft, Ruth. I told you we shouldn't have trusted him."

"You could have gone to your Elks dinner alone. I wouldn't have minded."

"Maybe I should have. Next time I will."

"Um, guys?" The boy—Jacob—seemed more aware of their audience than his parents were. He jerked his head toward Hank. "Could we focus here?"

Les pointed his free hand at his son. "Don't talk to your mother like that."

"Sor-ry," Jacob drawled, rolling his eyes.

"Jacob!"

He ducked his head. "Sorry."

The conversational pattern seemed well established. Hank decided he'd better jump in before it deteriorated further. "You guessed right, son. I did want to ask you about the painting. It was sold by mistake at the Goodfellows' yard sale."

"Yeah, that's what the chi—uh, lady said. She wants it back."

The woman called Ruth tilted her head, appearing thoughtful. Instead of fluffing her hair this time, she twirled a lock around one finger. "Is it valuable?"

"To be honest, the frame is worth more than the canvas, ma'am," Hank said. "The painting only has sentimental value."

"Is that so?" The man lifted his beer and took a long swallow, his version of being thoughtful. "Seems to me, Mr. Jones, it's got to be worth something for them to hire a private eye to look for it."

"I can understand how you'd assume that, but I'm working on my own time." He'd told Amelia the same thing, and it was perfectly true. To be exact though, since he was self-employed, *all* the work he did was on his own time. "I'm helping out the Goodfellows as a favor," he added. "I'm an old friend of the family." Which was sort of the truth, too, since they'd been friendly enough to him fifteen years ago.

"So there's no reward?"

"I wish there was. It would make my job easier."

"I don't know. Seems a lot of trouble to go to for something that's not worth anything...." Les snapped his fingers. "The redhead who came around here must have been Goodfellow's sister, right? The one who stole all that money!"

Ruth responded first. "It was her husband who stole the money," she corrected.

"Same thing."

"It is not the same thing, Les. A wife isn't responsible for her husband's behavior."

"Sure, I'll remind you of that next time

I'm driving. I could do without the speedometer readings every ten seconds."

"Well, I feel sorry for her. That man ruined her life."

"Hardly. She let her husband take the blame and got off scot-free."

Hank cleared his throat. "Excuse me? I think something's burning."

Les glanced at the barbecue. Smoke billowed from the hamburger patties. He swore as he scraped them off the grill.

"I can see you folks are busy," Hank continued, "so I'll make this quick. Did any of you go to the Goodfellows' yard sale?"

Ruth seemed about to say something but as had happened before, it was Les who replied. "No way. We've got enough junk in our house as it is."

Hank kept his gaze on the woman as he drew a business card from his shirt pocket and held it out. "If you remember anything later, I'd appreciate it if you give me a call."

"Sorry, we can't help you," Les said. "Got better things to do than worry about that spoiled rich girl's painting. If you ask me, she shouldn't be showing her face in public anyway. It was because of her all those reporters camped out in front of her brother's place last year. It was a disgrace for the neighborhood, brought everyone's property values down. Next thing you know we'll have a Hells Angels clubhouse at the end of the block."

Hank concentrated on not crushing the card. It wouldn't do Amelia any good if he lost his temper. If this was a sample of the kind of attitude she had to contend with in her own neighborhood, it was little wonder she'd seemed so tense when he'd seen her.

Ruth got up from the table and came over to take the card. She hesitated momentarily, then unlatched the gate and stepped through. "I'll walk you out, Mr. Jones."

"Burgers are ready, Ruth," Les called.

"I'll be right back." She led Hank to the front of the house and stopped beside the bed of petunias. Her gaze darted to the neighboring houses. "I don't want you to get the wrong idea about my husband. He has a low blood sugar condition and isn't himself when he's hungry."

He suspected that apologizing for her husband was another well-established pattern of conversation for this woman. "No problem."

"And we all think the Goodfellows are decent people. We feel sorry for Will's sister. It's nice you're helping them out."

"I'm doing my best, but so far I haven't

had much luck." He lowered his voice confidentially. "They've had their share of troubles, and with Jenny expecting again, I'd hate to let the family down," he finished. Then he waited. He could tell she had something else to say.

"I didn't go to the Goodfellows' yard sale."

He nodded encouragingly.

She leaned closer and spoke in a rush. "But I happened to be weeding my flowers on Sunday morning while that sale was going on, and I remember seeing a man putting something flat in his car trunk."

All *right!* "Could it have been a painting?"

"Possibly. It looked like a big, folded blanket, but it could have been wrapping something. Now that I think about it, it must have been the painting."

"How large was it?"

She held her hands about a yard apart. "It was around this long, maybe bigger. I don't normally pay attention to what my neighbors do, of course, but I couldn't help noticing that."

"Because of the size of the bundle?"

"No, it was the car that caught my eye. It was bright yellow. I suppose you could call it canary yellow."

"Do you remember the make or model?"

"I wouldn't know the difference. It was old."

"Was it rusted? Patched? Dented?"

"Oh, no. I didn't mean old that way. I meant it must have been from the fifties. It was one of those big, bulky sedans, like the kind that used to be used for taxis."

That certainly narrowed things down. The lead might not pan out, but at least it gave him a starting point. Hank smiled. "Thank you, ma'am. You've been a lot of help. If you remember anything else, please give me a call."

She put her hand on his arm. "Well, actually, there is something else I noticed after lunch that same day, while I was trimming the hedge...."

HALF AN HOUR later, Hank was climbing the steps to the Goodfellows' house when he had a flash of déjà vu. The porch light was shaped like a lantern, a popular design, and the screen door was plain, white-enameled aluminum, variations of which he'd already seen in this neighborhood. The inside door was varnished wood and had been left open to allow the evening breeze to help cool the interior, which wasn't unusual since most people around here would prefer to save the cost of running an air conditioner and let nature do the work. Yet the feeling of familiarity he was experiencing didn't arise from what he saw, it came from what he felt.

He'd undergone the same swooping sensation in his stomach when he'd been a teenager and had called on Amelia at her parents' house. Their front door had been painted forest-green, and the screen door had been a relic from the sixties, decorated with the silhouette of a flamingo. Rather than a square, cement stoop like the one he stood on here, their house had had a veranda along the front that had been large enough for a swing. Their porch light had been a high-wattage bulb in a glass globe, which had illuminated that swing—and anyone on it—like a spotlight, much to the disappointment of a teenage boy hoping to steal a few extra good-night kisses.

That place had been several miles from here, on the east side of the Ganaraska River that bisected the town. The neighborhood was much older than this one and had developed naturally, with no subdivision master plan. As a result, modest clapboard houses like the one where Amelia's family had lived were mixed in haphazardly with stately, three-story, brick century homes like his father's. It had taken Hank less than ten minutes to walk to Amelia's. Sometimes he would take the junker he'd fixed up in shop class. Amelia had claimed she'd been able to hear it coming a block away, so she'd often be halfway down the walk by the time he'd pulled up. It wouldn't have occurred to her to hide her eagerness to see him any more than he would have tried to hide his own.

But that was then, and this was now. He took a few deep breaths to calm his pulse, then pressed the doorbell.

Chimes sounded inside the house, followed by high-pitched yapping and the scrabbling of nails on hardwood. A small black mop of a dog skidded to a halt at the screen door. Barred from going farther, it spun in place and yapped faster.

Amelia appeared behind it, carrying a toddler on one hip. The boy was dressed in short pajamas and clutched a tattered yellow rabbit. The dog immediately lost interest in Hank and jumped at the stuffed toy.

"Toto, cut that out!" Amelia ordered, swiveling to turn the boy and rabbit away from the dog. She unlatched the door and moved back so Hank could enter. "Hi," she said. "What are you doing here?"

Hank pulled the screen door shut behind

him, enjoying the picture she presented. Amelia wore cutoff jean shorts that showed off her legs and a flowered blouse that was similar to the one she'd worn to his office, only this one had a smear of what could have been spaghetti sauce on the collar. Most of her hair was caught back by a scrunchie into a stubby ponytail at the nape of her neck. She wore no makeup, so her freckles stood out vividly against her cheeks, like sprinkles of melted cinnamon on warm pudding.

She had always managed to look beautiful to him, regardless of the circumstances. It used to leave him tongue-tied, or wishing he was so he wouldn't embarrass himself by making clumsy compliments. Cinnamon? He tightened his lips.

She grasped his arm suddenly. "Did you find it?"

The touch set off another stomach swoop. He reminded himself that her eagerness wasn't for him, it was for the painting. "Sorry, no. I was in the neighborhood and thought I'd give you an update."

The dog backed up, took a running leap and latched on to the rabbit, yanking it out of the boy's grasp.

"Mine!" the child yelled. He squirmed violently until Amelia shifted him to her shoulder. He arched his back and screamed. "No! My bunny!"

"Is this a bad time?" Hank asked.

"No worse than usual." She led him the few steps to the living room. Toys were scattered on the floor. On a corner table sat a computer that appeared even older than his. Bulky, brown leather furniture huddled around an oval coffee table, which was covered with stacks of neatly folded children's clothes. A wicker basket with more laundry sat on the floor beside it. The Goodfellows weren't well-off, as Hank had already learned when he'd done the credit check for his father. Nothing appeared to be new here, but the mess was from disorder, not dirt. The sofa set looked comfortable, and the wooden pieces were skillfully crafted from solid oak. The overall effect was inviting and homey.

"Will and Jenny went to the movies so I'm in charge of the circus tonight." Amelia nodded Hank toward the couch as she jiggled the boy in her arms. "Have a seat and I'll be with you in two minutes. I just need to get Timmy settled."

The two minutes stretched into ten. Hank used the time to observe what was visible from the living room doorway. Like the other houses of the same design on the block, this one had a kitchen and bathroom to the left of the hall that ran through to the back door. The staircase Amelia had carried Timmy up was in the center. Hank deduced the older boys were playing video games in the basement, since he heard phrases of the distinctive music from Super Mario emanating from the depths of the house.

Hank turned his attention to the room to the right of the stairs, which had to be the one where Amelia was staying. Through the open door he saw a table with a sewing machine and shelves crammed with folded lengths of fabric and small, plastic storage containers. Beneath the window was a toy box shaped like a treasure chest that stood next to a pine futon with a blue-and-white striped cover. The walls were bare, apart from an empty picture hook and smudged arcs on the paint where the lower corners of the painting would have rested.

He tried to imagine Amelia living here. It was difficult. She'd moved in months ago, yet he could see no trace of her personality in this room. Everything appeared to belong to her sister-in-law or her nephews. This was the room of someone who was passing through, who was marking time, getting from one day to the next. The look was familiar to him, since he'd lived that way himself during the years that had followed Amelia's departure.

His gaze returned to the empty picture hook. He didn't want to feel sorry for her, because she would hate that, but how could he help it? This cramped room was a giant step down from the luxury condo in Toronto where she used to live. Not that he had any firsthand knowledge of it—he would be the last person Amelia would have invited to visit. He'd seen pictures of the outside of the building on a newscast last year. None of the camera crews had been allowed past the lobby, but from what the reporters had described, the square footage of her apartment had been greater than this entire house. Amelia would have had closets that were bigger than this bedroom. She wouldn't have had spaghetti stains on her collar or needed to contend with screaming toddlers or yapping mop-dogs. She would have worn designer outfits and gone to operas or art galleries or wherever it was rich people hung out in the city. That had been the life she'd chosen, after all.

And she hadn't lived that life alone. She'd had her husband, the man she had chosen over Hank.

"Sorry to keep you waiting. Timmy wanted another story."

Hank started at Amelia's voice. He hadn't heard her approach, likely because she was barefoot. She had loved going barefoot during the summer when they were kids. She used to be self-conscious about the size of her feet, but he'd thought they were perfect, long and slender, with a particularly ticklish spot in the center of the arch. He'd loved hearing her laugh....

Hank pushed his memories aside as Amelia returned to the living room. "It sounds as if you settled the dog down, too," he said.

"He sleeps at the top of the stairs whenever Timmy's up there. He thinks he's a guard dog." She cleared the stacks of laundry off the coffee table by putting them in the wicker basket. "The other two boys have popcorn so they should be good for a while."

"You've got your hands full."

"It's Jenny and Will who are the busy ones. I try to give them a break when I can. It's the least I can do."

He waited until she sat, then took the chair across from her. "When do you expect them back?"

"Not for another hour at least. Why?"

"I was canvassing the neighbors tonight

and hoped to talk to your brother and sister-in-law, too."

"It would probably be too late. They both get up early, and Jenny needs lots of rest these days. We'll have to do it another time."

"I can talk to them on my own."

"It's no trouble. I'd prefer to be present. That way you won't need to bother giving me updates." She gripped her knees and leaned forward. "Speaking of which, have you made any progress?"

"I do have a lead I'll be pursuing. One of your neighbors believes she might have seen the car of the person who bought the painting." He summarized what he'd learned from Ruth.

"That's great!"

"It gives me a place to begin, as long as she actually saw what she claimed she did."

"Oh, you can believe Ruth Talmidge. She's a sweet lady. I see her busy with her garden most nice days. She always waves hello."

"She did seem observant."

"Jacob was the only one I talked to at the Talmidges'. He'd promised to ask his mom but I guess it slipped his mind."

"He likely didn't want to get into trouble for leaving the house. He was supposed to be grounded."

"I'm glad you went back. It's a good thing you were thorough."

"I'd like to talk to your sister-in-law to confirm what Ruth told me. Describing a car that distinctive might help trigger Jenny's memory."

"Yes, it might. I'll ask her as soon as they get home."

"You said it would be late."

"Well, yes, but that wouldn't take long. I'll call you tomorrow if I learn anything, okay?"

That was the second time she'd put him off, as if she were reluctant to have him talk to her sister-in-law himself, but that made no sense. It was true that Jenny would indeed need a lot of rest in her condition, as Amelia had said. "Sure. I'll see what I can do about tracking down the owner of that car. Even if he didn't buy the painting, he did attend the sale. That alone could prove helpful."

"There couldn't be many canary-yellow classic cars from the fifties around. The problem is finding it."

"Depends where you look."

"Can you hack into the Ministry of Transport database?"

He shook his head. "Hacking the MOT would be illegal. Besides, I do have another approach I could take. I heard there was an antique car show at the fairgrounds on the weekend."

"Last weekend? That couldn't be a coincidence."

"Probably not. Collectors tend to baby their cars, so they don't use them for everyday errands. I'm guessing the owner of that yellow car your neighbor saw brought it out for the show."

"Then you can contact the group who organized the show!"

"That's the first step. Odds are good that the person we're after is a member, or that I'll find someone who knows him."

Amelia closed her eyes briefly. She exhaled on a sigh. "Hank, this is wonderful. Thank you so much for helping me."

"I haven't found anything yet, Amelia."

"I know, but at least you've given me hope."

Her anxiety over the painting appeared as genuine as it had when they'd met in his office. Now that he'd seen for himself how she'd been living, he could understand how she might be feeling emotionally raw. That made it more difficult for him to broach the next subject. "Do you believe that Ruth's observations are reliable?"

"For sure. And with all the gardening she does, she likely knows everything that goes on in the neighborhood."

"Then I hope you could explain something to me. She was certain she saw your family celebrating on Sunday afternoon."

"What?"

"She said you had just gotten home."

Amelia wiped her palms on her knees. "Sunday?"

"In the afternoon. Ruth saw you hugging Jenny and Will. She said the boys joined in, too."

"That was before I found out the painting was missing."

"What was going on?"

"Jenny made more than five hundred dollars at the yard sale."

"Was that what you were celebrating?"

"Five hundred dollars is a lot of money."

"From what Ruth described, you appeared very excited. I just wondered whether there was more to it. Was there?"

"Why would you ask that?"

"You seem nervous, and you're not looking at me."

She rubbed her knees once more, then folded her hands in her lap. "Money's a sensitive subject for me."

"Sorry."

"And I don't appreciate being given the third degree. If I had a dollar for every time people have given me attitude about the fortune I lost, I'd be halfway to getting it back by now."

"I wasn't giving you attitude, Amelia, or the third degree. I was just trying to make sense of what I heard. That's how I work."

"Well, what Ruth observed had nothing to do with the painting. It wasn't until we came inside that I saw it was gone."

"I see."

"Good. Then let's concentrate on that. What happens next?"

"Hmm?"

"Once you find out who owns that yellow car."

"Then I go and talk to him."

"In person?"

"That's right. I prefer to speak with people face-to-face whenever possible. It gets better results. It's too easy to say no over the phone."

"I'll come with you."

"Why?"

"I could help. He might be more willing to talk to a couple than to a man on his own."

"I do have some experience conducting interviews."

"Why wouldn't you want me along? We both want the same thing, don't we?"

Hank always worked alone. It was one of the aspects of his profession that he truly enjoyed. He had never allowed a client to interfere with his methods, much less accompany him on an investigation. "What about your own job at Mae B's?" he asked. "Won't you be too busy?"

"They let me go."

"What? When?"

"Yesterday. They gave my job to the owner's niece."

"Amelia, I'm sorry."

She shrugged. "I'll find something else, but at the moment I have plenty of spare time so there's no reason why I shouldn't help you. It's only fair, since you're waiving your fee. And besides…" She smiled. "It would be more efficient if we work together. You wouldn't need to waste time giving me updates."

Her smile set off another flash from the past. It was the first full smile Amelia had given him in more than a decade, and like everything else she did, she put herself into it one hundred percent. Eagerness shone from her face. Her lips curved, her cheeks dimpled and her eyes gleamed the familiar, unique blue-green that made his brain shut down.

He'd never had any defense against that smile. His reasons for refusing her seemed trivial when weighed against the prospect of spending more time in her company. Sure, he normally worked alone, yet he'd known this case would be anything but normal from the moment Amelia had shown up at his office. It wasn't merely curiosity that had convinced him to help her. He would have gone along with whatever she'd asked, regardless of how slim the chances of success, because his knee-jerk reaction had been to make her happy.

It still was.

Terrific. Obviously, nothing had truly changed in the past fifteen years. Amelia was still smart enough to talk circles around him. She still had the ability to wrap him around her little freckled finger.

And apparently, when it came to Amelia, Hank was still a fool.

CHAPTER FIVE

A ROW OF ragged spireas grew along the side of the garage and partially blocked the only window. Amelia lifted her arms to keep them from getting scratched, twisted around and used her back to push her way between the bushes. Once she reached the wall, she discovered that the window was coated with several years' worth of grime. She cleared a peephole with the heel of her hand and leaned close to the glass. Although there was an hour to go before sunset, an ominously dark bank of clouds towered in the west, bringing an early dusk. "I can't see anything, Hank," she said. She cupped her hands around her eyes. "It's too dim."

"Hang on." Branches rustled as Hank joined her. He took a handkerchief from the back pocket of his jeans and expanded the circle she'd cleaned, then clicked on a small flashlight and angled it against the window. The narrow beam slanted through the shadows inside the garage to reveal a dull, flat expanse of pale blue fabric.

"That doesn't look like a car," she said.

Hank passed her the handkerchief, waited while she wiped off her palm, then folded the cloth dirty-side-in and returned it to his pocket. He continued his inspection of the garage. "It's a tarp. There's a car underneath."

She squinted. He was right. The fabric was draped over a large, bulky shape that could only be a car. "That's got to be it."

Hank continued to play his light over the tarp until he reached the lower edge. There was a sudden glint from a chrome bumper and the gleam of a highly polished fender. A yellow fender. "It's the right color, and the shape does correspond to a fifty-seven Chevy. Whether it's the right car remains to be seen."

She knew that Hank was cautious by nature—after all, what other man his age would carry a clean handkerchief in his jeans?—so she tried to contain her impatience. He must know what he was doing. He had been right about the car jogging her sister-in-law's memory. As soon as Amelia had described what Ruth had observed, Jenny had remembered how the man who had bought the painting had wrapped it in a quilt he'd had in his car trunk. She hadn't noticed what model of car it had been, since she'd had to deal with other customers at the same time, but she did remember glimpsing bright yellow.

Amelia had relayed the information to Hank immediately, but it had taken him two days to get a response from someone at the car club who had organized the show last weekend, and another two days to learn which members had a fondness for canary-yellow paint. Of the six who owned cars of the right era that came close to the right color, three lived out west and two were in Quebec. Only one, Kemp Forsythe, whose spirea bushes they were currently standing in, lived within an hour's drive of Port Hope.

"It's the car, Hank."

"Possibly."

Still don't like to make a commitment, do you? she thought. She swatted at a mosquito that hummed near her ear and turned to study Kemp Forsythe's house. According to Hank's research, the man owned a small computer repair business in town, and had lived at this address for twelve years. No one had answered the door when they'd arrived, and the windows were still dark, despite the rapidly deepening dusk. The ranch-style, brick bungalow appeared to be around thirty years old and was set well back from the road. A cornfield stretched out behind it and at least two acres of yellowed grass plus an apple orchard separated it from the nearest neighbor. The road itself was a winding, pot-holed length of tarred gravel that branched off a county road twenty kilometers north of the highway.

Hank had driven most of the way under the speed limit. Part of the reason for that might have been due to his choice of vehicle. For a man whose father owned a car dealer-ship, he drove a remarkably *un*remarkable sedan. It was sensible, gray and at least six years old. She likely could have coaxed more speed out of Will's old Chevette.

"We'll give him another half hour," Hank said. "If he doesn't show up, we'll come back tomorrow or next week. Tuesday evenings are usually good for finding people at home."

"Come back? No way. My painting's here. It has to be. We can't leave."

"Seeing how it's Saturday, we could have a long wait." Lightning flickered through the clouds, followed by a rolling grumble of thunder. Hank reached past her to push aside the branches that blocked her path. "Storm's going to break soon. We can't stay out here."

There wasn't much space between the bushes and the garage wall. His chest nudged her shoulder, his arm slid against hers, and instantly, warmth tingled across her skin.

The memory of another summer evening stole into her mind, when Hank had driven her to the lakeshore in the old jalopy he'd been so proud of. They'd left their shoes in the car and had gone to the water's edge to watch a storm roll in. The breeze had been heavy with the smell of seaweed, wet sand and impending rain. The air had crackled, both from the storm and from their own sense of something about to happen. Their typical teenaged garb of shorts and T-shirts had turned every casual touch into the delicious feel of skin against skin. That had been the night their friendship had entered new territory, one they'd both been enthusiastic to explore. They'd begun the journey by sharing their first kiss....

Hank eased farther to the side, breaking the contact.

More thunder, louder than before. Amelia could sense electricity in the air now, too. She exhaled slowly and maneuvered out of the spireas. She brushed herself off more briskly than necessary. It didn't work. The memories clung like static-charged lint. "We could try phoning him."

"Do you have somewhere else you need to be?"

"No, of course not. Finding the painting is my number one priority."

"Do you have an issue with the way I work?"

"No."

"But?"

She crossed her arms. "But I'm not good at waiting."

"Wow, really? You? Never would have guessed." He looked pointedly at her right hand.

She was tapping her fingers against her upper arm. She slid her hands into the pockets of her shorts. "We know where he works. We could have talked to him there."

"Sure, but if he's got the painting, it's more likely to be in his house. If he agrees to sell it back to you, we don't want to give him any opportunity to change his mind."

"*If* he agrees?"

"Another reason to speak with him in person. It's too easy to say no over the phone."

"Okay, you told me that before, and I understand your reasoning, but—"

"Relax, Amelia. There could be plenty of simple explanations why he's not here yet. He could have a date. He might have decided to work overtime, or he might have had a flat tire on the way home. Or he could have bitten down on a walnut shell in a muffin at lunch and needed emergency dental surgery."

Yes, there were lots of possible reasons why Forsythe wasn't home, more than fifty-two million of them. He could have found the ticket. He could already have gone to the lottery office to cash it in. He might have been burning rubber down Highway 401 to Toronto while Hank had been poking his way along the back roads as if he had all the time in the world.

Lightning forked over the line of trees beyond the cornfield. The crash that followed was loud enough to make her jump.

"We'd better get in the car," Hank said.

She resumed her study of the house. They had only knocked at the door—they hadn't tried the knob. They hadn't tried the windows, either. One of them might be unlocked. The orchard blocked the view of the neighbors, and the approaching storm was making it darker by the second.

"Don't even think it, Amelia."

"What?"

"We're not breaking in."

"It wouldn't hurt to take a closer look. We might be able to spot the painting through a window."

"And then what? We still need to wait for Forsythe. I said I would help you, but that doesn't extend to committing a crime." Fat droplets splatted in warning as the wind kicked up dust and bits of dried grass around them. He grasped her arm and turned her toward the driveway. "Come on. It's starting to rain."

Would he consider breaking in if he knew about the ticket? Would he be tempted to compromise his principles for fifty-two million dollars?

Knowing Hank, she doubted he would. The boy she remembered wouldn't have taken a risk like that. Neither would the hankie-carrying, slow-driving man he'd become. If she wanted to search the house for the painting, she would have to come back on her own.

They returned to Hank's car. Within minutes, the downpour was pelting the roof and streaming over the windows in silver sheets. The dampness made Amelia shiver. She pulled her heels onto her seat and wrapped her arms around her legs.

This was how that memorable evening by the lakeshore had gone, too. They'd been half-soaked by the time they'd reached Hank's car. They hadn't cared. They'd shivered together, keeping each other warm, laughing at the fogged-up windows and secretly wishing the storm would never end.

"You cold?" Hank asked, raising his voice over the drumming rain.

"I'm fine."

He reached into the backseat and retrieved a denim jacket. "Here. Use this."

"No, I'm okay."

He draped the jacket over her knees like a blanket and tucked it behind her shoulders. "It's all part of the service."

She breathed shallowly for a while, trying to ignore the scent that clung to the denim collar. It was no use. Even after more than a decade, she recognized the smell of Hank's skin, in particular the scent of his jaw and the back of his neck. It was pure…Hank, untinged by anything other than a trace of Irish Spring soap, which had been his favorite brand in the old days, too. He hadn't used any styling products in his hair—he wouldn't have thought of it—and he'd seldom used aftershave, on those occasions when he'd actually needed to shave. She couldn't detect any now, either.

Spencer had been the opposite. He'd been meticulous about getting his short hair trimmed every two weeks and wouldn't step out the door without inspecting his reflection in the mirror at least three times. He'd used a sandalwood-scented balm to minimize the irritation from his razor, since he'd shaved twice a day. He'd had a heavy beard, and had been concerned he would appear slightly piratical when his five-o'clock shadow set in. She'd thought his concern was groundless, because Spencer had been the picture of buttoned-down fastidiousness, and trustworthiness, and honesty.

She'd truly been an idiot.

"If you're still cold, I can run the heater awhile."

"No, thanks, really, I'm fine." She paused, then added, "As long as you don't count being stuck in a thunderstorm in the middle of nowhere while we wait for some computer geek to finish gallivanting around town."

"In my business, you get used to it."

She thumped the back of her head against the headrest a few times. "It's going to be a week tomorrow since I lost that painting."

"I'm doing all I can, Amelia."

"I realize that, Hank, and I appreciate your efforts. I'm just…"

"Not good at waiting."

"Me? Really?"

He chuckled. The car seat creaked as he shifted his weight to lean his shoulder against the door. He rested one elbow on the steering wheel. "This case is progressing pretty well, considering what we started with. We've made more headway than I thought we would."

"That's encouraging. I think."

"It is."

"I hope this isn't taking too much time away from your other cases."

"I can manage."

She held on to the edges of his jacket to keep it in place and turned her head toward him. Though the shadows hid his expression, his body language appeared relaxed. The Hank she used to know had been unflappable. She couldn't recall seeing him panicked over anything. That hadn't meant he didn't have feelings. He did, only he kept his deep inside. "I hope this isn't cutting into your social life, either," she said.

"Don't worry about that."

"I mean, it is Saturday night."

"I'm not seeing anyone, Amelia, if that's what you were getting at."

It was, but she'd really had no business asking. "I suppose your profession means you need to work odd hours."

"From time to time. Most of the stuff I do is pretty routine."

"Can you give me an example? Or is that privileged?"

"Not as long as I don't name names. Last week I got some video to prove a guy was faking a bad back. Week before that, I tracked down a woman whose brother needed her signature so he could close the sale on their family farm." He lifted his palm. "Port Hope isn't exactly a hotbed of intrigue."

"I heard you work for your father sometimes."

"Will told you about that loan, did he?"

"Yes, but he understands." It was only half a lie, since Will did grasp the reasons he'd been turned down. He just wasn't very understanding. She rested her chin on her knees. The jacket collar tickled her cheek. "What made you decide to go into detective work? I don't remember you mentioning it when we were kids."

"I kind of fell into it, I guess. I got started

by helping my father do credit checks. The business grew from there."

"Then you two must be getting along better these days."

He hesitated. "We do okay."

His tone had tightened, and she could tell there was a wealth of words left unspoken. "Does he still live in the same house?" she asked.

"Yeah. It's too big for one man, but he likes the space."

"You don't live with him anymore?"

"No, I have a place of my own. That's why we get along better."

Though she was tempted to pursue this, it would be wiser to leave the subject alone. Hank had been close to his father when he'd been very young—he'd often shared fond stories of things they'd done together during his early years. Their relationship had become strained when his mother had been diagnosed with cancer. After her death, Basil Jones had dedicated most of his time and energy to his business. He had worked hard to maintain a loyal customer base in the area, and he'd had a ready smile and a friendly handshake or slap on the back for everyone, yet he'd been distant and critical with his only son. Amelia hadn't witnessed any arguments—that hadn't been their style. They'd had a lot of silences instead. They'd shared a roof, but not much else. Hank had made sure to earn whatever he'd been given. The old car he'd driven around had been a good example. He'd preferred to rebuild a junker rather than get a vehicle from the family car lot at cost. Judging by the nondescript sedan they were currently sitting in, he still didn't take favors from his dad. Will had to be wrong about Hank's business being propped up by his father.

Amelia had often been troubled by the ongoing tension in the Jones house, since her own family had been so different. They had been too passionate to tolerate silences. They'd had their spats, but like any storm, the arguments usually blew over as quickly as they arose. There hadn't been any doubt about the love that lay beneath everything they said and did. Her parents had extended their warmth toward Hank, too. Her mother had felt sorry for the skinny, motherless boy, and had enjoyed pushing her homemade carrot cookies and granola bars at him every chance she got. Even Will had been friendly toward him, once he had gotten over his protective-big-brother glowering.

"I'm sorry about your mom and dad," Hank said.

The change of topic took her off guard. Then again, it wasn't that unexpected. His thoughts had likely paralleled hers, leading from his father to her family. She pulled his jacket more tightly around her legs. "Thanks."

"I was in Fort McMurray. By the time I heard about the accident, the funeral was already over. I'm sorry," he repeated. "I would have liked to have gone to it. They were good people."

She focused on the water that ran down the windshield. This was another subject she should leave alone. Although she and Hank had broken up several months before the car accident that had abruptly ended her parents' lives, she'd been hurt by his absence, which was crazy, because she'd already begun seeing Spencer. It was Spencer who had driven her home from the University of Toronto and stayed beside her during the service, had squeezed her hand at the twin graves, and slipped his arm around her waist to steady her steps on the snow-covered path as he'd led her back to his car. She'd still been angry at Hank, and wasn't sure she would have spoken to him if he'd been there, yet his presence would have helped ease the pain. Maybe if he'd been there, she wouldn't have been such a vulnerable, gullible fool over Spencer.

But it wouldn't be reasonable to blame Hank for not attending the funeral. After their breakup, he'd left town within weeks of her own departure, heading to Alberta to work on the oil sands. One local tragedy on an icy road wouldn't have made the news half a continent away. "It was a shock to everyone."

"I phoned the house, but you'd already gone back to Toronto."

"I didn't know you had phoned."

"Will answered."

She could imagine the conversation. It wouldn't have been a pleasant one. "You could have called my apartment. One of my roommates would have passed on your message."

"Will wouldn't give me your number."

No, he wouldn't have. He would have thought he was protecting her.

"Would you have talked to me if he had?"

She shrugged. "We'll never know, will we?"

"Well, I'm still sorry."

Lightning flashed through the darkness.

Thunder followed immediately, loud enough to shake the car and jolt Amelia's pulse. An afterimage of the lightning seared her retinas. She blinked at a sudden rush of tears. "Why did you go out west, Hank?"

"I got a job there."

"You could have had a job with your father."

"It wouldn't have paid as much."

"So it was only about a job, not about getting as far away from me as you could?"

He hesitated. "It was a good job. I earned a good wage."

"What did you need it for? It's not as if you spent it on clothes or cars or going on dates since you'd just dumped your girlfriend."

"I never dumped you, Amelia."

Had she thought the hurt was buried? The humiliation was over? Hank's patently false claim brought back the whole painful event as if it had happened yesterday. "Excuse me? What would you call it when a boy breaks up with a girl the day before she leaves for university?"

"I thought it was for the best."

"For you, sure. You strung me along all through high school, but as soon as I wanted more you backed off. You thought once I was gone, I'd be out of sight, out of mind."

"It wasn't like that."

"Oh, right. I remember now. You called it 'setting me free.' That's what you said. Of all the cheesy lines. That's as bad as when you're trying to get off the phone and you tell the other person, 'I should let you go,' as if you're doing them a favor when the truth is you want to watch the hockey game or make a sandwich or are just bored with the conversation. You dumped me, Hank."

"I'm not good with words. Not like you."

"You were that time. I got the message loud and clear."

"And I got yours. Especially the loud part."

"After the way you treated me, what did you expect?"

"You got over it fast. You sure found a replacement boyfriend in a hurry. What was it, three weeks? Two?"

"It was longer than that, but what would you care?"

"You said you loved me, Amelia."

"It wasn't love, Hank. It was teenage hormones and proximity."

"Sure, I realize that now, but for a while I'd sure thought it was love."

"It was a mistake. It ruined a perfectly good friendship."

"You got that right. Time proved that we wouldn't have suited each other, anyway."

"No, we wouldn't. We're too different. You're too...careful."

"You're too reckless."

"And you're afraid to take chances."

"I took a big one when I let you go. Look how well that worked out."

"Why are you doing this? Are you trying to rewrite history so you don't come off as the bad guy? You dumped me, plain and simple."

"Simple?" He leaned over and grasped her cheeks between his hands. "Nothing about you is simple, Amelia."

The sensation of his touch on her face scattered her thoughts. His palms were smooth and warm. His grip hummed with restrained strength. These weren't the hands of a boy; they were the large, capable hands of a man. He skimmed the ridges of her cheekbones with his thumbs. The caress wasn't hard but it wasn't tentative, either. It was...just right.

This was pleasure, not love. She was old enough to recognize the difference. But oh, it felt wonderful. She allowed herself to enjoy it for a guilty, crazy few heartbeats, then caught his wrists. "This isn't a good idea."

"I know."

"Hank…"

"Hey, I never pretended to be smart, especially where you're concerned." He leaned closer and eased his hands into her hair. Though his touch was gentle, a tremor went through his fingers. That held her in place more effectively than force.

More lightning flared beyond the windshield, painting harsh shadows in the angles of his face, making her more aware than ever of the changes time had brought. She could push him away if she wanted, but instead she curled her fingers around his forearms. His mouth was inches from hers. She felt his breath puff across her lips and she remembered that other storm, and the boy's kisses, and she wondered how a kiss from the grown-up Hank would feel.…

A car horn sounded behind them. It hadn't been lightning that had illuminated his face, it had been headlights.

She took longer than she would have liked to process what the headlights meant. She released his arms. "It must be Forsythe. He's home!"

Hank didn't move. "We need to finish this conversation."

"Not now."

"Amelia…"

"We've said more than enough already."

The headlights swerved as the approaching car pulled alongside them. The horn tooted again.

Hank drew back to his side of the car. He rubbed his face and muttered a short, pithy oath.

Amelia dragged his denim jacket off her legs and shoved it into his lap. She reached for the door handle.

He flung his arm in front of her. "Wait!"

She pressed back into the seat to avoid his touch. "We have to talk to him."

"Sure, but—"

"Hank, stop. This isn't the time or the place for a personal discussion. I shouldn't have dredged up the past. It's over and done and there's no going back. The only thing that matters is my painting. That's the reason we're here, remember? It's my top priority. It's the only reason I came to you. What I *need* is for you to stick to business."

"Yeah, but you're also going to need this." He completed his motion by leaning over her. His chest nudged her shoulder, his arm brushed her knees, and she was once again enveloped by his warmth. The sensations lasted only an instant before she realized he hadn't been reaching for her, he'd been reaching for the door. He pulled something from a recess beneath the handle and placed it in her hands. It was a collapsible umbrella.

Amelia swallowed, her throat tight. Of course, a man who carried a handkerchief would also be organized enough to have an umbrella. "Thanks."

"No problem." He opened his door, swung his jacket over his head and stepped into the rain. "It's all part of the service."

THE INSIDE OF the brick bungalow was what Hank would describe as a work in progress. Plastic drop sheets covered the living room floor and draped the furniture. Paint cans and a stepladder formed a crooked pyramid in the center of a rough archway that had been ripped through one wall. Except for scattered smears of white plastering compound, the other three walls were completely bare.

He glanced into the shadowed room past the archway. Lightning flickered through a set of patio doors, revealing more plastic sheets covering the floor and a bulky dining table and chairs. Nothing hung on what he could see of the walls there, either.

"You'll have to excuse the mess. I'm renovating the place." Kemp Forsythe peeled off his wet windbreaker and tossed it over a wooden coat tree beside the front door. He used the tail of his shirt to dry his glasses, then fitted them back on his nose and finger-combed his salt-and-pepper hair from his broad forehead. A thin beard skimmed down his cheeks and outlined his prominent jaw like a helmet strap. He appeared to be in his mid-forties, although he projected the energy of a much younger man. "This'll be one big room when I'm done."

"You'll have a great view of the countryside," Amelia said, turning in a circle while doing her own scan for the painting. "It won't matter where you sit."

"Exactly!" Forsythe beamed at her. His reaction to Amelia was another factor that made him appear younger than his years. He regarded her as if he'd never had a woman in his house. Maybe he hadn't. Hank suspected if he'd come to interview Forsythe without Amelia, he wouldn't have been invited inside as readily.

Amelia could have that effect on an otherwise rational man, make him do things that weren't all that sensible. Act like a fool who was starved for female companionship, regardless of the consequences.

"You folks want coffee or something?" Forsythe asked, his gaze still on Amelia. "I've got plenty of Coke, too. The real kind, not that diet, decaffeinated stuff. I mean, what's the point in drinking it if it doesn't kick back?"

"No, thanks, Mr. Forsythe," Hank said. "We wouldn't want to take up your time. I just wanted to ask you a few questions."

"Sure, sure. And it's Kemp. You're the first private eye I've ever met. Didn't know we had any around here. And you said you tracked me down through my car?"

"That's right."

"Incredible. Right out of a TV show. Come on back to the kitchen," he said, leading the way past the redecorating debris to a horseshoe-shaped alcove filled with kitchen appliances. He stopped at a counter that appeared to serve as his table and pulled out a stool for Amelia. "Have a seat. Don't worry about dripping on it. I covered the cushions with vinyl and put two coats of Urethane on the wood. This is some rain, isn't it? My uncle says the corn needs it. Good thing they already got the wheat in, or the rain might have flattened it. That happened two summers ago, left most of it in the mud." He opened the refrigerator, made a happy exclamation and hauled out a slender blue-and-white can. He popped the top and took a long swig. "I forgot I still had some Red Bull. There's plenty if either of you want one?"

Amelia smiled as she declined, giving the kitchen a careful perusal. The only thing on the walls here was a calendar from a John Deere dealer. She hooked her feet on the lowest rung of the stool. Her heels bounced up and down. "All the redecorating you do must be a lot of work."

"I don't mind. It's my hobby. Along with my car. I like fixing up old things. You should have seen this place when I bought it. What a wreck. People think a brick house doesn't need maintenance but there's the roof and the window frames, just to mention the obvious." He took another drink of the super-caffeinated soda, suppressed a burp, and used the can to gesture at Hank. "So, what's this about? Did someone see my car? Was I supposed to be a witness or something? I had it out last weekend for the show in Port Hope, but I don't remember seeing an accident or anything."

Hank hitched himself onto the stool beside Amelia's. "Actually, Kemp, we're hoping you could help Miss Goodfellow out. Her sister-in-law had a yard sale last weekend."

"*Miss* Goodfellow?" Kemp asked quickly. She smiled again. "Amelia."

"What a beautiful name. Like Amelia Earhart. My cousin's got a Cessna and sometimes he takes me up. He keeps it in the hay field back of the pig shed and he needs to cut a runway first if the hay's high. They baled at the start of June, so it's growing in again."

In the old days, if Hank and Amelia had encountered a character like Kemp, they would have shared a private smile over his pinball-style conversation. Or more likely, they would have avoided making eye contact with each other so they wouldn't laugh out loud. Hank found nothing amusing about the situation now, though. Judging by the continued nervous bouncing of her feet, neither did Amelia. She hadn't met his gaze since they'd left the car, so they wouldn't be sharing a smile or anything else.

It was just as well. Otherwise, he might get confused again about why they were together. "About that yard sale," Hank said, nudging the conversation back on track.

"I stopped at a yard sale while I was in town. It wasn't far from the high school.

House was a story and a half, white clapboard with black shutters. Looked as if some work was being done on it. I saw a pile of drywall in the garage. Pregnant woman in front of the house."

Amelia's heels slid off the stool and thumped to the floor. "Yes! That was my sister-in-law. You definitely *were* there."

"I didn't see you. I would have remembered if I had."

"I was at work."

"I used to open the shop on Sundays, but hardly anyone came in, so now I don't bother. It's just not worth it. I might around Christmastime when people are more inclined to open their wallets. Too bad you had to work on such a nice day. I hope this rain stops before tomorrow. One summer it rained every weekend and was sunny all week. That's enough to drive a working man nuts."

"Kemp?" Amelia's voice shook. "Did you buy a painting at that yard sale?"

"You mean that sappy landscape of the farm?"

"Yes!" She got to her feet. "Yes, that's the one!"

"No offense, but the artist wasn't much good. I liked the frame more than the painting. That frame alone was worth the thirty bucks I paid, since I planned to fix it up and use it on something else."

Amelia paled. "Did you take the painting out of the frame?"

"No, too busy. How did you know I bought it?" He snapped his fingers. "The car, right? Someone remembered my car. It was this washed-out shade of blue when I got it and you could see brushstrokes in the paint. Can you believe it? Using a brush to paint a car? Takes all kinds. It took me weeks to sand it down. I considered tangerine for a while but I settled on yellow."

"It's a great color," Hank said. "They made cars roomy back then, too. Must have been easy getting the painting in the trunk. Was it hard to get it in the house?"

"You kidding? I'm used to hauling lumber. The big stuff I bring in through the patio doors. I knew a guy built a rowboat in his basement one time but had to take it apart to get it out."

Amelia took three steps toward Kemp. Her hands twitched as if she wanted to shake him. "The painting you bought was sold by mistake. I would like to buy it back from you."

"Sorry, no can do."

"Please." She caught his sleeve. "You said you paid thirty. I'll give you fifty."

"Wish I could help you, but like I just said, I was too busy to fix up that frame. Once I got it home I could see it would have taken way too much work, so I got rid of it."

Amelia let go of Kemp and pressed her hand to her stomach. She looked sick. "You got rid of it? How?"

"I gave it to my aunt."

"You gave it to your aunt," Amelia repeated, her voice rising.

"What's your aunt's name, Kemp?" Hank asked. "We'd like to talk to her."

"Oh, she'd get a kick out of this story. She used to be a huge fan of *Magnum P.I.* She keeps saying how it was far better than the new cop show that's shot in Hawaii. Both her husbands had a mustache like Tom Selleck's. She'll be disappointed with your car, though. Ever thought of getting a red one?"

"Her name, Kemp?" Hank prodded.

"Hazel Blight. Blight's her second husband. She used to be a McClelland. Her first husband sold drilling rigs, traveled all over the world, built a snug little house near Coderington for when he retired but then they put the hydro lines through. Ended up with a tower right behind his back door that wrecked his view. I think the disappointment's what killed him."

Coderington was a dot on the map about thirty minutes farther east of here. "Does she still live in the same place?" Hank asked.

"No, her second husband runs a dairy operation on the Trent. He was a bachelor until she married him, never threw anything out. Talk about junk! The old farmhouse was packed to the attic and the barns hardly had room for the cows. There must have been four generations' worth of furniture and tools. Aunt Hazel's been cleaning off the good pieces and carting truckloads to the big flea market near Barrie every weekend for years and still hasn't hit bottom. That's why I gave her the painting, so she could add it to her booth. She knows about antiques and stuff like that, figured she'd get at least twice what I paid for it…" He broke off as Amelia stumbled backward to her stool. "Hey, sorry."

Hank stifled the urge to hug her. He squeezed her shoulder instead. "We'll drive up there first thing tomorrow."

Amelia nodded tightly. Her jaw flexed as if she were grinding her teeth.

"Good luck," Kemp said. "You never know, maybe the painting hasn't sold yet. It *was* pretty bad, no offense."

CHAPTER SIX

THE 400 MARKET got its name from the route number of the six-lane highway that went past it, which was the main thoroughfare running north from Toronto. Commuter traffic from the surrounding communities funneled through the road on weekdays, and at peak times on summer weekends city dwellers escaping north to their cottages in the Muskokas made the route resemble a slow-moving parking lot. Due in large part to its advantageous location, the flea market had undergone three expansions during its nearly forty years in business and now boasted over five hundred vendors inside its large indoor facility, plus more outside during the warmer months. Of the thousands of shoppers who went through it each weekend, only half came from the immediate area. Tourists, cottagers, passing truckers, families on their way to visit relatives...everyone loved hunting for bargains.

But Amelia was in no mood to appreciate the atmosphere or the merchandise. She wove her way through the slow-moving browsers, past racks of postcards, T-shirts and purses, glass cases crammed with sausages and beer nuts, shelves of potted plants and silk flowers, her attention fixed on the carved oak china cabinet she glimpsed near the end of the aisle.

Kemp had provided detailed directions to Hazel Blight's booth. He'd given them his aunt's cell phone number, too, but every call Hank had made yesterday evening had gone straight to voice mail. The same thing had happened during the drive here this morning. Of course, Hank's standard-model sedan wasn't equipped with options like Bluetooth or hands-free calling, so he had pulled over to the side of the road and stopped each time he'd used his phone. That, coupled with his careful driving, had pushed their arrival to well past noon.

She had restrained her urge to complain. After their blowup at Kemp's, she was grateful he was still helping her. But that was Hank. Even as a teenager he'd been responsible. Solid. Dependable. Until the time he had rejected her love and broken her heart…

No, she had to stop thinking about that.

The past didn't matter. Only the painting, and the future it would give her.

"That must be her in the green shirt," Hank said. He had no trouble keeping up with her pace. He moved so smoothly he didn't seem to be hurrying at all.

Amelia detoured around a couple pushing twins in a double baby stroller and spotted the woman Hank must have meant. She wore black jeans and a moss-green sweatshirt with a screened print of a loon on the front. Her salt-and-pepper hair had more salt than Kemp's, and she was several inches shorter than him, but there was a strong family resemblance in the broad forehead and lantern jaw. She and a thirtysomething, deeply tanned woman in white Bermuda shorts were standing beside a battered, galvanized-steel milk can.

"You don't see many of these cans anymore," the older woman was saying. "My husband's family used them back before the dairy started sending around the milk tanker, so it's a real collector's item."

"It's lovely, but I'm not sure what I'd do with it."

"I had an interior decorator come by here a few weeks ago. She was looking for a milk can just like this one to use for holding branches or flowers or some such. That's why I brought it in."

"Yes, I can see how that would work."

"She called it a focal point. Gives a room that professional touch."

"I'm still not sure. It seems a bit too rustic."

"I also have some earthenware crocks that might interest you. The interior glaze is a lovely chocolate-brown and the outside is a neutral tan, which would go with any decorating scheme."

Amelia tuned out the sales pitch and scanned the three-sided booth. Maximum use had been made of the limited space. The oak china cabinet that had drawn her attention initially, itself for sale, was packed with an assortment of teacups and glassware. A vintage quilt was displayed over a ladder-back chair. Antique tools and kitchen gadgets crowded a multitiered table in the center, while an assortment of old feed signs and sepia-tinted photographs hung from the dividing walls. The variety of items did appear to be a sampling of someone's barn and farmhouse attic, as Kemp had said.

She couldn't see her painting.

Maybe Hazel had changed her mind about

selling it, or had forgotten to bring it. Maybe this was the wrong booth.

"Mrs. Blight?" Hank asked.

The customer in the white shorts was moving away, cradling an earthenware crock in her arms. The woman with the loon sweatshirt zipped a pink fifty into a pouch at her waist and nodded to Hank. "That's me. What can I do for you?"

He introduced himself and Amelia. Hazel's eyebrows shot up when she learned of Hank's profession. She scrutinized his face, but if she was hoping for any resemblance between him and her TV hero, she kept it to herself. Hank got straight down to business. "We were talking to your nephew, Kemp. He said he gave you a painting last week?"

"Yes, that would be the Mathers."

Mathers? That must have been the scrawled signature that Amelia had never been able to decipher. "Was it an oil painting of a farm?" she asked.

"Yes, the scene featured a farmhouse and weathered barns on a hill."

That confirmed it. Hazel had the painting. Amelia's chest went tight. She clenched her hands to control their sudden trembling... and to stop herself from tearing apart Hazel's booth to find where she'd stashed it.

"I also have some excellent sepia portraits. They're real collector's items."

"We're more interested in the painting," Hank said.

"That surprises me. Jonathan Mathers isn't all that popular."

"You've heard of him?"

"I've run across a few of his canvases over the years, mostly at church rummage sales. He wasn't a real artist—he was a doctor in Brighton maybe fifty years ago or so. He painted rural scenes as a hobby and gave them as presents to his relatives. That's why the paintings show up at rummage sales. No one wants to keep them." She gestured toward a brass-framed, oval mirror that leaned against the rear wall. "Now that mirror is a true gem. It's been in my husband's family for several generations and would add flair to any room."

Amelia recognized the same kind of redirect that had been used on the previous customer. She cleared her throat. Even so, her voice sounded raspy. "Mrs. Blight, where is the Mathers painting?"

"It used to be right there," she said, tipping her head toward an empty space on the back wall. "I sold it first thing this morning."

"You *sold* it? You had no right! It was mine."

Hazel took a step back. "Excuse me?"

Hank laid a restraining hand on Amelia's arm. "There was a mix-up at a yard sale last weekend, Mrs. Blight. Your nephew bought the painting by mistake. I explained it to him. Didn't he call you?"

"He might have tried. My phone battery ran down, and I didn't bring my charger. I assure you, if there was any wrongdoing here, it was unintentional. I believed I had every right to sell that painting."

"We don't blame you, ma'am, but would you happen to remember anything about the customer who bought it?"

"I certainly do. He came around here last year, as well. I'm pretty sure it was in August then, too. He bought two small watercolor still lifes that time."

"Would you know how we could get in touch with him?" Hank asked.

Hazel patted the pockets of her jeans. "Let me see. I seem to remember he might have given me his business card. He said he's always in the market for interesting pieces by Ontario artists."

"We'd be grateful for any help you could give us, ma'am."

She bent down to retrieve a small strong-box from beneath the table, unlocked it and thumbed through the papers inside. They appeared to be receipts. "The card must be in here someplace." She gave them a sideways glance. "While I'm busy, why don't you two take another look at that mirror?"

Amelia tapped her foot. "We're really not interested in—"

"Sure, we are," Hank said immediately. He squeezed Amelia's arm in warning. "Weren't you telling me that Jenny had wanted to fix up a mirror for the back room?"

"It's a bargain at one-thirty," Hazel said, making a show of continuing to rifle through the strongbox. "But I'd be willing to let you have it for an even hundred."

"That's a fair price." Hank pulled his wallet from his pocket and counted out five twenties. "A hundred it is."

As soon as Hazel took the money, she handed him a small white card. "Because you seem like a nice young couple, I'm letting you know that my customer only paid seventy-five dollars for the Mathers. So be careful." She smiled as she zipped Hank's hundred into her belt pouch. "I wouldn't want you folks to get gouged."

THE TYPICAL SUMMER Sunday evening traffic jam on the highway had begun a few hours early. Another severe weather front was predicted to pass through during the evening, causing many cottagers to get a head start back to the city. Hank kept to the slow lane, as usual, but under these conditions it didn't make much difference. All the southbound lanes were snaking along well under the 100-kilometer limit.

"They need to widen this highway," Amelia said.

"The gallery doesn't close until five. We'll get there." He turned on the radio. A perky country song warbled from the speakers. "Why don't you relax and listen to the music?"

Relax? He had to be kidding. Amelia tapped the card Hazel had given them against her leg. It was no do-it-yourself card from a laser printer. The lettering was embossed, and the design was elegant and tasteful, no doubt the product of a professional. According to this, her multimillion-dollar ticket and the painting were now in the possession of Rupert Whitcombe, proprietor of the Whitcombe Gallery, which was located on Yonge Street in downtown Toronto. Business hours were noon to 9:00 p.m., Tuesdays to Fridays, and 11:00 a.m. to 5:00 p.m. on weekends. It appeared that Whitcombe's clientele didn't get up early or go shopping on Mondays.

During the early days of their marriage, she and Spencer had occasionally visited art dealers together as he built his collection, but she wasn't familiar with Whitcombe. On the other hand, there were plenty of dealers in the city she hadn't met, since she'd stopped accompanying her husband on those excursions after a few years. Besides not sharing his interest, she just hadn't found the time. She'd been too busy building their business to bother with peripherals, like the toys and perks their growing wealth could buy. She'd encouraged Spencer to go out alone. Trusting, gullible idiot that she was, it hadn't occurred to her to question what he did when she wasn't watching.

She flicked the card with her index finger. "This doesn't make sense. Rupert Whitcombe is a professional art dealer. Why would he scrounge around a flea market for a seventy-five-dollar painting?"

"For the same reason he would acquire any painting—to make a profit."

"Usually galleries don't pay an artist until

the work sells. They make their money from the commission they charge."

"I guess Whitcombe is confident he can find a buyer."

"From what Hazel said, Mathers wasn't good, and his work isn't in demand. If there was any chance of that painting being valuable, she wouldn't have parted with it so quickly."

"You've got that right. She's a pretty savvy businesswoman."

That was true. Hazel certainly had been slick about getting paid for her information. She'd gotten rid of the painting at the first opportunity, too. There was one positive aspect to the fast turnover, though. It meant she would have had less time to stumble on the ticket.

That might not be the case with Whitcombe. An art dealer would be inclined to inspect his new acquisition more closely than someone buying the painting on a whim at a yard sale, or someone accustomed to dealing with the contents of a hoarder's attics and barns. And when he did inspect it, Whitcombe was bound to notice the scrap of folded paper that was wedged underneath the frame.

Amelia glanced at her wrist, then gritted

her teeth at the reflex that she couldn't seem to shake. She looked at the clock on the car radio. "It's almost three. The gallery won't be open tomorrow. Can't you go any faster?"

Hank looked at her. "Tell that to the guys ahead of me."

"Maybe we should try phoning again. Whitcombe might be there by now."

"Chances are he's not going to put the painting up for sale right away."

"We can't be sure of that."

"We don't want to tip him off how important it is to you, either, or he'll jack up the price."

Amelia chewed her lip. He had a point. Until she got the painting back, her resources were limited. "Hank, please. I hate just sitting here."

He flicked on his turn signal.

"No, don't pull over! I'll call myself."

"I'm not pulling over, I'm taking a shortcut." He steered onto an exit ramp that led to a two-lane county road running perpendicular to the highway. When he had merged into the eastbound traffic, he took his phone from his shirt pocket and passed it to her. "Here."

She immediately dialed the number on the card. The woman who answered told her the same thing she'd told Hank earlier. The gallery owner was out of town on business but was expected back soon. She politely turned down Amelia's request for Whitcombe's cell number, recited their business hours and ended the conversation.

Amelia put the phone in the empty cupholder between the seats, crossed her arms and thumped her head against the headrest.

"No luck, huh?"

"No."

"Feel better?"

"Marginally. Thanks for humoring me, Hank."

"No problem."

Amelia focused on the countryside that paraded past. It didn't seem as green here as it did around Port Hope. Mats of yellowed grass spiked by chicory and tufts of goldenrod choked the ditches, and rusty wire fences bordered the fields. Clusters of houses dotted the hillsides wherever the land was too steep to plow. There was a steady stream of vehicles heading east, but it was moving more quickly than the traffic they'd just left. "And thanks for getting off the highway," she added.

"I prefer country roads anyway."

Of course, he would. "I'll pay you back."

"Mmm?"

"The hundred bucks you gave to Hazel."

"Forget it. It's all part of the service."

"Hank, you said you'd donate your time, but that bribe was a direct expense. I'll reimburse you for that, as well as for the gas you're using."

"This car doesn't burn much gas. Sometimes I go more than a week without needing to fill up, so it would be hard to keep track of how much I'm using on this case."

"Don't you normally keep a mileage log when you're working on a case?"

He shrugged. "I'm not officially working. Besides, the hundred wasn't a bribe, it was the cost of a true gem of a mirror, a real collector's item."

She glanced behind her. Hank's trunk had been full of fishing gear, so he'd put the mirror on its side and leaned it against the backseat. Seeing it in full daylight hadn't made it look any better. The silver backing was worn off in blotchy streaks, and fly specks dotted the glass. "Don't expect me to believe you actually wanted that thing."

"Tell you what. Give the mirror to Jenny for her next yard sale. You can give me whatever she gets for it."

"No, I'll pay you what you spent."

"You don't have to, Amelia."

"I insist."

"I told you that tracking down your painting was my gift to you. I haven't changed my mind."

"Thank you, but I don't want to take advantage of you. I'd like to keep our relationship as businesslike as possible."

"Why? Because of what happened yesterday while we were waiting for Kemp?"

They'd avoided the topic all day, but that didn't mean it hadn't been there, under the surface. She should have known it would pop up eventually. "Are you referring to our argument or to the almost-kiss?"

"Both."

"Well, both were mistakes," she said. "I thought we had that straight."

"So did I."

"Then why did you try to kiss me?"

"Good question. Would you have let me if Kemp hadn't shown up when he did?"

"Maybe. I don't know. We had stirred up the past. I was confused."

"Yeah, I guess that's what happened with me, too. The storm and all. Sort of got me thinking about the first time we kissed."

"Same here."

"But you're not confused now?"

The song currently playing on the radio

was a rousing, foot-stomping bar song. It wasn't the least bit romantic. Neither was the hot glare of sunshine that bounced off the car hood or the monotonous drone of the engine. The circumstances weren't tugging loose any memories of their past encounters. Nevertheless, she was maddeningly aware of how close Hank sat, of how his scent drifted through the car, and how his short-sleeved golf shirt clung to the curve of his biceps and his large hands held the wheel as confidently as he'd cradled her face.

No, she wasn't confused. She knew perfectly well that he was an attractive man, as any female would attest, whatever her age happened to be. That wasn't the issue. It also wasn't relevant. "No, Hank," she replied. "I know exactly what I want."

"Your painting."

"Yes. That's all I can focus on."

"I'm not expecting anything in return, Amelia."

"What do you mean?"

"There are no strings to this gift."

"Maybe not for you, but I don't want to feel as if I owe you," she said. "I'm already in debt to too many people."

"Still sensitive about the subject of money, huh?"

"Yes, that tends to happen when you lose everything you own, on top of losing the life savings of people you promised to help."

He eased his foot off the accelerator as they came up behind an RV that was towing a boat trailer. "What happened with your company was a tough break, Amelia, but it wasn't your fault."

"Yes, it was. I should have seen what Spencer was doing. I was inexcusably naive to have trusted him."

"Hindsight's twenty-twenty."

"Hindsight sucks."

"Sometimes it does, but you have to stop blaming yourself over what he did. If the cops and their forensic accountants couldn't recover the money, you can't expect to have been able to yourself."

She glanced at him. "It sounds as if you kept track of the story."

He lifted one hand from the wheel briefly. "Some. Enough to say again that it wasn't your fault."

"Thanks, but—"

"No, Amelia. We can't predict what someone else will do, even people we think we love."

Was he referring to her marriage, or to their own failed romance?

There was really no comparison. Hank's betrayal had hurt, yet that pain had been private. Spencer's betrayal had been viewed by millions when some enterprising bystander at Pearson Airport had captured his arrest on her cell phone. The footage had played over and over, first on the internet and then on TV. After all, it had everything guaranteed to up the ratings: crime, violence and sex.

Amelia hadn't been blind only to her husband's embezzlement of their clients' funds. She'd also been blind to his unfaithfulness. He'd been attempting to leave the country with his mistress when the police had moved in. He'd resisted arrest and been wrestled to the floor in front of the gate while his blonde trophy bimbo had defended her man by jumping on one officer's back and swatting him with her purse. It had made for great television. Once the footage had done the rounds of the news shows, it had found new life on the late-night comedy programs.

She ought to be grateful to the bimbo. She might not have been able to prove her innocence otherwise. As her lawyer had argued in court, since Amelia had been oblivious enough not to realize her husband was having an affair, it stood to reason that she had been equally oblivious to the fact he was bilking their clients.

The stupidity defense. The judge had believed it. Lucky her.

Yet for one precious hour a week ago, she had believed her luck had changed. It had felt incredible, like stepping outside and taking a deep breath of fresh air after being locked in a prison cell. The past had lost its grip and she would be able to start anew, atone for her mistakes, take care of her family, have a clean slate and a future....

She rubbed her eyes. "I have to get that painting."

"There's a good chance we will now, Amelia. We know who bought it, and we know where it's going."

"As long as we get to the gallery before it's sold again." *Or before Rupert Whitcombe stumbles on the lottery ticket.* She dropped her hands as she felt the car decelerate. They were traveling more slowly now than they had been on the highway. She glared at the back end of the ski boat on the trailer in front of them. It was a large, fiberglass number with two huge black outboard motors clamped to the stern. The blades of both propellers turned lazily in the wind, as if mocking them. "Can't you pass him?"

"That RV plus the trailer takes up the space of about four regular cars, and I can't see far enough ahead here. Besides, it's a double line." As he spoke, a van pulled out from behind them and sped by on their left. Tires squealed as it cut directly in front of them just as a dump truck rumbled past in the oncoming lane. Hank tapped the brakes, backing off farther. "It's only a few more kilometers before we turn south anyway. Hopefully he'll keep going straight."

Amelia turned her glare on him. "Let me drive. I'll get us past him."

"No."

"Hank…"

"I realize the painting is important to you, Amelia. I get that. But whatever it symbolizes, it *is* just a painting. It's not worth taking dumb risks for."

"Sure, but—"

"It's not going to change your life by itself. You're the only one who can do that."

"Since when did you get so philosophical?"

"Just being realistic. Chasing the painting is the same thing as you wanting to phone the gallery a few minutes ago. It's not practical but it makes you feel as if you're getting somewhere."

"Isn't that the whole point?"

"Sometimes patience can pay off."

"Not in my experience."

"All I'm saying is there's no shortcut to the future. You've got to get there one step at a time."

"Fine, Mr. Socrates, but where does it say those steps have to be a slow walk? I'd rather sprint."

"Yeah, that's you, all right."

"I told you we're different."

He made a noise similar to one of Will's grunts. "Have you given any thought to what you'll do once you get the painting back?"

Oh, yes, she'd thought about it. Every night for a week, she'd dreamed of little else. New cars and a new house, an education fund for the boys, a vacation cruise and spiffy wardrobes for Will and Jenny plus a generous reward for Hank...all of that wouldn't put much of a dent in fifty-two million. She would have plenty left to establish a trust fund for her former clients. It wouldn't make up for what they lost, but it would be a good start. "Some," she said.

"You might need something to tide you over since you lost your job at Mae B's."

"Are you offering me a loan?"

"If you need it, sure. I have a lot of contacts in town, too. I could ask around and see who's hiring."

So much for feeling free and breathing fresh air. Guilt rolled over her in a choking, sticky haze. The pit she'd dug for herself when she'd lied to Hank just kept getting deeper. She sighed and nibbled the inside of her lip.

The truth was going to come out as soon as they reached the Whitcombe Gallery and she retrieved the ticket. Giving Hank a reward wouldn't stop him from being furious when he learned how she'd deceived him. He would also be hurt. Is that how she wanted to repay him for his help? Regardless of the pain he'd caused her when they'd been teenagers, he'd proven through his actions during this past week that he'd grown up to become a sensitive, decent and considerate man. The more time they spent together, the more she had to admit that he truly was nothing like Spencer.

He patted her knee. "Don't go getting all sensitive about the money again, okay? I just want to help."

His touch made her jerk.

He sighed and withdrew his hand. "Don't get all sensitive about that, either. It was just a friendly pat."

Tell him! her conscience screamed.

But tell him what? That she'd lied to him and was using him?

Or should she tell him that she was still attracted to him and wished Kemp had arrived home a little bit later yesterday so she wouldn't have to keep wondering how the grown-up Hank kissed?

Or maybe she should simply tell him the whole truth, that she was a complete mess and didn't trust herself to decide anything.

He took his gaze off the road to look at her.

And because he was looking at her, he didn't immediately notice when the van that had cut in front of him pulled out to pass the RV with the boat trailer.

A horn blared. Brakes screeched. Amelia shouted a warning.

Hank whipped his gaze back to the road just as the van met a pickup in the oncoming lane.

CHAPTER SEVEN

IF THE TRAFFIC had been moving only a fraction faster, the outcome would have been tragic. As it was, both drivers had a chance to avert a head-on collision. The front bumper of the oncoming pickup truck merely clipped the back end of the van. Nevertheless, the strength of the impact was enough to spin the van onto the opposite shoulder. The pickup careened off the side of the RV and sent the oversize vehicle into a twisting skid that jackknifed the boat trailer.

Hank instinctively hauled the wheel to the right and steered for the ditch to avoid being caught in the accident. A thudding crash sounded from the road behind them, along with more screeching tires. Momentum carried his car down the grassy embankment and up the other side until the front right fender crumpled against a fence post.

It was more of a hard bump than a crash, but it was enough to shatter a headlight and set off the airbags. The force of the plastic hitting his face stunned him. He shook it off and clawed the deflating bags aside, his thoughts only on his passenger. "Amelia!"

The car was tilted up on her side. She was held in place by the seat belt, her head lolling. She wasn't moving. His heart stopped for an instant, but then she turned her head and looked at him, her eyes wide with shock, her breathing fast and shallow. "Hank?"

The engine had cut out at the impact, but the radio was still on, the announcer droning a news report. Hank shut it off and pulled the key out of the ignition, then unlocked his seat belt and twisted toward her. He kept one foot against his door to maintain his balance. "Are you okay?"

"I'm fine."

He ran his hands over her arms, her shoulders, everywhere he could reach. "Do you hurt anywhere?"

"No." She blinked hard. As soon as she focused on him, her breathing steadied. "Hank, you're bleeding!"

"I'm all right."

"No, you're not! You're bleeding!" She braced her feet against the console between the seats and stretched her arm to touch the corner of his lips.

He tasted blood. He probed his mouth

with his tongue and realized the tip stung. He swallowed, then kissed her fingers. "It's nothing. I must have bitten my tongue when the airbag hit me. Which is better than tripping over it, like I usually do. My tongue, I mean, not the airbag."

She made a noise that was closer to a sob than to a laugh. Her eyes filled with tears. "If you can joke, you must be okay." She stroked his hair from his forehead, then glanced past him. She gasped.

Hank followed her gaze.

The RV had come to a stop crosswise to the road, blocking the traffic in both directions. Glass and scraps of metal littered the pavement. People had gotten out of their cars and were already converging on the accident scene. The driver's door of the van that had caused the accident hung open and a dazed-looking woman was being helped outside. A cut on her forehead was her only visible injury. Beside the pickup truck, a thin blond man, likely the driver, sat on the pavement holding his wrist to his chest. An elderly couple leaned against the RV, their expressions bewildered as they surveyed the destruction behind them. The trailer they had been towing was empty—the boat had been knocked loose and had crashed to the pavement.

It was precisely where Hank's car would have been if he hadn't taken the ditch.

Amelia pulled the handle on her door. It was jammed shut by the fence and didn't budge. Hank tried his own door. The lower edge hit the ground before the door could open completely, leaving just enough space for him to squeeze through. He reached back for Amelia. At the motion, pain bloomed in his left shoulder. He rotated it cautiously, decided it was merely bruised, and helped Amelia slide out of the car and get to her feet.

A plump woman wearing a Jays baseball cap jogged along the edge of the road toward them. She shouted as she drew near to ask if they needed help. When she saw they didn't, she spoke into the cell phone she was holding and continued past them to the couple beside the RV.

With so many people milling around the road, Hank decided it would be best to remain out of the way until the authorities arrived. He leaned against the trunk of his car and curled his arm around Amelia's waist. He could feel her trembling. Or was that him? She pressed her head to his shoulder.

It was his unbruised one, but even if it had been the other, he wouldn't have cared. Right now, he needed the contact. He didn't want to lose her. Sure, he'd lost her once before, but not…forever.

Something shifted inside him at the thought, like a lens finally adjusting to the right focus. No, he didn't want to lose her again. He shouldn't have let her go fifteen years ago. If he hadn't, maybe she wouldn't have married Spencer. Then she wouldn't have had her life stolen from under her, and she wouldn't have been so emotionally strung out that she'd become obsessed with a meaningless painting.

He rubbed his cheek against her hair, immersing himself in sensations he'd never thought he would feel again, but had always hoped he would. There was no point deluding himself any longer. He'd never gotten over Amelia. Otherwise, he wouldn't have taken on this ridiculous case.

If that made him a fool, well, so be it. There were too many things he should have told her years ago, more he wanted to say now…but even he wasn't idiotic enough to confess his feelings while they leaned against a wrecked car in the middle of a ditch.

Yet even if they'd been surrounded by soft music and candlelight, that wouldn't have helped. It didn't take a genius to see that Amelia was still healing from the scars Spencer had left her with. Her determination to pursue the painting made that obvious. Declaring his feelings might make Hank feel better, but it wouldn't make her happy. She might not believe him, anyway, and he couldn't blame her, considering the mess he'd made of it the last time. Right now, there was only one thing she wanted from him, which she'd made abundantly clear. "I'm sorry," he said.

"Why? Hank, look at that boat. Your driving saved our lives."

"I mean I'm sorry this had to happen. We'll need a tow truck to get the car back on the road. It could be a while."

A siren wailed in the distance. She shuddered. "At least we don't need an ambulance. No one else seems badly hurt, either. I can't believe how fast it all happened."

"The damage doesn't seem that serious, but if my car's out of commission, my insurance will pay for a rental."

"It could have been a lot worse. We were lucky." She turned her head to look at the car. "Oh, no!"

He followed her gaze. Through the rear windshield he saw the mirror Hazel had sold them was no longer leaning on the backseat. The brass frame was intact, but the rest was in jagged pieces.

"I didn't think my luck could get worse, but that's another seven years..." Amelia's words trailed off. She inhaled sharply. "Hank, my painting!" She pulled out of his embrace. "The gallery!"

"We'll go tomorrow."

"We can't! The gallery's not open tomorrow." She put her palms on the car, as if she meant to push it back on the road herself. "We have to go now. We have to get there before it closes!"

"That's what I'm apologizing about. Doesn't look as if we'll make it there today."

"You lied to me."

"No, I never lied. I just didn't tell you everything."

"Why? Did you think it didn't concern me? I had a right to know."

"I'm sorry, I never meant to hurt your feelings."

"What did you think I would feel when I found out? Gratitude? For being deceived?"

The words were mere whispers, scarcely

loud enough to wake her. Amelia opened her eyes groggily. Dawn was inching into the corners of the room. The tops of the maples in the backyard glowed golden in the rising sun. It couldn't be morning already, could it? She felt as if she'd just gotten to sleep. She must be dreaming the conversation. She'd imagined plenty of variations of it while she'd lain awake last night.

"Please, don't get upset. I had hoped it would have only been for a few days, a week at the most. I hadn't wanted to tell you until it was over."

"I thought we were a team."

"We are. I love you. I worry about you. I didn't want you to be stressed out."

"And I'm not stressed now?"

Amelia blinked. This wasn't how her imagined conversations had gone, because the issue of love hadn't come up in those. She forced herself fully awake. The whispers weren't inside her head. They were coming from the other side of the door.

"Carolyn had no reason to email you about the layoffs. My job is none of her business."

"Carolyn's my friend and was concerned. I'm glad that she told me because apparently, you don't believe your job is any of *my* business, either."

"Don't say that, Jenny. You're everything to me."

"You made a fool out of me, Wilbur."

"Baby—"

"Don't you 'baby' me. Summer hours, my foot. Lancaster Cabinets never did that before. I should have known it was a crock. A charade. A *lie*. But like a fool I kept packing your lunch every morning. I should have realized why you hadn't been finishing it. You hadn't done anything to work up an appetite."

"Sweetheart—"

"How long have you been laid off? Tell me the truth."

"Since the end of June."

"That's six weeks!"

"They said we should be called back to work any day now."

"Fine. Until they do call you back, *you* can do *my* job. I'm going out."

"Jenny…"

Footsteps retreated down the hall. Moments later, the back door slammed. The noise woke Timmy, who wailed crankily for his mother. Will's footsteps pounded up the stairs.

Amelia wouldn't have intentionally eavesdropped, but there was little privacy in a house as small as this one. She lay motionless as she sorted through what she'd overheard. The mere fact that Will and Jenny had been arguing was difficult to absorb. She'd never seen them argue before. They seemed like the perfect couple, functioning as true partners in all aspects of their lives. Their love for each other and for their children was obvious. It surrounded them like a warm, fuzzy aura.

Then again, even people who loved each other argued. Her parents used to from time to time. Their arguments had tended to be loud, though, and frequently had involved breaking crockery.

The floor overhead creaked. Timmy's complaining tapered off at the sound of Will's voice. There was a sudden thud, which she recognized as Eric jumping down from his bunk bed. Owen's taunts echoed from the stairwell as he raced his brother downstairs to the bathroom. The older boy won, as he did most mornings. Eric pounded on the bathroom door while his brother laughed. Toto's nails scrabbled on the stairs as the dog added his barking to Eric's complaints. The daily circus was beginning, whether Jenny was here or not.

Amelia rolled off the futon and reached

for her clothes. At the movement, pain shot through her right shoulder and down her chest. She took shallow breaths until it receded, then carefully pulled off her nightgown. A bruise in the shape of a seat belt angled across her skin. The discolored area had enlarged overnight as the line of purple had gone blue along the edges. At least the swelling had subsided. She'd been lucky to get away with such a minor injury. It could have been much, much worse.

Hank had been wonderful. His sensible driving had likely saved their lives. He couldn't have understood her desperation to reach the Whitcombe Gallery, yet he'd remained patient and calm and solid as a rock throughout the accident's aftermath. His car hadn't been fit to drive—the engine was fine, but the collision with the fence had jammed one of the front wheels against the wheel well so it couldn't be steered. He'd talked the owner of the garage where it had been towed into renting him another car, but it had been well after five by then. He'd driven her home, walked her to the door and instructed Will and Jenny to keep an eye on her overnight, just in case she suffered any aftereffects.

Amelia yanked on her clothes and tugged

a brush through her hair, despite the pangs the motions sent through her shoulder. She would have liked to blame her insomnia of the previous night on the physical effects of the accident, but she'd known her conscience had been the cause. She'd come close, oh, so close, to telling Hank the truth about the ticket, but in the end she'd chickened out. It hadn't seemed like the right time. They'd just been in an accident. He had enough to deal with. He'd claimed he wasn't hurt, but she'd noticed the stiffness in his movements, so he was probably as bruised as she was. And he'd been so kind, so considerate, she couldn't bring herself to disillusion him. She couldn't think of any way to tell him without hurting him.

If that seemed like some heavy-duty rationalizing, it was. She'd thought of plenty of excuses why she should remain silent. Number one on the list was the possibility Hank would quit before she actually recovered the ticket. He'd left her high and dry once before, hadn't he? All right, that relationship had been personal rather than professional, but she couldn't risk having him dump her again. Too much was riding on this. Regardless of how her conscience twanged, she couldn't reveal the truth until it was over.

No wonder her brother had reacted so gleefully to the news that she'd won the lottery. His need for money was more urgent than she could have imagined.

There. Another excellent excuse.

Without Jenny's stabilizing presence, breakfast was an ordeal. Will put up a good front as he doled out cereal and juice for the boys, and Amelia helped as much as she could, but the children sensed there was trouble. Neither Owen nor Eric seemed comfortable with their father's claim that their mom had simply gone for a walk. The older boys were quarrelsome, and slunk off to the backyard to work on their fort. Timmy was too fussy to finish his breakfast. Even Toto was subdued, snuffling disconsolately as he licked spilled cereal from the kitchen floor.

Amelia cleared the dishes from the table and set them beside the sink. The dishwasher had gone on the blink three weeks ago. She understood now why Will had put off getting it repaired. "Want to talk about it?"

Will shook his head. "It's Jenny I need to talk to."

She stepped to the kitchen doorway so she could see into the living room. Timmy was sulkily building a lopsided tower of blocks on the coffee table. "Just so you know, Will," she said, speaking quietly so there was no chance of the child overhearing, "I heard your argument through the door this morning."

He grimaced. "Then you know I was laid off last month?"

"Uh-huh. And you pretended to go to work each day."

He fitted the plug into the sink, added a squirt of dish detergent and turned on the taps. "I know it's lame, but I didn't want Jenny to worry. It's not good for the baby or for her."

"You wanted to protect her."

"That's right, only she doesn't see it that way." He watched the sink fill. Morning stubble bristled as he flexed his jaw. "I never meant to hurt her. I hadn't meant to make her feel like she didn't count. She's the glue that holds this family together. I love her more with every year—" His voice cracked. "I hope she's okay. She sure was mad when she left."

Amelia rubbed his back. "Jenny loves you, too. And she wouldn't do anything that would endanger the baby, no matter how mad she was. She'll cool down."

"I bet she went to Carolyn's. That woman's a busybody. Ever since her divorce her favorite pastime has been man-bashing."

"Well, a divorce does tend to leave a person cautious."

"Now I've hurt your feelings, too. I didn't mean to."

"You didn't, I'm not that fragile. And we're not talking about me here. If Jenny did go to her man-bashing friend's place, then at least she'll be able to blow off some steam."

"Yeah."

"But from what I know of my sister-in-law, she's more likely to be lighting into Carolyn for stirring up trouble than to be criticizing you."

That brought the hint of a smile from Will.

"I wish I could help," Amelia said. "Do you want me to call her for you?"

"Not yet. Let her punish me a while longer. I deserve it." He transferred the pile of dishes to the sink. Cutlery clattered against the stainless steel. He plunged his hands into the suds. "I knew she'd find out the truth eventually. Too bad it had to be like this."

Amelia's conscience stirred, but she batted it back down. "You had your reasons for what you did."

"Yeah. It's just that once I started to lie, I couldn't see how to stop."

"Believe me, I understand that all too well."

"I see how you would. Does Hank know about the ticket yet?"

"No."

"You still don't trust him."

"I can't afford to, but that doesn't mean I feel good about deceiving him. Actually, I'm feeling worse about it every day." She took a tea towel that had been hanging from the stove handle and lifted a bowl from the dish rack. "But as I said before, this isn't about me. Jenny thinks the world of you. You two will get past this."

"I hope so. She got really anxious when I was laid off the last time, and I didn't want to put her through it again."

"It wasn't your fault if the factory didn't have enough orders. Times are tough everywhere."

"Tell me about it. I wasn't pretending to go to work. I *was* working a lot of those days, only not where Jenny thought. I delivered telephone books for a while. I cut grass down at the fairgrounds once. Last week I skimmed algae clumps off the water around the yacht club. Yup, I worked with pond scum. Talk about low! But money's money."

"Why didn't you tell Jenny about that?"

"It would have worried her, too. She would have known as well as I did that my unemployment insurance checks and a few part-time stints wouldn't be enough money to support the family indefinitely. And the only reason I got those jobs was because I knew the guys who were hiring."

"At least Jenny's medical bills won't be an issue."

"Yeah. Good thing the government covers health care whether I have a job or not. That's one thing I don't mind paying taxes for." He took a deep breath and blew it out in a man-sized sigh. "Anyway, we'll ride it out. I've put in job applications everywhere. If the factory doesn't call us back, something else is bound to turn up."

"I'm sorry that I've added to your burden, Will. You didn't need another mouth to feed."

"Forget it. You've bought more groceries for us than you've eaten, and don't think I didn't notice how you had your meals at Mae B's whenever you could. And that's not even counting the help you gave us with the furnace when you moved in."

"I should have found a place of my own

weeks ago. At the very least I should have insisted on paying you rent."

"If you paid rent, then we'd have to pay you for all the housework and babysitting you've done. Believe me, we're getting the better end of that deal. The word's gone out about those two mechanics and the rug rat, not to mention the dog. The last teenager we talked into watching them wanted hazard pay."

"I love my nephews. I wouldn't take a cent for spending time with them."

"And I wouldn't take a cent for giving my little sister a roof."

"But, Will," she began.

"No buts." He rinsed off the last cereal bowl, dried his hands on the towel she held and crossed his arms. His chin angled forward in what she recognized as his stubborn pose. "I know you don't like when I bring this up, but that doesn't mean I've forgotten. It's because of you that we have a roof in the first place. By rights you should have taken half the money from the sale of Mom and Dad's house. Their will split everything fifty-fifty between us."

He was right. She didn't like to talk about that period of her life—it had been too painful. But this was the second time in two days she was recalling it. "This issue was settled ages ago. My scholarship covered my tuition and my living expenses. You needed the money more. You and Jenny had just bought this place. It made economic sense to decrease your liabilities by paying down your mortgage. You got to use what you earned instead of making the bank rich on interest."

"Absolutely, it did make a lot of sense. That was the best financial advice I ever got. It's because of you that we could manage on one salary and Jenny could stay home and raise the boys. The way I see it, this house is half yours."

"No. Will—"

"We're family, Amelia. You have a place with us for as long as you need it, so that's the end of the discussion."

His generosity humbled her. Now, more than ever, she had to get that ticket back. It would solve not only her own problems, but her family's.

There's no shortcut to the future.

Hank's words from yesterday drifted through her mind. His approach to driving might have proved to be right, but when

it came to the future he was dead wrong.
Fifty-two million dollars would pave quite
a shortcut.

CHAPTER EIGHT

THE WHITCOMBE GALLERY was in the center of a three-story commercial building with yellow stucco walls and oversize, round windows on the ground floor. More round windows dotted the upper stories in a random pattern. It was probably supposed to be sophisticated, cutting-edge architecture, but it reminded Hank of a road sign that had been used for target practice.

He drove past slowly while he searched for a parking spot. The location was a good distance from the office towers that clustered in the downtown core, but apparently the site was close enough to a subway stop for a developer to consider it worthwhile to invest in a high-rise condominium complex. The billboard across the road pictured a soaring structure with lots of blue glass and balconies, although nothing was visible beyond the boards that had been set up along the sidewalk except the top of a construction crane.

Unfortunately, because of the construction, there were no vacant parking spaces along the street. The parking garage Hank found two blocks away was almost full—he had to wind his way to the fifth level before he found an empty spot. As soon as he'd eased the rented car into the space, Amelia picked up her purse and grabbed the handle of her door.

"Hold on a sec, will you?" Hank asked. He pulled a coiled tie from the pocket of his sport coat, flipped up his shirt collar and looped the tie around his neck.

"What's that for?"

"Credibility, seeing as how we're planning on buying some art. Whitcombe's not running any flea market."

"You look fine already."

He couldn't tell whether she meant it or whether she was being polite. He peered into the mirror on the visor as he fumbled with the knot of his tie. He'd taken extra pains with his appearance this morning, since the rumpled shirt-and-jeans look wasn't the best way to impress a woman who used to run a multimillion-dollar business. And yes, that's what he was trying to do. He wanted to impress Amelia more than he wanted to appear solvent for some gallery owner. At least he was being honest with himself and could admit it now—that was one thing the accident had been good for. He cleared his throat. "Thanks. You look terrific, by the way."

That was an understatement if there ever was one. Like him, she had opted for less casual clothes today. City clothes. Her suit was made out of soft, cream-colored fabric that must have been custom tailored to fit her figure. She wore it over a shiny, scoop-necked blouse that was a shade of rich brown. The combination somehow subdued her red hair into the auburn she liked to claim it was.

She seemed surprised by his compliment. She brushed at a wrinkle in her skirt, then set her purse primly on her lap. The purse was another item he hadn't seen before. It matched her shoes, which were strappy, tan leather and had heels at least three inches high. They made her legs look shapelier than usual, if that was possible. "Thank you," she said.

"Is that outfit from before?"

She thought it over a beat, but she must have known what he meant. "Good guess. I didn't get rid of my entire wardrobe when I moved in with Will and Jenny. I put a few of my favorite outfits in a Rubbermaid tub and stored it in the attic."

"You look classy. Like one of those fancy pastries with whipped cream and chocolate in the middle."

"Uh, thank you again."

"How does it feel?"

"What?" She smiled. "To be dressed like a chocolate éclair?"

He extended his tongue between his teeth and pretended to bite down on it a few times. "Yup. Still tripping over it. I meant how does it feel to be back in the city?"

Her smile faded. "I'm not sure. I hadn't thought about it."

"You lived in Toronto for close to fifteen years. Don't you miss it?"

"I miss some things."

"Like going to ritzy restaurants and concerts?"

"Not really. Going out was nice, but I doubt if I'll ever be completely comfortable in a restaurant again. Not unless I give the waitstaff huge tips."

"So what are the things that you do miss?"

"My job mostly."

"This might be a dumb question, but what exactly does a financial advisor do?"

"Essentially, I helped people make the

most of their money. To do that, I got to know each individual client so I could devise an investment plan that suited their income and their needs. That's one part of the job I really enjoyed. I liked the challenge of trying to outguess the market, too."

"You were always good at math. You must have been a wiz at investing."

"Sure, I made oodles of money for my clients. All the more for Spencer to steal." She tapped her fingers on her purse, then twisted to reach for his tie. "Here, let me do that or we'll be here all day."

He dropped his hands and tilted up his chin. He hoped she hadn't noticed his sudden intake of breath as her knuckles brushed his throat. She was just trying to be helpful. She seemed to know what she was doing, too. Her fingers made quick work of the knot that he'd skewed. She must have had plenty of practice tying Spencer Pryce's ties.

The resentment that usually arose at thoughts of Amelia's ex-husband didn't happen. That was too bad. It made resisting the urge to kiss her that much harder. Her scent surrounded him. Her face was only inches from his and she still had the old habit of pursing her lips as she concentrated on her task. It wasn't an invitation, but…

Her gaze met his. "Too tight?"

"Mmm?"

"Is the knot too tight? You groaned."

"No, it's fine. Are you done?"

She folded his collar back down, then as naturally as breathing, she smoothed his hair off his forehead.

Hank remembered she had done the same thing after the accident on Sunday. She used to enjoy running her fingers through his hair when they were teenagers. And this was one thing she hadn't practiced on her ex-husband, because in every picture of Spencer that Hank had seen, the man had sported an almost military-short haircut that wouldn't have allowed one strand to be out of place. He'd also had a receding hairline.

Hank smiled. "Thanks."

Her gaze lingered on his mouth for a tantalizing moment, but before he had a chance to close the gap between them—or to debate whether or not he should—she retrieved her purse and stepped out of the car.

Whitcombe's sat between a store advertising vintage books and a furniture shop that displayed a stark, Scandinavian-style dining room set in the front window. The gallery's window display consisted of a framed painting on a wooden easel in front of a draped backdrop of white velvet. To Hank, the art seemed to be an incomprehensible collection of blobs—maybe the artist was trying to match the bullet-hole theme of the building. Another, smaller easel held a gilt-edged sign advertising an upcoming charity gala and auction.

Amelia didn't pause to regard the window. She went straight for the door. Hank lengthened his stride so that he could pull it open for her. Though it was made of glass, it was heavier than he'd expected. The weight was likely due to the thick slabs of steel that surrounded the edges of the glass. A distant chime sounded as they crossed the threshold.

The showroom was a cool expanse of pale, hardwood flooring and white walls. Classical music played softly from speakers that had been painted white to blend into the decor. Small spotlights in the ceiling provided cones of illumination for each of the paintings that hung on the walls. There were also a few pedestals with sculptures on top of them. More art was displayed on vertical panels that had been arranged in a zigzag configuration across the center of the floor. An empty, glass-topped desk stood in front of an arched doorway at the rear of the room that appeared to lead to a hall. Aside from the two of them, there was no one else around, which wasn't surprising, since it was just past noon and the place had been open for only a few minutes. The staff had to be aware of their arrival—the low-tech security of the entrance chime was supplemented by several darkened glass domes that likely concealed surveillance cameras.

"I don't see it!" Amelia hissed, whipping her head from side to side.

Hank proceeded more slowly, checking each painting as he made his way around the room. He saw another blob painting and a few that seemed to be composed of spatters from an overloaded paintbrush, but there were also more true-to-life canvases. One depicted a bowl of fruit on a windowsill. Another was a portrait of an old man with a pipe. There were several framed ink drawings of flowers that he thought were pretty good, considering they were only done in black and white. He saw some landscape paintings, too, but nothing that matched the description of Amelia's.

A tall woman with poker-straight black hair appeared from the doorway behind the desk. She glided toward them, her footsteps swallowed by the flowing black dress she wore. She offered them a subdued smile.

"Hello, I'm Evangeline. Welcome to the Whitcombe Gallery."

Amelia seemed about to blurt a question, so Hank spoke before she could. "Thanks," he said. "You have quite a selection here."

"We pride ourselves on maintaining an eclectic mix." She flashed long, scarlet-tipped nails as she wafted one hand toward the group of ink drawings. "I noticed the Drummonds caught your interest. They're beautifully executed, aren't they?"

"For sure." Hank tilted his head, as if he were studying them. From the corner of his eye he sensed Amelia shift impatiently beside him. He tapped the back of her waist in a silent message.

They'd discussed their strategy on the drive here and had decided it would be wise to heed the parting advice Hazel had given them at the flea market. The direct approach might not work very well with a professional art dealer, so they had decided to pose as a couple out shopping. If Whitcombe realized how important Amelia's painting was to her, it would be far too tempting for him to set an exorbitant price. From what Hank had seen on the small, discreet information tags that were mounted beside each painting, he considered the prices already exorbitant. There was nothing under a thousand dollars, and he'd spotted a few in the five-figure range.

He could only hope the price of the Mathers would be set at the low end of the scale. Although he was willing to fork out as much as he needed to in order to make Amelia happy, he didn't have a whole lot of spare cash lying around. Spending a few hundred was one thing, but a few thousand would involve rejigging his budget. She would probably still insist on reimbursing him, too. Not that he wanted her to, but her sensitivity over money issues was genuine, and he would hate to saddle her with yet another debt she wouldn't be able to pay.

"We're very fortunate to have the whole series," Evangeline said. "Shanna Drummond was quite prolific a few decades ago, but I understand her arthritis has taken a terrible toll, both on her work and her psyche."

"That's a shame," Hank said.

"It is. A great loss for all of us who treasure Shanna's work." The woman lowered her voice, as if imparting a confidence, even though they were still the only ones in the gallery. "We don't anticipate this series will remain on the market for long. It's a fabulous investment."

Hank lifted an eyebrow as he turned to Amelia. "What do you think, honey?"

"I would prefer something with color, darling." She made a show of looking around the gallery. "What about a landscape?"

"We have an interesting Levesque watercolor of the Gaspé peninsula over here," Evangeline said, swishing toward one of the panels.

Hank put his hand on the small of Amelia's back as they followed. She was so stiff, she was practically vibrating. He brought his head close to her ear. "Relax. We're getting closer."

"If she mentions sepia portraits or mirrors, I may have to hurt her," she whispered.

"You might not want to tangle with her. Those nails are pretty scary."

She bared her teeth, but turned the expression into a smile as Evangeline stopped beside a painting and glanced back over her shoulder.

"It's quite accomplished," the woman said. "At the same time, it conveys the artist's unique sense of playfulness."

"I see what you mean," Hank said, although he didn't see anything except lots of white paper with a few streaks of blue and green around a brown cliff. Since the price of the painting was two and a half thousand, that meant each brushstroke was worth at least several hundred.

"You said it was painted in the Gaspé?" Amelia asked.

"Yes, Rob Levesque lives in Montreal but has a summer home near the coast. That's where he does much of his work."

"Do you have any Ontario landscape artists?" Amelia asked.

Evangeline lifted her eyebrows.

"We like the idea of supporting local talent," Hank added.

"As do we," Evangeline said. "The Whitcombe Gallery has discovered and promoted many artists from the area." She hesitated. "As a matter of fact, Mr. Whitcombe returned from one of his periodic scouting trips to the hinterland just this past weekend."

"Did he have any success?" Hank asked, slipping his arm behind Amelia's waist. It didn't seem possible for her to feel any tenser, but she was.

Evangeline's hesitation was longer this time. "He would be able to tell you more than I would. Excuse me, I'll see if he's free." She pivoted swiftly, her dress swirling around her ankles, and disappeared through the doorway in the back wall.

Amelia stepped forward as if to follow.

Hank placed himself in front to block her path. "Cool it, Amelia. We don't want to make them suspicious."

"This is killing me."

"Want to wait in the car?"

"Not a chance. The painting's here. It has to be. They weren't open yesterday, and we're the first customers today."

They were still the only potential customers six minutes later when a man approached them from the doorway Evangeline had departed through. He was as tall as Hank and at least eighty pounds heavier, judging by the overall snugness of his navy blue suit. Though he appeared to be only in his mid-fifties, his hair was completely white. He wore it pulled back in a ponytail that dangled well past his shoulders. Gold cuff links gleamed beneath the cuffs of his sleeves and heavy, jeweled rings adorned three of his fingers. His hands were pale and disproportionately large. "Good afternoon," he said. "I'm Rupert Whitcombe."

Hank didn't often make snap judgments, but he did about this man. He didn't like him. It could have been the tone he'd used as he introduced himself, as if he were bestowing a huge favor, or the way he angled his head back as he spoke, as if he wanted to look down his nose at them or had smelled something bad. Or maybe it was that ponytail. Not that Hank cared how long a man wore his hair, but on Whitcombe it appeared like a prop, as if he wanted to project an artsy image over a thug's body.

Whitcombe gave them a subdued smile that teetered on the edge of condescension. "My assistant informed me you're interested in Ontario artists."

"Yes, we are," Amelia said. "I'm also very fond of landscapes."

Not subtle, but at least she wasn't grabbing him yet.

"How fortunate." Whitcombe's smile expanded to reveal teeth as white as his ponytail. "It just so happens I've recently collected a number of pieces that feature our lovely province."

Amelia pretended to scan the gallery. "Do you have them on display somewhere else?"

Whitcombe continued to regard Amelia. "Excuse me, but have we met?" he asked.

"I don't think so."

"Your face looks familiar."

"No, I'm sure we haven't met. Would you

tell me more about these pieces you collected recently?"

"I'll do better than that. Would you care to see them?"

"Certainly," Hank said.

Amelia nodded, clasping her hands under her chin. "Yes, please."

Whitcombe turned and walked to the desk. He bent down to open a carton that was on the floor beside it and withdrew what appeared to be a small, glossy booklet. "These are the catalogs for the auction," he said as he returned to them. "We had a few last-minute changes, so they just came in from the printer's this morning. The finishing touches always end up being such a rush."

"What auction?" Amelia asked.

"We host the event annually. I'm sure you must have heard of it. The *Globe* did a lovely feature on last year's gala and auction. We donate the entire proceeds to charity, of course."

"That's admirable," Amelia said. "But you were going to show me your new pieces?"

Whitcombe held out the booklet. "They're all in here."

Hank reached for it but Amelia was faster.

She plucked the booklet from the gallery owner's hand and opened it.

The pages were filled with photographs of paintings accompanied by what Hank assumed were written descriptions of each work. He couldn't tell for sure since she was flipping through them too quickly for him to read. She stopped suddenly. The paper rattled in her grasp.

He looked at the photograph numbered fifteen. It was a rural scene of a farm on a hill, with fields and old barns. The artist was Dr. Jonathan Mathers. The medium was oil on canvas. The dimensions given were ninety-two centimeters by sixty, about three feet wide by two feet high. Every detail was exactly what Amelia had described, right down to the ornately carved wooden frame. That was her painting, all right.

"How much do you want for it?" Amelia asked.

"Excuse me?"

"For this landscape," she said, pointing to the photo.

Whitcombe's smile wavered while his eyes narrowed. The artsy demeanor slipped. "You have interesting taste," he said slowly. "What attracted you to that particular item?"

"We're redecorating," Hank said, drawing the gallery owner's attention away from Amelia, who was beginning to tremble. "Lots of wall space to fill."

"I see. Jonathan Mathers isn't widely known, although he is enjoying a resurgence of popularity. His work doesn't come on the market often so we were thrilled when we acquired one of his canvases. No one quite captures the primitive feel of the rural regions as well as Mathers did."

"What's the price?" Amelia persisted.

"I'm sorry. That will be determined at the auction. You're welcome to attend." Whitcombe did another of his down-the-nose glances. "The gala is black tie, of course."

She rolled the brochure into a tube and tapped it against her skirt. "What if I wanted to buy the painting now?"

"Oh, that would be impossible."

"Why?"

"As you can see, the catalog has been printed. It would be unfair to our other patrons if I didn't give them an equal opportunity to bid on every piece."

"When's the auction?" Hank asked.

"It takes place on the twenty-third."

"The twenty-third?" Amelia's voice rose. "That's almost two weeks from now."

Hank eased the brochure from her grasp,

slipped it into his jacket and took her hand. He had the feeling she was about to lunge. "We'll check our schedule, honey."

She looked at him. Her lips pressed into a tight line.

"I know how busy you are," he continued, "but an auction and gala sound like fun. And it's for charity, after all."

"Indeed," Whitcombe said. "I hope to see you both there."

Hank began to turn her toward the front door, hoping to get her outside before she completely lost her cool, when she pulled free and moved back to Whitcombe. She glanced toward the desk and the doorway behind it. "Excuse me, but do you have a washroom I could use?"

AMELIA OPENED THE first door on the left, as Whitcombe had directed her. The room was small, windowless and smelled strongly of lavender air freshener. Light from the corridor gleamed on a white toilet and a small vanity. After a quick glance to ensure she was still alone, she hitched her purse onto her good shoulder and pulled the door closed without going inside. She could still hear the sound of Hank's and Whitcombe's voices from the showroom, so she slipped off her shoes, hooked the straps through her fingers and padded silently down the hall on her bare feet. From a partially open door to her left came the chug of a fax machine and Evangeline's voice. It was likely the gallery office. She was speaking softly, probably on the phone since the conversation was one-sided, and her heels clicked on the hardwood floor, so she must be pacing as she talked. Any second now her pacing could bring her into the hall.

Moving as quickly as she dared, Amelia grasped the knob of the first door on the right and swung it open. It turned out to be a closet containing cleaning supplies and a large fuse box. She returned to the hall. The only other door was almost directly across from the office. The odds of getting in there and out without being noticed were slim, but she had to try. The painting had to be around here someplace. All she needed was a few seconds alone with the frame.

"Yes, the arrangements for payment and delivery after the auction will be the same as last year." Evangeline's tone firmed, as if she were preparing to terminate the call. "Excellent. We'll courier the special catalog to you within the hour, Emilio. We look forward to doing business with you again."

It was now or never. Amelia ran on her tiptoes to the remaining door and tried the knob. It didn't turn. On impulse she gave it a push. The door swung open with a soft snick—apparently the knob had been locked but hadn't been closed enough to latch completely. She slipped inside and shut the door behind her.

Blackness enveloped her. She groped for a light switch. A pair of plain, fluorescent bulbs flickered on overhead. This was evidently a combination storeroom and workroom. She saw piles of flat, wooden packing crates next to a long worktable littered with tools and scraps of lumber. Brackets on the wall supported lengths of framing in various styles. Beneath them was a rack of glass panes. Several colorful canvases leaned haphazardly against more crates at the rear wall of the room where there was another door. That one was made of steel and had two dead bolts plus a riveted hasp with a chunky padlock. If her painting was in there...

But it wasn't. Her heart thumped as she caught sight of the familiar scene. She hadn't noticed it right away because it was tilted sideways and propped on end, as if it had been casually discarded where it leaned against an open wooden crate next to a roll of bubble wrap.

Yes. *Yes!* She half ran, half slid across the floor.

The door smacked against the wall. "What are you doing in here?"

Amelia started at the sound of Evangeline's voice, but she didn't turn around. She couldn't see the ticket. Had it fallen out? Had someone taken it? "I'm sorry," she mumbled. "I think I got turned around. I was looking for the washroom." She pressed her hands to her stomach and staggered closer to the painting. "Oooo. I don't feel well."

Evangeline moved forward swiftly and grasped her arm. "You have to leave, miss."

"I'm really sorry. I… Oh, no!" Amelia doubled over and pretended to retch. Her shoes dropped to the floor while her purse swung forward from her shoulder and smacked her in the cheek. The motion also brought her face within inches of the painting. She scanned the frame feverishly. There! She spied a telltale, pale sliver of folded paper. It was in the narrow gap where the wood had warped away from the canvas.

All right. It was still in place, wedged into the lower left corner beside a tuft of weeds in the painted field, exactly where she'd put it almost two weeks ago, except it had gotten worked deeper into the gap. That's why she hadn't spotted it immediately. That's why no one else evidently had, either. Less than a millimeter of the paper was showing, and it was camouflaged by the streaks in the old wood frame. Unless you knew where to look, it would be easy to miss.

The woman shouted for help, then dug her nails into Amelia's sleeve and dragged her upright. "Please, control yourself!" she exclaimed. "You mustn't be sick in here!"

Amelia heard the men approaching from the showroom and knew she had only a matter of seconds. She stumbled sideways, flailing her free arm as if trying to regain her balance. Her knuckles rapped the frame. She spread her fingers and brushed the edge of the fold with the tip of her index finger, but her nails were too short and the ticket was wedged in too far for her to grip. Evangeline's persistent tugging wasn't helping, either. Her elbow struck the roll of bubble wrap, which unfurled as it fell, burying the painting in yards of pockmarked plastic.

"Miss, please!"

Amelia groaned as she tried to claw aside the bubble wrap. Before she could get past it, a pair of strong arms went around her and she was scooped off her feet.

No! *No!*

"Darling!" Hank said. "Are you all right?"

No, she wasn't all right. Her face was mashed against his chest, the bruise on her shoulder was throbbing like crazy and her ticket was so close, it hurt, too. Like an empty ache deep inside. She'd seen it, she'd touched it. All she'd needed was another few seconds....

"Honey?"

She wanted to scream with frustration. Why did Hank have to be so strong? Most men couldn't have picked her up like this. She clenched her jaw to keep the scream inside, tipped back her head and looked at his face.

The concern in his gaze seemed genuine. "What happened?"

"I'm sorry. I got dizzy. I think I might have momentarily blacked out."

He bent over to kiss her forehead. "I should have realized this was too much for you."

The kiss was tender, as if he really meant it. Same with his embrace. Though his arms were flexed hard, he cradled her gently. The sensation wasn't unpleasant. In fact, it went along with the pounding of her heart...

She blinked. *Focus!* This was *not* the time to notice Hank's muscles.

Whitcombe moved behind Hank to scowl at her. "This area is private. I must ask you to leave immediately."

"It's my fault," Hank said. "I thought she only got morning sickness in the morning." After another forehead-kiss, he turned and started for the door. "Let's get you some fresh air."

This time her stomach really did roll. She flung her arm backward. "No!" She gasped. "Wait!"

"Your shoes," Hank said. "Oh, you poor, brave girl. Were your ankles hurting again?" He glanced at Whitcombe. "Her obstetrician counseled her to wear flats, but you know how women are."

Evangeline picked up the shoes, her expression icy. She held them out, along with Amelia's purse, which had somehow become hooked on her wrist during their brief struggle.

Hank shifted the arm that supported her back, adjusting his hold with as little effort as she did when she lugged Timmy around. He snagged her shoes and purse with one hand, then angled sideways to carry her through the door. He continued to the front of the gallery, all the while babbling solicitous nonsense about her fictitious pregnancy and its accompanying health concerns.

It was an excellent improvisation. Judging by their pinched expressions, it was hard to tell whether Whitcombe and his sidekick were skeptical or merely disgusted at her gauche behavior. Whatever they believed, they unbent enough to invite them to return when she felt better.

Hank set her on her feet once they reached the sidewalk. "Okay, what was all that about?"

This was the second time his quick thinking had averted a potential disaster. But that was Hank, wasn't it? He was a good guy. Who smelled like Irish Spring soap and the boy she used to love. Whose arms had been strong and warm and felt like home.

But she had no home. Her only hope of regaining one was wedged into item number fifteen of the Whitcombe Gallery's auction catalog.

And on that thought, the tears finally came.

"Hey, don't cry."

She sniffed as she took her shoes from his grasp and put them on. "I almost had it."

"Amelia…"

"Another minute, even another thirty seconds, and I would have held it in my hand."

"What?"

"Didn't you see the painting?"

"No. Was it in the storeroom?"

"Yes! It was right in front of me. Morticia knocked the bubble wrap over it. That must be why you couldn't see it. I don't know how she found me so fast." She wiped her eyes with the back of her wrist, then took her purse from him and dug inside to search for a tissue.

Hank beat her to it. He took a white handkerchief from his sport coat and gently dabbed beneath her eyes. "Morticia?"

"Suits her better than Evangeline," she muttered.

His lips twitched. "Amelia, you heard what Whitcombe said. He wasn't going to sell you that painting, and going hunting for it on your own sure wouldn't have made him change his mind. We'll come back for the auction."

She hitched her purse on her shoulder. Out of habit, she'd put it on her right shoulder, which was the bruised one. She switched it to the other side. "We wouldn't need to come back if I'd had another thirty seconds."

He regarded her closely as he returned his handkerchief to his pocket, then put his hand at the small of her back and guided her away from the gallery. He didn't speak again until they reached the next block. "What did you mean? You couldn't honestly have thought you'd steal it."

"It's mine. It wouldn't be stealing."

"I'm serious, Amelia."

"So am I."

His steps slowed as they passed a small coffee shop where tables had been set up on the sidewalk in the shade of the building. He caught her hand and reversed direction. "Let's get something to eat before we head back, okay?"

She was glad to see that the coffee shop was cafeteria style, so she didn't feel uncomfortable about being waited on. Hank filled a tray with egg salad sandwiches and cherry Danishes and carried it to one of the outside tables while she followed with glasses of iced coffee. He took his time chewing, spending more time watching her than talking. She recognized the look—he was mulling something over.

He waited until she finished her pastry,

then stacked their dishes back on the tray, crossed his forearms on the table and leaned toward her. "I'd like to ask you a question, Amelia, but I don't want you to get mad."

"That's quite a preamble."

"Or offended," he went on. "I'm only asking because I'm concerned and I—" He hesitated. "I care about you."

"Hank…"

"As a friend. We were friends, once. Good friends."

"Now you're worrying me. What's your question?"

"Have you seen a doctor?"

She gave a self-conscious laugh and rolled her right shoulder. "I should have realized you'd notice. It's just a bruise from the seat belt. It's already getting better."

"I'm glad to hear that, but I didn't mean seeing a doctor since the accident Sunday. Did you go to anyone last year, after your husband's arrest? After you lost your company and all your money?"

"Why would I do that? It was a financial problem, not a medical one."

"I'm not explaining this right."

"Then what are you getting at? Maybe you better just spit it out."

"Fine. Amelia, have you seen a psychiatrist?"

"What?"

"A therapist. A shrink. Have you talked to anyone about the things you've lost?"

"I talked to plenty of cops and lawyers. My problems didn't happen because I was crazy, they happened because I was stupid. As far as I know, stupidity isn't a mental disorder."

"No, you're the smartest person I know. That's why I'm worried. I'm not saying you're crazy, but you've gone through a lot in this past year. I know it's bothering you because you keep bringing up your troubles, but you only talk about them in fast quips. Like punch lines."

"Thanks to the media, my life *is* a punch line. It got laid bare for everyone to see. There's not much to add."

"That's not true. What about your feelings?"

"I don't like to dwell."

"Sure, that's how you've always been. You race right past the stuff that you don't like."

"We already established that I'm short on patience. What's your point?"

"I think it would be healthy to take some time to work things through. It would help you heal. You've been under a lot of stress. It might do you good to talk to a professional."

"Why? A shrink won't get my money back."

"No, but neither will a painting."

The light dawned. She had a sudden urge to laugh. The concern on Hank's face quashed it. "You're bringing this up because of what I did at the gallery, aren't you?"

He nodded. "Trying to steal that painting wasn't rational behavior, Amelia. The Whitcombe Gallery isn't some isolated house out in the country. You had to have realized that you couldn't possibly have gotten away with it. For one thing, the painting's too large to carry out without someone noticing. Even if you had thought you were alone, there are security cameras throughout the interior. For another—"

"I appreciate your concern, Hank, I really do, but I'm not nuts."

He reached across the table and took her hand in his. "I understand that you've focused on that painting as the first step in regaining your life. You told me yourself that losing it was the last straw, it was where you drew the line."

"I know that's what I said, but you're reading too much into it."

"I don't think so. I believed finding your painting would help you, but the closer we've gotten to it, the more...oddly you've been acting." He squeezed her hand. "And that's why, as your friend, I think you need help."

For the second time within an hour, her eyes filled with tears. She blinked hard, annoyed that her emotions were so close to the surface. She'd managed to shove them aside for more than a year. He'd been bang on about that. But that's the way she'd always been—he was right about that, too. "You really are a good man."

"I only want you to be happy, Amelia. And the truth is, taking this case wasn't only a gift to you, it was a gift to me."

"Hank..."

"I'm enjoying the time we're spending together. I want to get to know you again. And maybe once you're feeling better and you have a chance to get back on your feet—"

"Hank, stop. Please."

He closed his eyes as he inhaled deeply, then shook his head and gave her a lopsided smile. "Sorry. For once I was the one rushing things."

She couldn't do this anymore. Not one more day, not one more minute, regardless of the consequences. She glanced around the adjacent tables to make sure no one was within earshot, then leaned forward and pitched her voice as low as she could. "Hank, I didn't want to take the painting from the gallery."

"Okay. That's progress."

"I only wanted to take the ticket."

"Ticket?"

"I won Lotto 6/49. I had left the ticket in the frame of that painting."

"Sure."

"I'm not joking, Hank. I really did win the lottery."

His smile dimmed. "What?"

"Jenny didn't know I'd put the ticket in the painting. She sold it before I found out I had won. That's why I have to get it back, and that's why I came to you."

"How…" His voice rasped. "How much did you win?"

"Fifty-two million."

He released her hand and fell back in his chair. "Fifty-two…*million?*"

"Shh. Dollars. Rounded off. It's actually a bit more."

"I don't believe this," he muttered.

"I always play the same numbers. They're our family birthdays. I was at work when I saw the results of the draw in the Sunday paper."

Though he didn't move, every muscle in his body seemed to tense. He was drawing into himself before her eyes. There was no longer any trace of a smile in his gaze. His expression was rigid. Guarded. He was mulling again.

Amelia hurried to fill the silence. "I know it's a lot for you to take in all at once, and I'm sorry to spring it on you like this. I appreciate your concern about my mental health, but as you can see now, I do have a completely rational, logical reason to want that painting back."

He nodded once, a tight dip of his chin.

"And getting that painting really is the first step in reclaiming my life. I didn't lie about that. I can build a great future with the money from that ticket."

A motorcycle roared past on the street. Dishes clattered somewhere inside the coffee shop. A group of women took seats at a nearby table amid the sounds of laughter and scraping chair legs. Hank's gaze didn't waver from hers. It was as impenetrable as flint.

"Hank, I'm sorry. I understand that you're mad, and you have every right, but please, talk to me. I didn't set out to hurt your feelings. I've been wanting to tell you about the ticket for days."

"Why didn't you?"

"At first, I didn't think it was necessary."

"Not *necessary?* You didn't think I needed to know exactly what I was tracking down?"

"I realize it wasn't fair to let you work for me without telling you the whole truth, but—"

"That won't be a problem now."

"Oh, thank you! I—"

"Let me finish, Amelia."

No, she didn't want him to finish. She could tell by his tone that she wouldn't like what he was about to say. "Hank…"

"It won't be a problem because I'm no longer working for you."

"Hank, please!"

"You're on your own, Amelia." He rose to his feet. "I quit."

CHAPTER NINE

HANK ROUNDED THE corner and headed for the parking garage, jerking his tie from his neck as he walked. He rolled it into a ball and lobbed it at a nearby trash can. Amelia's high heels clicked along the sidewalk as she struggled to catch up to him, but he didn't shorten his strides. He didn't attempt to rein in his temper, either. Some detective he'd turned out to be. So much for being thorough and methodical. This was what happened when he listened to his heart instead of his head. There had been plenty of clues, only he hadn't put them together. Until now.

At their very first meeting in his office, he had suspected Amelia wasn't telling him the whole story. He'd swallowed her lies and ignored his misgivings because he'd wanted to make her happy.

It was obvious to him now that the neighbor, Ruth Talmidge, had seen the Good-fellow family celebrating the lottery win. Amelia's explanation about Jenny netting five hundred dollars had seemed thin, but when he'd questioned it she'd become touchy about the topic of money. He'd backed off because he hadn't wanted to hurt her feelings.

Amelia had dragged her feet about letting him interview her sister-in-law. That should have raised a red flag, but rather than pursue the issue, he'd convinced himself he was mistaken. After all, he and Amelia wanted the same thing, right?

Then there was the way she had talked him into letting her tag along while he worked on her case. Part of him had been flattered that she'd wanted to keep him company. He'd even secretly hoped she had been drawn to him as much as he'd been drawn to her. It had never entered his head that she was sticking with him because she had been worried he might stumble on the truth.

Yeah, right. Fat chance of that. Not while he'd been blinded by the old infatuation. He'd found an excuse for everything. He'd blamed the inconsistencies in her behavior on her emotional fragility. How she'd managed not to laugh in his face, he'd never know. On the other hand, she'd become pretty good at acting, hadn't she?

To top it off, he'd already heard about the

unclaimed ticket. The DJs on the local radio station had been joking about it this morning while he'd been on his way to pick up Amelia. According to the lottery office, the winning ticket had been purchased in Northumberland County, which included Port Hope. At the time, Hank hadn't paid any attention. He'd felt the story had nothing to do with him. He didn't play the lottery because he didn't like to gamble.

But Amelia did. She loved taking chances.

Idiot. Imbecile. Glutton for punishment. He'd *known* she could hurt him again, but he'd walked right into it anyway. How pathetic was that? Even now, he found himself searching for more excuses. She was still healing from Spencer's betrayal and was too raw to trust anyone. She truly was emotionally fragile. She hadn't set out to hurt him....

If anyone needed a shrink, he did.

"Hank, I'm sorry!"

He walked into the garage. He still had too much steam to work off so he bypassed the elevator and pulled open the door to the stairs.

Amelia caught the door before it could swing shut. "Hank!"

He started to climb without looking back.

She ran up the stairs behind him. "Please, wait up."

He pulled his wallet from his pocket and withdrew three twenties. He paused when he reached the landing for the second level and held the bills out to her.

She didn't touch them. "What's that for?"

"The eastbound Greyhound leaves around six. The Yonge subway line should take you close to the bus terminal. But you would know that. You used to live in Toronto."

She put her fists on her hips. "So you just plan to maroon me here?"

"I did mention I'm no longer working for you, didn't I? That means no more free rides."

"I know, but—"

"This sixty bucks isn't a gift. Let's get that straight. I expect to be paid back when you redeem your lottery ticket."

"But I don't have the ticket."

"That's not my problem. You only asked me to find the painting. I did. I'm done."

"Look, I realize you're angry with me right now…"

"Angry?" He returned the cash to his wallet and jammed it back into his pocket. "Why should I be angry? Just because I've been used and lied to? Made a fool of? Because I've been donating my services to help an old friend I thought was destitute but who turns out to be a millionaire?"

"I offered to pay. I never asked for your pity."

"You didn't have to. You knew I was a soft touch, same as I realized what you were like when I took this case." He snorted a laugh. "And here I thought I was getting to know you again. I shouldn't have bothered. You're still the same. You had me going with that act about how important the painting was to you, but I should have realized a woman like you would never be motivated by sentiment."

"What does that mean? A woman like me?"

"It was about the money now just like it was about the money then."

"Then? What are you talking about?"

He started up the next flight of stairs. "That's why you married Spencer, wasn't it? Because he was rich?"

"He wasn't anywhere near as rich when I married him." She followed, keeping one step behind him. "And my ex-husband has nothing to do with us."

"No? Then why didn't you tell me the truth about the ticket? And don't say you didn't think it was necessary."

"Okay, yes, I lied because of Spencer. After what he did to me, I wasn't eager to trust anyone with my money."

"Including me."

"Especially you."

"Why?"

"Because you had already proved I couldn't trust you."

"How did I do that?"

"Because you dumped me. But that's your pattern, isn't it? As soon as the going gets rough, you quit."

He stopped where he was. She bumped into his back. He turned and reached for her shoulders to steady her, but released her just as quickly when she winced. He cursed himself for forgetting her bruise. "I never dumped you, Amelia."

"Don't start with the word games again, Hank. You dumped me then just like you're dumping me now."

Her voice echoed hollowly from the cinder block walls of the stairwell, along with the muffled sound of a distant car alarm. The air smelled of oil and cement and city humidity. White bulbs glowed starkly behind metal safety grates. This was hardly the place to hold a conversation that had waited fifteen years. As settings went, it was even worse than standing in a ditch next to a car wreck. But Hank was done being patient. He'd waited long enough. "For a smart woman, you really didn't see it, did you?"

"See what?"

"I broke up with you to set you free, Amelia."

"You're still sticking with the cheesy lines."

"Put aside all that resentment you've been carrying around and think this through, for a change."

"Believe me, I've thought about it."

"I doubt that. It's not your style. You skim right by anything that hurts."

"So you've mentioned."

"So I did. You must have busted a gut to keep from laughing when I tried that intervention back at the coffee place."

"No, Hank, I appreciated your concern, I really did, but—"

"Save it for someone who'll believe you, Amelia. We can't keep avoiding talking about what happened between us. It's time to settle things, once and for all."

"Fine. You want to dredge up the past? Let's start with how you broke my heart."

He hesitated, attempting to order his thoughts, but it was no use. The words had been bottled up so long, they tumbled over themselves to get out. "No, let's start with that scholarship you won."

"What's that have to do with... Wait. Were you envious? Was that it?"

"You know me better than that. Don't you remember how proud I was? How proud your whole family was? You were the first Goodfellow to go to university. With your brains, you could have become anything you wanted to be. That scholarship was going to open up a whole new world for you. It was your chance to leave Port Hope and spread your wings. I didn't break up with you because I didn't love you. I loved you too much to hold you back."

"It wasn't love."

"Yeah, we already got that straight, but at the time, we believed it was. Remember the day before you were supposed to leave home? You said you wanted to forget school and get married?"

She winced again, but it wasn't from any physical discomfort. "Of course, I remember it. Vividly. It was the most humiliating moment of my life."

"And I handled it about as clumsily as a teenage boy could."

"I scared you off. I figured that out. Asking for a commitment like that would send most boys running, but I had been laboring under the delusion that we really were in love."

"So was I. I might have been a teenager, but I was old enough to realize we weren't in any position to get married. Neither of us had jobs, we couldn't even have afforded a place to live. What had you expected, that we would stay with my father and bum our meals off your parents? That's no way to start a life together, and more than anything, I wanted to make you happy."

"By dumping me flat and breaking my heart?"

"By ensuring you had a choice. I didn't want you to throw away your big chance just to stay with me, and if I'd agreed to get engaged, that's what would have happened. I know you wouldn't have waited. That's how you are. That's why I had to make the break. It was for your sake."

"But you never said…"

"I trusted you, Amelia. I trusted our love. I was more than willing to wait the four years while you got your degree. I was willing to wait forever, because I was certain you would come back to me. Shows you what a fool I was. The next thing I knew, you were dating some rich old professor."

"Spencer wasn't my professor, he was a guest lecturer in my Introduction to Economics course. And he was only six years older than me, hardly ancient."

"But he was rich."

"He was well-off."

"Now who's playing word games, Amelia? Idealistic fool that I was, I hoped you would come back to me if I had more money. That's why I moved out to the oil sands. I worked like a dog and lived in places that would make Will and Jenny's back room look like a palace. For a while I even lived in my car. I saved every penny. I did it for us. For our future."

She descended a step, grasping the handrail with both hands. She shook her head. "I never guessed."

"No, you wouldn't. You were too busy getting wined and dined by the charming, sophisticated, *well-off* Spencer Pryce. You forgot all about the ordinary guy you'd sworn you loved a few months before."

"I was hurt. I was vulnerable. He was there and you weren't."

"Like I said, you had made your choice."

"That's not fair. Why didn't you tell me?"

Hank stretched his hand toward her hair, but he stopped short of touching her. "I tried, but you refused to talk to me."

"You couldn't have tried very hard."

He dropped his hand. "That's right. Blame me. Don't blame your habit of jumping in with both feet before you bother to look where you're going."

"Oh, and your penchant for not making a move until you've analyzed it to death had nothing to do with what happened?"

"You're too impatient."

"And you hide behind your caution like a kid under his security blanket."

He moved down until he stood on the step beside her. "You should be grateful that one of us did think ahead. If I'd agreed to get married when you'd asked, it never would have worked out."

"That's right. It would have been a colossal mistake."

"We needed to grow up."

"And we have. And clearly, you haven't changed."

"Too bad you haven't, either." He grasped the handrail, placing his hands next to hers and caging her between his arms. He leaned closer until he could feel her body heat. "Yeah, some things just don't change."

Her eyes darkened in an obvious if involuntary response to his proximity. She pressed her back to the railing. "You're still afraid to take chances."

"Not always." He looked at her mouth. "Depends on the stakes."

"What about fifty-two million? Are those stakes high enough?"

He closed his eyes and inhaled slowly through his nose, trying to fight off the next spurt of anger, only this time it was directed at himself. As he'd just explained to her, he'd known what kind of woman she was. He'd reminded himself countless times. Once she decided on a goal, she pursued it one hundred percent. Why shouldn't she bring the topic back to the only thing that really mattered to her?

Her palm settled on his chest. She began to push him away, then stopped and spread her fingers. The caress was tentative, unsure, almost as if they were teenagers again. And just like every time she touched him, his common sense took a flying leap from his rapidly emptying brain.

There was something else that had waited for fifteen years. It had nothing to do with words, which was good, because Hank didn't have any left. Besides, actions always spoke louder. He lowered his head. Though his eyes were still shut, he had no difficulty finding Amelia's lips.

AMELIA KNEW SHE was in trouble. She was a thirty-four-year-old woman who had been married for nine years and divorced for more than one. She wasn't some inexperienced teenager in the throes of first love. The physical aspects of a man-woman relationship no longer held any mystery for her, and yet...

Oh, could Hank kiss! His mouth moved over hers, whisper-soft at first, letting her savor the contact and his warmth. He didn't push, he didn't lead, he invited. He gave her the same tenderness she'd felt in his chaste pecks at the gallery, only this time she also felt the masculine power beneath the surface. Apart from her lips, he touched her nowhere else, which only made her excruciatingly conscious of all the places that longed for his touch.

She understood the kiss was merely a side effect of their argument. It was the sort of thing that could happen when passions got aroused. In the heat of the moment, barriers were dropped. Inhibitions were bypassed. Nerves that had been frazzled and raw reacted to any sensation far more intensely than otherwise.

But the pleasure that zinged through her blood and curled her toes was from more than a mindless response of her body. She was old enough to know that this connection was more than physical.

And that's why she was in trouble.

She didn't want this. Getting involved with any man at this point in her life was the last thing she needed. Getting involved with *this* one would be insane.

But oh, could he kiss....

"Come on, buddy. Get a room."

At the muttered comment, she gasped and jerked back. Hank lifted his head to look over his shoulder.

A pair of middle-aged men in business suits were descending the staircase, shifting into single file to get around them. The man in front carried a salesman's sample case tucked high under one arm and kept his gaze on his feet. The man who followed leered at Amelia and waggled his tongue lewdly as he passed, then quickly caught up to his companion. They rounded the corner at the next landing and disappeared from view, but the scuffing of their shoes on the concrete—and their low laughter—remained.

Hank released his grasp on the handrail, raised his palms and retreated to the other side of the step where they both stood. He shook his head like a swimmer just surfacing. "Amelia…"

"Don't you dare apologize."

"I shouldn't have—"

"Forget it," she snapped. She tugged the hem of her jacket to straighten it. "We're both grown-ups. These things happen. It was no big deal."

"I'm not apologizing for the kiss. I'm apologizing for the lack of privacy."

"It makes no difference, because it isn't going to happen again. I've told you repeatedly that this isn't what I want."

"Just so we're clear, define *this*."

She waved her hand back and forth between them. "You and me. I don't want to revisit the past or rekindle it or however you want to put it. We were a mistake then just like we would be a mistake now."

"Right. You only want your money. That's what you value. That's all that matters to you."

"Stop trying to make me feel guilty. I have plenty of solid, practical reasons for pursuing that ticket. Anyone would."

"How much is it worth to you?"

"How much?" She glanced down the stairwell. The men's voices had faded, but someone else could happen by at any second.

Hank seemed to guess her thoughts. He made a move as if he were about to take her hand, then closed his fingers into a fist and dropped his arm. He climbed the remaining steps to the next landing and opened the door to the garage. He motioned her to go through. "This is our level. Let's talk in the car."

"What more is there to say? I'm taking the bus home, remember? You quit."

"I changed my mind."

"Why?"

"I'll get you what you want, but my help comes with strings attached."

She eyed him cautiously. "What kind of strings?"

"Consider me your new partner."

"Partner?"

"I don't want a fee, I want a share," he said. "When we get the ticket, I take twenty percent." He waited for a response. When she gave none, he shrugged and entered the garage.

This time it was Amelia who shook her head like a surfacing swimmer. She grabbed the door before it finished swinging shut and raced after him. She caught up to him as he unlocked the car. "That's outrageous!"

He opened the passenger door, waited until she was seated, then slammed her door, rounded the car and slid behind the wheel. "Outrageous? You of all people should be careful about using that word, considering the charade you've been putting on for the past eight days. I'm offering you a fair deal."

"I'm not giving you twenty percent of my money. What on earth makes you think I would agree to a deal like that?"

He backed out of the space carefully and wound his way through the garage and down the ramps to ground level. He didn't answer her question until he had paid the attendant and merged into the traffic on the street. "You'll agree because it doesn't take a mathematical genius to figure out that eighty percent of the money is better than none of it."

"I don't need you. I can get the ticket myself, now that I know where it is."

"Can you? Do you think Whitcombe's going to let you wander around the gallery on your own again after what you just pulled?"

Probably not. She might not find the storeroom door unlatched next time, either.

"And you can forget the auction. Unless you've got another secret lottery ticket stashed away somewhere, you'd never be able to win the bidding."

That was true, too. The three hundred and fifty dollars in her first-and-last fund wasn't even close to the price range of the paintings she'd seen today. She ground her teeth.

They neared the yellow building that housed the gallery. Hank jerked his head toward it as they passed. "Another thing to keep in mind—I know where that ticket is, too. If you don't take my deal, what's to stop me from getting it myself?"

"No! You wouldn't! That's blackmail!"

"Why are you acting so shocked? I'm just doing what you expected. That's what you were worried about from the start, wasn't it? That I would steal your money the way Spencer did?"

Yes, that was what she'd told herself, but in her heart she'd wanted to believe Hank was a decent man. His actions during the past week had proved it. Or so she'd thought. Then again, she knew better than to trust her judgment, didn't she? She'd made one doozy of a bad choice fifteen years ago. The past she'd assumed she'd understood had been turned upside down. There was too much to sort through right now, but one fact was clear. She'd made an even bigger mess of her life than she'd realized.

"Lucky for me you didn't take the time to sign the back of the ticket."

"How did—" She caught herself too late. She banged her head against the back of the seat and completed her question, since she'd already given it away. "How did you guess?"

"You wouldn't have been acting this desperate if you'd taken the time to sign it, which I guessed because I'm taking time to think things through." He slowed to a stop at an amber light. Cars honked behind him. "There are consequences to always being in a hurry."

He was making an effort to sound calm and reasonable, but his knuckles were white where he gripped the wheel and the tendons stood out on the backs of his hands. She turned to look at him. A quick flick of his eyes was the only indication that he sensed her regard. He kept his attention fixed on the road. If anything, his expression was even harder than it had been in the stairwell. He was still furious.

She laid her fingers on his sleeve. Beneath his jacket, his arm felt like steel. "Hank…"

A muscle in his jaw ticked. "Don't try it."

"What?"

"This," he said, lifting his hand from the wheel to wave it back and forth between them, mimicking the gesture she'd used minutes ago.

The motion also shook off her touch. She clenched her hands in her lap.

"I won't pretend that I'm not physically attracted to you, Amelia," he said. "And from the way you participated in that kiss a few minutes ago, I'd say the attraction's mutual."

She couldn't argue with that so she remained silent.

"But the chemistry or hormones or *history* or whatever you want to call it that's going on between us is irrelevant," he said. "We both have our priorities straight now. Our partnership isn't personal, it's strictly business."

His declaration should have pleased her. She'd wanted their relationship to be professional from the beginning. She didn't need any more complications. No, indeed. She'd told herself countless times to focus on the ticket. "I can't believe you're serious about taking twenty percent."

"Why not? Sentiment doesn't pay the bills. Only a fool would pass up a chance at getting that kind of money." He waited until the light had changed, looked both ways to ensure the intersection was clear and drove forward. "You see, I may be slow on the uptake, but I do learn my lesson eventually."

She wished she could say the same about herself. This was the second time she was about to lose a fortune to a man.

Yet she still couldn't equate Hank to Spencer. Her husband had left her with nothing. Hank wanted to leave her with the lion's share, and he was being up front and honest about it.

And eighty percent of fifty-two million was still a fortune. It would be more than enough to help her family and put her on the path to a promising future. Now that the truth was out, she and Hank could direct their efforts to recovering the ticket itself rather than the painting, and thus had a better chance of actually succeeding.

Regardless of what it would cost her, this deal was her best bet.

So Amelia suspected the sense of loss she felt during the long, tense trip back to Port Hope wasn't entirely due to the money.

CHAPTER TEN

The Mystery Millionaire

1, 3, 4, 17, 23, 29 are someone's lucky numbers, but the $52,485,720 prize in the August 3rd Lotto 6/49 draw remains unclaimed. According to the Ontario Lottery and Gaming commission, it is not unusual for lottery winners to delay coming forward, particularly in the case of a near-record jackpot. Many winners wish to ensure they have a financial plan in place in order to deal with their newfound wealth, as well as measures to address media interviews and personal security issues. Meanwhile, speculation as to the identity of the winner continues to build. An OLG spokesperson confirmed that the single winning ticket for the August 3 draw was purchased in Northumberland County, a region located east of the Greater Toronto Area. Ticket holders are urged to check their numbers—if the prize is not claimed within one year, the winnings are forfeited and the money is returned to the pot.

HANK SCROLLED TO the end of the article, but didn't bother following any more links. All the Toronto papers had posted similar stories on their websites. So had the TV networks. Sure. Who wouldn't be interested in $52,485,720?

Or in his case, $10,497,144?

He leaned back in his chair, stacking his hands behind his head as he contemplated his office's thrift-store decorating scheme. Once he got his share of the money, he could spring for new furniture and maybe some real art on the walls. Those ink drawings he saw at the gallery yesterday weren't half bad. He could get a faster computer with a bigger screen that would make the research he did easier on the eyes. For those jobs that involved surveillance, he could use a more powerful telephoto lens for his digital camera, a few more of those miniature video cameras and maybe a portable DVR to monitor the feeds. He could move to a better office, one with an air conditioner that could keep up with the midday heat.

But he liked this building. It had character that money couldn't buy. He liked the dips in the wooden stairs that had been worn down by more than a century of passing feet. He enjoyed the sense of history that permeated the age-darkened mahogany trim in the hallway. The funky, old doors with the frosted-glass windows could have come straight from the set of an old black-and-white detective movie. That appealed to him, too. This office might be hot in the summer, but in the winter when the leaves were down, if he angled his head just right, he had a great view of the lake. And he'd just gotten this chair nicely broken in.

On the other hand, if he had ten million dollars, would he bother coming to the office at all? He wouldn't need to work. He could go fishing every day if he wanted to. He pictured his favorite fishing spot, up a trail a few miles north of town, where a grove of willows overhung the riverbank. Nothing much would be biting at this time of day, but it would be cool in the shade. Quiet, too.

Fishing wasn't complicated. That's why he liked it. You chose your bait, you made a cast, you reeled it back in. Sometimes the hooks might snag on a tree branch or on a rock on the bottom, but if the line snapped, it was no big deal, as long as you weren't foolish enough to have risked a lure that you really cared about.

It was smart to be cautious. Otherwise, you left yourself open for disappointment and pain. He'd believed he'd learned that lesson solid—it was how he'd led his life from the day his mother had died—but obviously he'd needed a refresher course.

You hide behind your caution like a kid under his security blanket.

The image of the fishing spot winked out. So did the daydream about money he didn't yet have. Instead, he saw the look on Amelia's face when she had agreed to take his deal. Her jaw had been tight with anger. His threat to retrieve the ticket on his own had left her no choice, and she would have hated being finessed. He'd expected that. What he hadn't expected was the hint of pain in her gaze. It had been easy to recognize. He'd seen the same thing in the mirror more than a decade ago.

Hank rocked his chair forward, propped his elbows on the desk and tunneled his fingers through his hair. He'd long ago accepted the fact that he was a fool over Amelia. It was no coincidence that her parents had named her after the famous aviatrix. She'd been born to fly, to soar, to dare, to push the limits. She'd fascinated him in large part because they were so different. There was just something about her that made him put his common sense on standby.

Not anymore. It had been crazy to hope, even for an instant, that he might have a second chance for a future with her. He was a grown man. It was high time to let go of the past. They had been a mistake the first go-around, and nothing had changed.

But he wasn't going to compound that mistake by walking away from a chance at ten million dollars. That would be downright certifiable.

"What are you running in here, a sauna?"

Hank resisted the urge to sigh. He lifted his head. "Hi, Dad."

Basil Jones loosened his tie as he looked around the office. Despite his complaint, he didn't appear to be suffering from the heat. His shirt was crisp and wrinkle-free. No hint of dampness marred his graying hair or gleamed on his forehead. He was remarkably fit for a man of sixty-four, and he worked out regularly to keep his body trim and his posture straight. He was the same height as his son, and people often commented how alike they looked, but the resemblance was purely superficial.

Their values and temperaments clashed constantly. The older they got, the more apparent those differences became. It was true, as Hank had told Amelia, that matters had improved after he had moved out of his father's house. That's because the less Basil saw him, the fewer opportunities he had to find fault with him.

"You need a new air conditioner," Basil said.

"I'm working on it. How are you doing?"

"Busy. We're always swamped this time of year, clearing inventory off of the lot before the new models come in. I don't know why everyone wants to take their vacation time now."

"It is summer, Dad."

"That shouldn't matter. A man's got to set his priorities, especially in this economy."

"The kids go back to school in a few weeks. Most people want to spend their holidays with their families."

"Most people could use better time management."

Hank pictured another fishing spot, not on a riverbank, but on a long, shallow lake that was bisected by an old, sunken rail bed.

The shore was ringed by swamps. He and his dad used to go trolling for pickerel near one particular bay dotted with rafts of cattails. They would load the gear in the station wagon and hook up the boat trailer the night before, and then leave the house before dawn so they could be out on the water by sunrise. Their lunches usually consisted of sandwiches his mother had made, washed down by cans of root beer or cream soda. Whatever they ate always tasted better when they were out on the lake. Sometimes they would stay out until dark, talking about hockey or football or just listening to the slap of the waves against the aluminum hull.

But that had been a long time ago, back in the days when his father did take vacations during the summer, when he'd had different priorities.

Basil brushed off the seat of the leather visitor's chair and sat, pinching the creases of his trousers to keep the fabric from stretching over his knees. "How about you? Keeping busy?"

"I'm doing okay."

"You didn't look too industrious when I came in. If you put your mind to it, you could take on a lot more cases than you do."

"As a matter of fact, the case I'm working

on now is fairly promising. It should bring in a substantial amount of money."

"Good, good," he said absently. "I should have some credit checks for you to do next week. That should help."

"Sure, whatever you want."

Basil glanced around the office. "Do you remember Ian Taylor? Hammond Taylor's boy? You went to high school with him."

"He was a few years behind me. I didn't know him well."

"He's a real go-getter. He's expanded his uncle's real estate company. Doing great, from what I heard. Specializes in commercial properties."

"Good for him."

"You might want to give him a call."

"Why?"

"He could find you a better location." Basil lifted his hand toward the wall behind the filing cabinet. There was a rough patch in the corner near the ceiling where the plaster had been repaired last spring. "This place is old, and the office could use some sprucing up. You wouldn't want to leave the wrong impression on your customers, would you?"

"And what impression would that be? That I happen to like historic buildings?"

"You know very well what I'm talking about, Hank. If you want to be successful, you should make an effort to look as if you are."

He'd heard variations of this speech before. It was usually preceded by the mention of someone else's son who had become a dentist, or was running for mayor, or was tearing down a corner grocery store and building a Tim Hortons franchise. Or was expanding his uncle's real estate company. In other words, sons who made their fathers proud.

Normally, the jibes rolled off him. Today, they stung just as badly as when he'd been a teenager. He strove to control his temper. "Is there anything else you wanted to talk about, Dad?"

His father readjusted the creases of his trousers. "In point of fact, yes. I heard you've been seeing that Goodfellow girl again."

"Amelia's hardly a girl anymore."

"Don't be difficult. Do you think that's wise?"

No, it wasn't wise. It had been one of the dumbest things he'd done in fifteen years. He shrugged.

"In your kind of business, it's important to maintain a good reputation," Basil continued. "Your clients are relying on you to be trustworthy. It makes no difference that Amelia beat the charges against her—her reputation is still stained. This is a small town, and people talk. You should be keeping as far away from her as possible."

It wasn't funny, but Hank had a sudden desire to laugh. His father wasn't worried that Amelia might tramp all over Hank's heart, he was only worried she might be bad for business. But that was Basil Jones, wasn't it? If something couldn't be valued in dollars and cents, it held no worth. In that way at least, his father and Amelia had something in common.

Would Basil change his tune if he learned about Amelia's ticket? Would he be proud of the way his son had coerced her into agreeing to split it? Probably. He would have ridiculed Hank's initial decision to work for free. He would be pleased to hear he'd smartened up. "Don't worry about me," Hank said. "I've got my eyes open as far as Amelia's concerned."

"Good." He slapped his knees once, then rose to his feet. "One more thing. About that father-son golf tournament this Saturday?"

Hank nodded. He didn't particularly care for golf, but his father did, so he'd made sure to keep the date open. A few hours straight in each other's company was a rare occurrence, and one of them had to make the effort. Besides, playing golf gave Basil something neutral to focus on. "Starts at ten, right?"

"I'll have to cancel."

"Why?"

"A leasing company rep I've been trying to make a deal with is going to be in town for the weekend. Saturday morning's the only time he's got free."

"Sure, no problem." Hank picked up a pen, opened his day planner and drew a line through the entry for Saturday.

"We'll play a few rounds some other weekend."

"Uh-huh."

Basil seemed uncomfortable with Hank's even responses. Or maybe he was simply hot. He flashed a tight smile. "You understand, don't you, son?"

"Yes, I understand."

"We'll get together for lunch sometime soon. I promise."

Hank nodded a goodbye and watched him leave, then methodically scratched more lines through the calendar entry. He didn't stop until the pen wore a hole in the paper.

AMELIA SMOOTHED THE pieces of foam-backed, insulating fabric along the length of the futon, lining up the selvages carefully. She had learned the rudiments of sewing in Miss Weir's grade eight home-ec class, but hadn't made anything since the gingham apron that had been her final project. It had rated a B-, which had been the lowest mark she'd received in any subject throughout her school years. Fortunately, curtains were fairly simple, which was why Jenny had allowed her to help. She took the box of pins from the sewing table and sat cross-legged on the floor.

"What are you going to do now?" Jenny asked.

"I'm going to pin this seam."

"I meant about Hank."

She leaned over the curtains-to-be and inserted a pin. She had told her sister-in-law that Hank had learned about the ticket, but she hadn't told her what he'd revealed afterward about their personal history. She wasn't ready to talk about that. She was still sorting through it herself. "He said he wanted to do some background research on Whitcombe and his gallery. We've scheduled a meeting tomorrow to discuss our next step."

"You don't sound happy about it."

"It's *my* ticket, Jenny. I don't like having to split it."

"If it wasn't for his help, you wouldn't know where it was. Giving him twenty percent sounds fair. It's like a commission, or a finder's fee."

"He did it to get back at me."

"Can you blame him? I told you not to lie."

The next pin lodged in Amelia's fingertip. She jerked her hand back and stuck her finger in her mouth.

"You're lucky he's still willing to work with you."

She withdrew her finger, watching a bead of blood form on the tip. "Don't start with me. Please. I feel rotten enough about deceiving him, but I thought it was the right thing to do at the time. And I was planning to pay him a reward, a really big reward, but not as big as ten million dollars."

Jenny's trademark *hmph* was lost in the whir of the sewing machine as she stitched up the hem on a set of panels that were already joined. She had bought the heavy material a few months ago, designating it for the windows in the new bedroom Will had built in the basement. Owen and Eric would be moving into it as soon as the drywall was sealed and painted, which was likely what Will was doing now, since the smell of primer was wafting through the house.

He'd skimmed pond scum at the yacht club again this morning and had gone to work on the basement renovation immediately after lunch. The older boys had joined him, eager to help their dad with what they called "guy" stuff. Though it was questionable how much help a ten-year-old and a six-year-old could actually provide, Will had made sure to find small tasks to make them feel useful.

Naturally, Toto had somehow acquired skunklike stripes of white primer down the center of his back, and Timmy had taken an extra hour to calm down for his nap after his brothers had pretended to use his yellow bunny for a paint rag, but that just meant the family was back to normal. Will and Jenny's argument had blown over as quickly as a summer thunderstorm, and like a storm, it had cleared the air. The two of them seemed closer than ever. The kids had relaxed again, too. It was amazing that they could be so happy, since nothing else had changed. Will didn't have steady work, Jenny's baby was due in a matter of weeks, and the about-to-expand family was still packed into this house like sardines, in spite of the extra basement bedroom.

The sewing machine whined to silence. Jenny picked up a pair of scissors, snipped the threads and transferred the finished curtain section to the ironing board she'd set up beside the table. The pile was growing at an impressive rate.

Amelia popped her finger back in her mouth to get rid of the blood, then dried it on her shorts before she handed the fabric she'd pinned to Jenny. "You're really good at sewing," she said, hoping to change the subject. "I think it's great how you and Will can do things yourselves."

"I made every curtain and drape in this house myself because it was a fraction of the cost of buying them ready-made."

"Well, whether they're cheaper or not, they look terrific."

"Did you ever make curtains for your condo, Amelia?"

"Uh, no. The decorator handled that."

"Do you think Eric and Owen would be happier if their curtains were custom-made by a professional decorator?"

"I doubt it would make a difference."

"I do, too."

"I hope this isn't leading up to a speech about money not buying happiness."

"Well, it doesn't. The really important things in life don't come with a price tag."

"Sure, but everything else does. You need the money from my ticket. With my brother still laid off and your baby due in less than three weeks—"

"We'll manage, Amelia."

"But…"

"Haven't you seen what Will is doing?"

"Do you mean his part-time jobs?"

"For starters, yes. There aren't many men who would take those jobs when they have the kind of skills that Will does. He's like an artist with wood. Some of the furniture he's made are works of art in their own right." She smiled in the direction of the basement stairs. "But does he complain? Does he moan about his fate or sit around waiting for some magic solution to drop into his lap? No, he's out there busting his butt. He worked all morning out on the water, but instead of taking it easy when he got home, he jumped right into his reno project so he could make life more comfortable for his children."

"He's a good father."

"And he's a wonderful husband. If he was a millionaire, I wouldn't love him any more than I do now."

Amelia had tried loving a millionaire, but no amount of wealth would have made Spencer Pryce a good husband. She frowned over something else Jenny had said. "Is that what you think I'm doing? Waiting for a magic solution to my problems?"

"Aren't you?"

"There's nothing magic about a lottery ticket. It's just a series of numbers, and winning it was a matter of beating the odds. I could show you the mathematical formula for calculating them."

"But what if that ticket hadn't won?"

Amelia shifted on the floor, drawing up her knees to lean her back against the edge of the futon. "You're one tough lady."

"What makes you say that?"

"I keep trying to avoid the lecture but you're not backing off one inch, are you?"

"If you know it's coming, why are you trying to avoid it?"

"Because that's what I do. I skim right by anything that hurts, or so I've heard."

Jenny set aside the pinned curtains, grasped the sewing table to push herself to her feet, and moved the two steps to the futon to sit beside the place where Amelia leaned. "You know I love you, Amelia," she said softly. "You've been the sister my parents never gave me."

A lump the size of a ping-pong ball formed in her throat. First Will, now her sister-in-law. The generosity of her family was truly humbling. "I feel the same way about you, Jenny."

"And I hate to interfere, but I think you're making a mistake with Hank."

"Hank? Why? I'm not lying to him anymore. He knows the truth now."

"Does he know you still love him?"

"Love? Jenny, it's your pregnancy hormones talking again. I don't love him. How could I? I never did in the first place. We were kids. It was a crush. We didn't know what love was."

Jenny waited until Amelia's rush of words ran down, then stroked Amelia's hair, the same way she stroked the boys' hair when they were upset. "I don't know why so many people assume there's a minimum age for falling in love. I met Will when I was nineteen. I've been in love with him ever since. Mind you, what I feel now isn't the same fluttery, over-the-moon infatuation I felt then. Love changes as it grows, like any living thing. When Owen was born, it stretched to include him. It expanded to include Eric and Timothy, too. Sometimes, when we deal with problems, our love can get pulled awfully thin, yet afterward we realize the stress made it deeper, as if another layer's been added to strengthen and protect it."

"What you and Will have is very special."

"It's not unique to us, but yes, it's special. It's why we can be happy in spite of our troubles."

"It's also why you can get over your arguments so fast."

"That comes with practice. Just because I love my husband doesn't stop him from driving me crazy at times. I'm well aware of his faults, and he knows all about mine, too. We've learned to deal with them. Neither of us expects the other to be perfect. Otherwise, it would be fantasy, not love."

The low rumble of Will's voice came from the basement, followed by the higher-pitched voices of the boys. Though the words were too muffled to make out, their tone was calm and easy. Homey and ordinary. Amelia slid around on the floor to face Jenny. "Well, whatever you call it, you two were meant to be together."

"I'm not saying we haven't had our share of disagreements over the years. Married couples who claim they don't are either in denial or aren't really sharing a life. But no matter which of us is to blame initially, it takes both of us to work it out. The key is trying to see things from the other person's point of view."

"You make it sound simple."

"It is, once you cut through all the peripherals. Take our latest spat over Will's layoff. He was a real sweetie for trying to spare me the worry and handle the burden on his own. He did it because he was trying to make me feel better. The main reason I got mad was because he hadn't let me share the load and make *him* feel better." She sighed. "I also got annoyed by how Carolyn put the news in an email. She could have waited to tell me about Lancaster face-to-face. But I'm over that now, too. She did mean well."

"How did you know you and Will were right for each other?"

"That's hard to answer. We just did, I suppose. It was instinct. Neither of us could imagine a life without the other."

"That was obvious at your wedding. You both were practically glowing, and that was before Will got into the champagne."

Jenny laughed, then crossed her legs suddenly, a pinched look on her face.

Amelia twisted to her knees. "What's wrong? Is it the baby?"

Jenny shook her head, inhaling deeply through her nose. She exhaled slowly through her mouth, her expression easing. "Nothing's wrong. Sometimes when I laugh, the baby does a tap dance on my bladder. You'd think with the fourth I would know better." She rested her palm on top of her protruding stomach. "But let's not change the subject. We're talking about you and Hank."

"I'd rather talk about my new niece or nephew."

"I remember how you smiled when you caught my bouquet. You were so happy. And Hank was totally smitten. He couldn't take his eyes off you. I was sure the two of you would be inviting us to your wedding one day."

So had she. Catching the bouquet, dancing with Hank, seeing how blissful Will and Jenny were…all of that had made her eager to get started on her life with the boy she loved. She hadn't believed they'd been too young—her own parents were married at twenty and twenty-two, and they'd been a perfect example of how a couple could grow together. Amelia hadn't wanted to go to university and leave Hank. She'd waited all that summer, hoping he would ask her to stay. When there was one day left and he had yet to broach the subject, she'd taken matters into her own hands and proposed.

She'd been certain he would say yes. She'd believed that when someone said they would love you forever they really would. Why else would they have talked about the kind of house they would live in, and the number of children they would have? Being an only child, he'd wanted at least three kids. She'd envisioned a houseful of redheaded boys and blonde girls. And the house would have a big, sunny kitchen and a wraparound porch and plenty of trees in the yard for the kids to climb....

The memory of his refusal still hurt, but the source of the pain had changed. It didn't spring from what had happened, but from what might have been. If only he'd told her the truth. If only she'd *seen* the truth. If only she had been patient, had trusted her feelings....

But she wasn't good at waiting. And Hank wasn't good at venturing out of his comfort zone. Besides, if she'd really loved him, would she have fallen for Spencer? If Hank had really loved her, wouldn't he have tried harder to win her back? Their dreams for the future had been hopelessly naive. Their relationship might have been doomed, anyway. They probably would have broken up sooner or later, just as Hank had said.

Probably. If only. Might have been. Were there any sadder words in the English language?

"Hank was a nice boy," Jenny said. "I was surprised when you two broke up. I was absolutely astonished when you married Spencer Pryce. You never looked at him the way you looked at Hank."

No, she hadn't. She'd considered herself older and wiser by then. She got to her feet, contemplating escape. The ironing board blocked her way to the door.

"Tell me," Jenny persisted. "What did you feel when you saw Hank last week for the first time after so many years? Were there any sparks?"

"That's irrelevant."

"Were there?"

She shrugged. "You've seen him lately, haven't you? The man's a six-foot-three, blond-haired, brown-eyed, steel-jawed, broad-shouldered hunk of eye candy."

"Aha. So you admit there still is something between you."

"It's only a physical…" Her words trailed off. She couldn't complete the lie. She'd known the moment Hank had kissed her there was more between them than a physical attraction. At least there'd been more for her. "It's too late. If love is a living thing, like you said, then it can die."

"If love isn't nurtured, of course it can die. But I don't think it has with you and Hank."

"Jenny—"

"I think it's just been lying dormant, waiting for the right time to bloom again."

"Did anyone ever tell you that you're a hopeless romantic?"

"How do you think I got all these kids?"

"Well, you're definitely seeing things through your pregnancy hormones again. Hank and I agreed that our relationship is strictly business, and that's how it's going to stay. There's more than fifty-two million dollars at stake here."

"Did money make you happy before?"

Amelia threw up her hands. "You're as bad as Toto with a bone. You just won't let it go."

"Think about it, Amelia. That's all I ask."

"I'll think about it after I get the ticket."

CHAPTER ELEVEN

"RUPERT WHITCOMBE opened his gallery five years ago. He's put on his so-called charity gala and auction each August since then. It's grown in size every year." Hank pushed a plain, buff-colored folder across his desk. It bulged with paper. "Here are the details I've gathered so far. It's all I could get without taking another trip to the city."

Amelia dragged her chair closer to the desk, opened the folder and leaned over to leaf through it. Some of the pages were printouts of newspaper articles. Pertinent sections were marked with a yellow highlighter. The sheets containing information on Whitcombe himself were paper-clipped together and neatly subdivided by headings. Evangeline, whose real name turned out to be Gillian Edwards, had a few paper-clipped pages of her own. There were also what appeared to be transcripts of telephone conversations Hank had made to artists and to customers who had dealt with the gallery.

The volume of information impressed her. So did the speed with which Hank had assembled it. She tapped the stack of paper. "You've been busy."

"I didn't find as much as I'd like on Whitcombe."

She dug back through the pile and pulled out the paper-clipped sheets. "Seems like more than enough to me," she said as she scanned the printouts. "You've found where he's from, where he went to school, his employment history…" She paused. "It says here he worked at the Art Gallery of Ontario for twelve years. His art expertise is for real."

"I suppose."

"You don't sound convinced."

"He worked for the AGO as an authenticator. His job involved determining whether or not a painting was a forgery, not whether or not it was any good."

"Still, that would give him the idea of what would sell."

"Maybe. He was involved in one high-profile case where someone claimed a piece on display at the gallery had been stolen from a private collection. According to Whitcombe, it was a forgery, so the AGO wasn't guilty of receiving stolen property, but they had made a public blooper by accepting it in the first place. He left to open his own gallery a few months later."

Amelia lifted her gaze from the folder to Hank's face. He must have been working nonstop from the time they'd gotten back from Toronto in order to put together this report, and it showed. He had never been a man who fussed with his appearance, but his shirt was beyond rumpled. She suspected he'd slept in it. His eyes were red-rimmed and shadowed. His hair stood up in finger-combed ridges. He looked tense and exhausted. She had a crazy urge to get out of her chair, stride around the desk and take him in her arms....

She stamped out the impulse before she could move. Until now, she had been careful not to regard him too closely. That had been easy to do, because he had seemed to avoid looking at her since she'd entered his office. He'd closed the door behind her, waved her toward the chair she'd used the other time and taken his seat behind his desk. There had been no polite inquiry about her health or banal observation about the weather. He hadn't commented on the fact that she'd turned up ten minutes early for their meeting, either. Instead, he'd gotten right down to business.

Well, she'd wanted to keep their relationship professional, and he was definitely doing that. She returned her attention to the documents in front of her. "I don't understand why you're worried about Whitcombe's background."

"Something's not right with him. He seems shady. And why would his assistant use an alias?"

"She probably decided that Evangeline sounded more artsy than Gillian. What difference does any of this make to getting the ticket?"

"I don't like surprises."

"Yes, you've made that crystal clear."

"Making impulsive decisions seldom works out. I prefer to be fully informed before I decide on the best way to proceed."

She closed the folder and crossed her arms. "Since we're partners, you meant to use the plural there, right?"

"What?"

"If there are any decisions to make, *we* make them."

"Fine. I believe *our* best option for recovering the ticket is to attend the auction next Friday and buy the painting."

"Why wait until then? We know where it is."

"Evangeline is a full-time employee at the gallery, and Whitcombe spends most days there, as well. Both of them would be sure to recognize us. After Tuesday's fiasco, they probably won't allow us to go wandering past the showroom again, especially not you. And if you're contemplating breaking in after hours, forget it."

"We wouldn't steal anything. We'd only be taking the ticket."

"From what I observed, Whitcombe has an impressive security system. I don't have the skills to get past it, even if I wanted to. My field of expertise is gathering information, not breaking and entering. Which *is* a crime, whether we take anything or not, and I don't intend to risk getting arrested and losing my P.I. license just because my partner's got the fidgets."

"Fidgets? You sound like Mrs. Milsom, our grade five teacher."

"Then stop sounding like a fifth grader. Breaking in," he muttered, shaking his head. "I'm surprised you didn't suggest dressing up in disguises and masquerading as customers again."

Not for a million dollars would she admit

the thought had crossed her mind. "Going to the auction has an obvious drawback. What if we don't win the bidding?"

"We'll have to make sure we do." He pulled open the top drawer of his desk and withdrew the brochure Whitcombe had given them at the gallery. The edges were still curled from when Hank had rolled it up to slip in his pocket. He smoothed it out and tossed it on top of the folder. "You went through it too fast before. Take another look, and this time pay closer attention to the other pieces of art."

She picked up the brochure and flipped straight through to number fifteen. Her pulse bumped at the sight of her painting. She rubbed her fingers over the photo. Even this much contact helped solidify the possibility of recovering it.

"Amelia?"

She lingered over the picture for another moment, then went back to the beginning to study the other entries more thoroughly. There were twenty in all, including some street scenes done in oil and several abstract paintings that appealed to her. There were also some poorly composed watercolor studies of garden flowers, a sleeping dog on a rocking chair, and still lifes done with wildly bright acrylics.

"Notice anything?"

"Well, I'm no art critic, but a few of these are pretty bad."

"I agree. It's an odd mix. None of them were on display at the gallery when we were there. I didn't see any in the storeroom, either. Did you?"

She thought back. "I think I saw some of those acrylics. There were a lot of packing crates, so other paintings could have been in those. Some could have been behind that door."

"What door?"

"The steel one with all the locks. It was in the back wall."

"I missed that. I guess I was distracted by the swooning lady."

Just as she had been distracted by being swept into Hank's arms. Her gaze drifted back across the desk. He'd left the top two buttons of his shirt unfastened. It gaped limply to one side, revealing the edge of one collarbone. His square shoulders stretched the rumpled fabric deliciously. So did his broad chest. A quiet tingle crept over her skin as she remembered his embrace, how good it felt to be held, how good he smelled....

Her eyes met his. He was scowling. She matched his expression. "I didn't swoon," she said. "I was improvising."

"Uh-huh. You're good at putting on an act, I'll give you that."

She exhaled slowly, striving for patience, and returned her gaze to the catalog. "I wonder if Whitcombe acquired all these pieces specifically for his auction."

"From what he said to us at the gallery, it seems that way."

"The proceeds are supposed to go to charity." Amelia read the front of the booklet. "To send underprivileged kids to camp."

"The charity's legit. I checked that out, too."

"It explains why he cruised a flea market for art. He minimized his cash outlay for the auction. It also could be why he bought my painting from Hazel outright instead of going the commission route with her. He anticipates recouping his costs through the increased business the publicity from his event will bring in."

"Guess you would know about all that stuff."

"It's basic economics. There's nothing

shady about any of this. Making it a charity event will give him a tax deduction, as well as some good PR from the newspaper write-ups."

"Not exactly a philanthropist."

"So what if he's not a philanthropist? He's a businessman."

"I did an internet search for other paintings by Jonathan Mathers. I found two for sale at a gallery in Warkworth and three in Kingston, and they'd been there for months. Whitcombe lied about Mathers's work being in demand."

"Who cares? He was giving us a sales spiel, like Hazel did with her milk cans and her mirror."

"Why are you defending him?"

"I don't see why you're digging into all this, anyway. Or do you have a general grudge against people who try to make money?"

"Not me. That's what we're here for."

"Fine."

"Good."

"I believe you were trying to make a point about the art up for auction?"

He stretched his arm across the desk and pulled the catalog back. "Since none of it was on display at the gallery, none of it had been priced, so it's hard to predict what any of it will sell for. To that end, I did some research on the other artists in the brochure besides Mathers. They can be divided into two groups. Six of the artists had paintings for sale at other galleries that were priced in the hundreds. The paintings of the other fourteen were selling for around ten thousand."

"That's a big gap. What were the prices of those Mathers paintings you mentioned?"

"They were all priced under two hundred."

"Less than two hundred? That's great! That means we should be able to win the bidding!"

"There's a good possibility, yes."

"Why didn't you just say so at the start?"

"I thought you would want to know how I reached my conclusion, seeing as how you seem to have a problem trusting me."

And you still avoid making a commitment. Amelia had to dig deep for more patience, but somehow, she managed to hold back the automatic retort. Trying to approach this from Hank's point of view helped. She had taken months, no, years to cool off after he had hurt her in the past. It had only been two days since she'd dropped her bombshell on him. "I realize you're probably still a bit annoyed with me for bending the truth," she began.

"Bending?" He snorted. "That's one way to put it."

"And it would be easy for both of us to keep sniping at each other, but we need to focus, okay? Let's keep this professional."

"Fine."

"Good."

Hank curled his fingers around the arms of his chair.

She did her best not to fidget as the silence grew. She knew he was waiting for her to break it, because she usually did, and she didn't want to wait all day. Her gaze strayed to her wrist.

"You've done that before," he said.

"Okay, we've already established that I lied. There's no need to keep harping on it."

"That's not what I meant. I've noticed you often look at your wrist but you don't have a watch. What happened to it?"

"I sold it. I sold all my jewelry."

"Guess it was a Rolex or something fancy like that, huh?"

"No, it was the gift my parents gave me when I finished high school."

Hank's cheek flexed, as if he were gnawing the inside of it. "I remember that watch. It was gold, wasn't it?"

She nodded. "With a diamond at twelve o'clock. It wasn't worth anywhere near as much as a Rolex, but I always wore it. I hated having to sell it."

"Yet you hung on to a Rubbermaid tub full of fancy clothes."

"Sure, go ahead and judge me, Hank. Everyone else has. Don't bother stopping to think that a watch can be sold a lot more readily than used clothes that fit a woman my height."

"It would be worth more, too."

"Much more. The watch was precious, not because of what it cost but because it was the last thing my parents gave me. I cherished it. I hung on to it as long as I could. Deciding to let it go was like losing a piece of myself, but as you pointed out the other day, sentiment doesn't pay the bills. Gold wouldn't have kept me as warm as a new furnace."

"Wasn't the heat included in your condo..." He trailed off. "You weren't in the city by the time you sold that watch, were you? The furnace was for Will and Jenny."

"That's right. It broke down in February, a week after I moved in. Do you remember how cold last February was?"

He nodded. "It set records."

"They don't know where I got the money." She rubbed her bare wrist. "I'd appreciate it if you didn't tell them."

Another silence threatened. He was the one to break this one, too. "No problem," he said gruffly.

"Fine. Now, if you're done poking into my finances, could we get back on topic?"

"Actually, that's the next thing we should discuss. Finances." He tipped his head toward the brochure. "The auction's cash only."

"Seriously? For a charity fund-raiser? No checks or credit cards?"

"That's what it says on the front page."

"That's nuts. I've never heard of such a thing."

"Chalk up something else that's strange about Whitcombe."

Hank was right. The cash-only stipulation was very strange. But since she didn't have a credit card or a checking account, cash would be her only option, anyway. "I have three hundred and fifty dollars," she said. "To be more precise, I saved three hundred and fifty-one dollars and eighty cents during the time I worked at Mae B's. Jenny really did bring in more than five hundred at her yard sale. I didn't lie about that. And she did offer to let me use it, but that was before Lanc—" She stopped. "Three hundred and fifty should be enough to buy the Mathers."

"I wouldn't count on it, not if there's a bidding frenzy. I've seen auctions before where people care more about winning than actually getting the thing they're bidding on."

She'd seen that happen, as well. "You offered to give me a loan a few days ago, so I'm assuming you can get your hands on some cash. Not to put too fine a point on it, how much would you be able to chip in for the auction?"

His chair creaked as he rocked back toward the window. He didn't reply right away.

"We'll keep track of the amount each of us puts in," she said. "We should be recording any other expenses incurred as well, like your gas money and the tickets for the gala. We'll divide those eighty-twenty and deduct them from our respective shares of the winnings. Does that sound fair to you?"

"Yes, it sounds fair. What happened at Lancaster? That was the word you were about to say, wasn't it?"

"Excuse me?"

"You don't want to use Jenny's money. You were about to mention Lancaster Cabinets. I'm guessing Will was laid off again. Am I right?"

She squinted. His change in position had put the light from the window at his back so she couldn't see his expression. "Yes," she replied.

"That's a tough break. When's the baby due?"

"Less than three weeks."

More creaking as he rocked his chair a few more times. "By the end of the month, I'll have around twenty-two hundred left in my savings account."

"That should be enough, don't you think?"

"Maybe. I'd prefer to bring at least ten thousand in case something unexpected happens."

"*Ten?* Could you get that?"

"I'll do my best to scrape it up."

"But what could happen? It's just a charity fund-raiser put on by a minor-league art dealer, and besides, no one's going to bid that much for a Mathers."

"We have to hope not."

"And since the payment has to be cash, there's a limit to how much anyone would be comfortable carrying. That works to our advantage. I'll bet the selling prices for all the pieces are going to be on the low end of the scale."

"Just trying to be…"

"Cautious," she said.

"I thought we were done with the sniping."

"Who's sniping? I'm just stating a fact."

"Uh-huh. It's a good habit to get into, telling the truth."

Does he know you still love him?

Amelia shook off the memory of Jenny's words and got to her feet. Why was she quibbling? Hank was right to be careful. Ten thousand dollars might be out of reach for her now, but not long ago it wouldn't have made a dent in her budget. It wouldn't mean much to the kind of people who collected art and attended charity galas, either. With so much at stake, it would be a good idea to have extra money available. She and Hank had both learned the hard way that life didn't always go as planned.

THE WHITCOMBE GALLERY Annual Gala and Auction was being held at the Dalton Place Hotel. It was on the fringes of Yorkville, which was a section of Toronto's downtown that was known for chic shops, fancy, over-priced restaurants and serious art galleries that were miles out of Rupert Whitcombe's league. The boutique hotel had only a few dozen guest rooms and was small in comparison to the major chains that had locations throughout the city core. Its primary business came from hosting corporate meetings and events such as Whitcombe's auction, and the staff were well trained to keep things moving. Within seconds after Hank had pulled up beneath the arched portico in front of the red sandstone building, a maroon-coated teenager had driven off with his car.

"Don't worry," Amelia said drily. "You'll get it back. They call this valet parking."

"Uh-huh, I've heard about that. I think I might have seen it in a movie once." He craned his neck to look in the direction his car had disappeared. The repairs had been more extensive than he'd thought at first, and he'd only had it back for a few days. "I hope the kid doesn't ding the new fender."

"After tonight, you can get yourself an entirely new car."

"Why? I like that car." He offered her his arm as they moved toward the entrance. "It's good on gas, and the gray paint hides the dirt."

She made a *tsking* sound, hitched the

chain of her beaded evening purse on her shoulder and placed her hand in the crook of his elbow. "You have no imagination," she said.

The comment didn't bother him. Since their big fight, they'd progressed from criticizing each other to trading something closer to banter. He suspected it was one of Amelia's ways of coping with her anxiety. She'd never been good at waiting, and the closer the auction drew, the jumpier she'd become. Even through the sleeve of his rented tux, he felt the tremor in her fingers. He covered them with his free hand, pressing them gently against his arm. "That's me, all right. Thick as two planks nailed together. Now, relax and smile for the camera."

"What?"

"There's a closed circuit video camera to the right of the door."

"Near the Incredible Hulk?"

There was no question who she meant. The man was enormous, and had the no-neck, puffed-chest shape of a serious bodybuilder. At first glance, Hank had assumed he must be standing on a step, but the entrance was wheelchair-accessible and dead level. He was simply that big. While he was dressed in a black tux, the earpiece and dark glasses marked him as a security guard. Another two guards were positioned just inside the entrance. They weren't as large, but their demeanor alone was menacing. By contrast, the succession of maroon-jacketed hotel staff who directed Hank and Amelia across the lobby were as smilingly perky as a cheerleading squad.

A good-sized crowd had already gathered in the hotel lounge. Along the far wall, a long, linen-covered table held a colorful array of hors d'oeuvres. Thick velvet drapes the same shade as the staff's jackets covered another wall, the only one where there might have been windows. Although groupings of low-backed, white leather sofas and chairs were scattered throughout the room, few people sat. They stood in small groups or milled around the intricately patterned parquet floor, champagne flutes and tiny white plates grasped in their manicured and beringed hands. Piped-in classical music mixed with the hum of conversation. Though crystal chandeliers glittered overhead, the overall lighting was dim.

Whitcombe stood near the maroon drapes in the midst of a knot of people. He was easy to spot—his ponytailed white hair gleamed like a beacon. His assistant, clad in black again, lurked beside him. Amelia had been right: the name Morticia suited her better than Evangeline or Gillian. In spite of the poor lighting, Hank recognized one of the men in the group as a former goalie for the Leafs. To his left was a box-shaped woman who used to head a national political party. Whitcombe's art might not be high quality, but his guests were. Hank scanned the rest of the room, noting the exits. Apart from the archway to the lobby, there were only two. One was behind the food table and likely led to the hotel's kitchen. The other led to the room where the auction would be held, according to the sign on the easel beside it. As he expected, a pair of security guards was posted beside each exit. With high-profile attendees carrying so much cash, Whitcombe would have needed to ensure there was a large security presence. Which made the cash-only stipulation even more puzzling, since it added significantly to the cost of the event.

On the other hand, maybe these people were getting an added thrill out of the guards' air of silent menace. Hank was no expert when it came to functions like this one. Social events for him usually involved beer, barbecues and jeans. The only other time he'd worn a tux had been at his senior prom. Amelia had been with him then, too.

He braced himself for the inevitable flash of memory—they'd been getting more and more frequent over the past few weeks. Anything could trigger one: the tilt of her head, the way she said his name, or like now, the twin tendrils of red hair that had escaped her French braid and corkscrewed down her neck. For their prom, she'd worn her hair piled on top of her head and had tried to keep it in place with hair spray and countless pins, but those tendrils had defied her then, too. He'd been glad. He'd thought they'd made her even more appealing. He remembered how springy they'd felt when he'd twined them around his fingers, and how silky they'd felt against his lips when he'd kissed her neck.

And that memory naturally led to the one of their most recent kiss. In a smelly cement stairwell. In the middle of an argument.

He wished he could still be angry. That would have been simpler. He'd stretched it out as long as he could, but staying mad was exhausting. Besides, it interfered with their goal. That was one thing they were in complete agreement on. Getting hold of that lottery ticket was the only reason they were together. To that end, they had to pretend to be a happy couple, out for an enjoyable evening.

Hank didn't have to pretend very hard, though. Amelia looked beautiful tonight. Her dress was gray, but the shade bore no resemblance to the color of his car. Gauzy layers of smoky fabric surrounded her body like mist around a waterfall, flowing delicately over her curves to curl in uneven waves below her knees. The dress gave off a liquid shimmer as she moved, lending her the air of a magical being, an illusion only the lucky could see.

A waiter glided up to them with a tray of champagne flutes. Amelia released Hank's arm and reached out to pluck one.

Hank declined with a shake of his head, waited until the man had moved on, then took the glass from Amelia. "Thanks."

"Hey, that's mine," she said. "You could have taken one for yourself. It's an open bar."

"You shouldn't be drinking in your condition."

"Are you kidding? The alcohol will be good for my nerves."

"Did you forget that Whitcombe knows our secret?"

"What?" she whispered.

"That you're pregnant, darling."

She pressed her lips together, her nostrils flaring as she inhaled. "Right."

"Amelia? Oh, my goodness! Is that you?"

At the woman's voice, they both turned.

A small, painfully thin blonde in a sparkly pink dress grasped Amelia's hands. "I don't believe this," she said. "It *is* you!"

Amelia curved her lips into a smile that didn't get anywhere close to her eyes. She leaned down to bring her cheek next to the woman's while they exchanged air kisses. "Hello, Cecelia. How nice to see you again."

"Yes, it's a wonderful surprise. How long has it been?"

"Since Spencer's arrest, I believe."

"A terrible, terrible time," she said, shaking her head. The string of pearls that hung around her neck swayed over her protruding collarbones. "I was just thinking about you the other day. I'm so glad that you've decided to circulate again. I had heard that Rupert's parties have become the place to be."

"Yes, we've been looking forward to it." She gestured toward Hank. "This is Hank Jones, a very old friend of mine. Hank, Cecelia Steinman. She used to be Spencer's and my neighbor. Her apartment was on the same floor as ours."

"Delighted to meet you, Hank," Cecelia said. She let go of Amelia and held her fingers out for Hank. "And what do you do?"

He took her hand carefully. It was like squeezing a sack of sticks. "Right now, I'm hoping to collect some art."

Cecelia laughed. "Aren't we all? Normally I spend August at my Muskoka house, but this year I was determined not to miss the fun. And it's all for such a good cause," she added.

"Then you must like kids," Hank said.

"Kids?"

"The good cause? Sending kids to camp?"

"Of course. I adore them." Cecelia laughed again, glancing from Hank to Amelia. "I must say, you're looking marvelous, Amelia."

"Thank you, Cecelia."

"I've always liked that dress. Didn't you wear it to the symphony benefit a few years ago?"

"Yes, it's one of my favorites."

"And it suits you so well, I can't blame you at all for bringing it out again. This season's fashions are so problematic for anyone who isn't a size two." She moved her gaze down to Amelia's stomach. "And it's draped so cleverly you barely show."

"Show?"

Cecelia leaned closer. "Congratulations."

"For what?"

"I admire you for getting on with your life, especially after how publicly Spencer humiliated you with that woman." Her lips pursed, as if she were savoring something tasty. "Has he heard yet?"

"Cecelia, I really don't know what you're talking about."

"Why, your pregnancy, of course."

Hank quickly deposited his full champagne glass on the tray of a passing waiter and slid his arm around Amelia's waist. "It seems our secret's out, darling. Obviously, Cecelia heard us mention the baby."

She opened her mouth, but nothing came out. She looked at Hank.

He smiled. "Will you excuse us, Cecelia? I see someone I promised to talk to." Firming his grip on Amelia, he guided her away before either woman could say more. He didn't stop until they reached a relatively vacant spot between a lush, potted fern and one of the room's central pillars. "Are you okay?" he asked softly.

"Oh, just peachy." She pulled away from him. "As if the gossips needed another tidbit to pass around."

"Maybe she won't say anything."

"Yeah, right." She looked down at her stomach and frowned. "I *barely* show?" she muttered, smoothing her dress over her hips.

"I hadn't meant to make things awkward."

"Doesn't matter. And leave it to Cecelia to point out I'm wearing an old dress."

"I thought she was giving you a compliment."

Amelia rolled her eyes. "Men can be so dense."

"Well, I think you look great. Like one of those creatures that lives in the bottom of a stream."

"You're saying I look like a salamander?"

"That's not what I meant. I remember this picture I saw in a mythology book when I was a kid, of a water sprite or fairy or something. The mist flowed around her like a dress. She was...memorable."

"Thank you, Hank." Her gaze moved along his shoulders and down his chest. "You clean up pretty well yourself."

"That's nice of you to say, but I know I look dull next to you. I'd had my heart set on one of those powder-blue tuxes with the ruffled shirt like the one that Bobby Caruthers wore to our prom, but they were all out of my size."

Her lips twitched. "I remember Bobby's tux. I couldn't even look at you when he was around or we'd both burst out laughing. And we were trying so hard to be cool."

"That blue outfit would have livened up this bash. The only one I could find that fit was this old black one. I shouldn't have left it till the last minute, but as you pointed out, I've got no imagination."

"Uh-huh. You manage okay for two thick planks."

He skimmed his knuckles down her arm. "I hope I didn't embarrass you with your friend."

"She wasn't my friend. As I said, I hadn't seen her since Spencer was arrested. She hadn't been one of our clients, so she hadn't lost money because of him, but that didn't stop her from avoiding me like the plague."

"That was rotten."

"Most people I had considered friends did the same, since they assumed that I was as guilty as my husband. The one person who *did* want to associate with me was my lawyer, and that's only because he was getting three hundred bucks an hour."

"I find that hard to believe. Seriously, you must have had some real friends who would have stood by you."

She hesitated, her gaze playing over the crowd. "You're right. Some did. They ended up being the target of the same kind of harassment and suspicion that I was going through, so I stopped talking to them, too."

"For their sake."

"What else could I do? It was bad enough that my reputation was in tatters. It wouldn't have been fair of me to spread the contagion to people I cared about. Why do you think I waited as long as I did before moving back to Port Hope?"

He remembered the reporters who had nosed around town when the story had broken, and the comments from the folks down the street from the Goodfellows about the siege of their neighborhood. "You wanted to spare them the hassle."

"It worked, too. Aside from the odd comment, most people don't mention my troubles, as you called them, anymore. I've gotten used to being normal again. It's been great. I should have realized what would happen if I came back to the city."

"Do you want me to punch her for you?"

"What?"

"Cecelia. Not that I want to strike a woman, especially one without any padding to take a hit. I've never hit anyone, come to think of it. In Cecelia's case, maybe all I'll need to do is wave my hand and the breeze will knock her over."

"Why on earth would you do that?"

"She was mean to you."

The laugh she couldn't stifle seemed to take Amelia by surprise. She swatted his arm. "Now who's sounding as if they were back in Mrs. Milsom's class?"

He caught her hand and twined their fingers together. "You do look beautiful tonight, Amelia."

"Hank…"

"But it's not because of your dress or what you did to your hair. I'm sorry…" He stopped talking when he noticed the approaching figure. He wasn't sure what he would have said, anyway. Was he sorry that she'd had a rough time? Sorry she'd lost the life she'd known? He'd already covered that. Sorry that he couldn't have been there for her? They'd both been responsible for that situation. Sorry he didn't want to admit that she was a warm and generous person? That she wasn't the hard-hearted, mercenary-minded, money-grubbing woman that his injured pride had wanted her to be?

The questions ricocheted through his brain. There was no time to find answers before Rupert Whitcombe was standing in front of them.

"I see you two made it after all. Splendid!" He scrutinized Amelia. "I hope you're feeling better?"

"Yes, thank you, Mr. Whitcombe." Amelia gave him the same lips-only smile she'd given Cecelia. "It appears as if you have a good turnout."

"Indeed we do. The event has expanded every year since its inception," he said, a smug expression on his face as he surveyed the crowded room. "I anticipate this evening's contribution to the Kids' Camp Fund will surpass all our expectations. And please, call me Rupert."

Her gaze dropped to her bare wrist momentarily before she caught herself. "I'm looking forward to the auction. When does it start?"

"It won't be long now. And I hope I may call you Amelia?"

Hank was certain they hadn't introduced themselves at the gallery. He'd deliberately used endearments instead of Amelia's name.

"I finally realized why you seemed so familiar when we met," Whitcombe said. "You're Amelia Pryce. Spencer's wife."

"Amelia Goodfellow," she corrected. "Spencer and I are divorced."

"My apologies. Under the circumstances, cutting your legal ties to him was prudent."

Hank was still holding Amelia's hand. He gave her fingers a squeeze and tucked them into the crook of his elbow, hoping to spare her another round of veiled barbs. "Will you excuse us, Rupert? Amelia tries to be brave but she shouldn't be on her feet too long."

Rather than stepping aside, Whitcombe gestured toward the lobby. "I have just the spot where you can rest," he said. "The hotel has provided a suite for my use. Please, come with me."

"Thank you, Rupert, but that's not necessary," Amelia said. "There's a couch right over here."

"No, I insist." Whitcombe signaled to the guards who were positioned near the exit. They appeared to come to attention. "There's something we need to discuss," he said. "It's regarding your visit to my gallery last week."

Hank didn't like this. He shifted closer to Amelia. "Let's talk here."

"No, I'm positive this is a conversation you would prefer to hold in private," Whitcombe said, looking squarely at Amelia. He smiled. "I understand why you were so eager to buy the Mathers. Let's put our cards on the table, shall we?"

CHAPTER TWELVE

THEY CROSSED THE lobby in silence. It was a good thing that Amelia was hanging on to Hank's arm, because otherwise she might not have made it out of the lounge. Her knees had turned to jelly. Her lungs were still drawing in air because her senses were still functioning, but she didn't have enough breath for speech. That was a good thing, too, because otherwise she might have given in to the urge to scream.

She could think of only one explanation for Whitcombe's actions. He must have stumbled on the ticket.

Well, why wouldn't he? Just because it had been in the frame when she'd last seen the painting didn't mean no one would have noticed it during the ten full days that had passed since then.

Ten days. She'd known she shouldn't have waited.

And she'd been so close. If only she'd found the storeroom ten seconds sooner, or if she'd kept her fingernails a few millimeters longer, or if Hank hadn't grabbed her so quickly...

The enormous security guard who had been stationed at the hotel entrance joined them as they reached the elevators. He got on first, went to the back of the car and turned, his gaze easily passing over their heads. Her stomach lurched as the elevator whooshed to a stop at the top floor. Whitcombe led them down a short corridor lit with shell-shaped glass wall sconces and stopped at a set of double, maroon-painted doors. "We can talk in here," he said, inserting a key card into the slot over one of the door handles. He swung the door open and swept his arm dramatically to invite them inside.

Not that she and Hank had much choice in the matter. The guard remained on their heels until they entered the suite, then backed into the corridor and closed the door. It creaked a moment later, as if he had leaned against it.

Whitcombe moved into the sitting room. It was done in plush, gold carpeting, glass tables and more of the white leather furniture that had decorated the lounge. Lights of neighboring buildings twinkled in the darkness beyond the floor-to-ceiling windows.

Momentarily, anyway. Whitcombe picked up a remote control unit from one of the end tables, pressed a button, and a set of vertical blinds slid over the windows. He continued across the room to a set of French doors through which she glimpsed a bed and a desk. "Make yourselves comfortable," he said. "I'll be right with you."

The moment he was gone, Hank pulled her to the nearest couch. "Don't say anything until we know what's going on," he whispered.

"We know what's going on. He found the ticket!"

He sat, tugging her down beside him. "I don't think so. If he did, he wouldn't need to talk to us, would he? He wants something."

"Maybe he wants to offer us a share of the winnings."

Hank just looked at her.

No, Whitcombe would have no reason to offer them anything. He wouldn't need her permission to cash the ticket, since she had no way to prove it was hers. "Maybe he wants to gloat," she said.

"Whatever he wants, it's important enough to motivate him to leave his guests."

"And to bring the Hulk along."

"I have a feeling something else is going on here. Let's listen to what he has to say."

She dropped her purse on the cushion next to her and clutched Hank's fingers. "You think he *didn't* find it?"

"Before we jump to any conclusions, we need to consider all the possibilities."

"Like what?"

"Well, for one, he might have talked to Hazel again, since she said he'd bought paintings from her before. She could have mentioned that we told her the Mathers was sold by mistake. He might be concerned we'll make a claim on it."

Some of her panic ebbed. "You really think so?"

"We can't be sure of anything until we learn more. We need to draw him out."

"How?"

"Listen to what he says and take our cue from that. He mentioned putting our cards on the table, so let's bluff."

"*Bluff?* This isn't one of your penny-ante weekend poker games. We're playing with fifty-two mill—"

"Shh." He brought their joined hands to her mouth and pressed his thumb to her lower lip. His gaze bored into hers. "Just stay cool and work with me on this, okay? It's not over yet."

She wished he wouldn't touch her like that. It made concentrating difficult.

Whitcombe returned moments later. He was holding what appeared to be one of the auction catalogs. "I must admit," he said, seating himself in one of the armchairs that faced the couch, "I was puzzled by your behavior initially. With so many exquisite works on display, why would you be so insistent about purchasing the Mathers landscape? It is clearly the work of a second-rate amateur."

After the gushing Whitcombe had done in the gallery, his sudden honesty surprised her. Amelia curled what nails she had into her palms. "Perhaps I saw something special in it."

Whitcombe laughed, as if she had said something particularly witty. "Yes, undoubtedly you did, but I hadn't understood how you would be able to. Your interest was, ah, troubling. It was only when I saw you tonight and someone mentioned who you were that I put the pieces together."

"Amelia prefers to keep a low profile," Hank said. "That's why we were reluctant to pursue matters at our initial meeting. We felt it best to be cautious."

"Completely understandable, considering her recent legal difficulties. It's a shame you couldn't have been more forthright with me, though," Whitcombe chided. "It would have saved time."

"We could say the same about you," Hank responded. "You brought us here to talk, but we haven't yet heard anything we don't know."

Irritation flicked across Whitcombe's face. He returned his gaze to Amelia. "How much did Spencer tell you about my auctions?"

Spencer? This was the second time he had brought up her ex-husband's name. Hank could be right. This conversation might have nothing to do with the lottery ticket.

The notion energized Amelia, giving her new hope. She thought fast, searching for cues in Whitcombe's words. He sounded as if he'd known Spencer personally, and given Spencer's fondness for collecting art, it wasn't unreasonable to assume that they'd met. Even though her ex-husband's tastes ran to more established—and much more expensive—artists than the ones featured at the Whitcombe Gallery, it was quite possible he had attended one of the previous auctions. Simply because she didn't remember hearing about it meant nothing, since there were many things he'd done without her knowledge. She hadn't been totally oblivious, though. She would have noticed if he'd brought home a new painting.

She chose her words carefully. "As you know, Spencer was a discerning collector, so you can imagine how very disappointed he was after he lost the bidding on a particular piece that he'd hoped to buy. He was frustrated. He likes to win."

The silence that followed couldn't have lasted more than a split second, but it felt like an hour. To her relief, Whitcombe reacted as if he knew what she was talking about. He lifted a palm. "The terms of the auction were made clear to him. Everyone has an equal opportunity to bid on each work, including the special items."

Special items? Why did that word ring a bell? She had a vague memory of a voice, but it wasn't a man's voice, it was a woman's. It was Evangeline! She'd been talking on the phone while Amelia had been tiptoeing down the corridor to the storeroom. She'd been saying something about the auction....

The arrangements for payment and delivery after the auction will be the same as last year. We'll courier the special catalog to you within the hour....

Amelia regarded what Whitcombe was holding. At first glance, it had seemed to be one of the auction catalogs, but now that she looked more closely, she realized the paper wasn't as thick or as glossy as the copy that he'd given her at the gallery. It could have been made up in someone's office rather than being produced by a professional printing firm. She still had no idea what was going on, so she took Hank's advice and decided to bluff. "That's true, Rupert. Even though Spencer came away empty-handed, he had been impressed by how well organized your event was. Is that the special catalog?" she added, as if it was an afterthought.

Her question seemed to please him. "Then you do know about it?" he asked.

"Of course. I was with my husband when you had the special catalog for one of your previous auctions couriered to him."

He seemed pleased by her answer, too. "Yes, we always have them hand-delivered to our elite clients. They're meant to be kept confidential."

"That's perfectly understandable," she

said, even though she understood zero. What on earth was going on?

"But evidently, someone allowed you to see this year's copy before you came to the gallery."

"Don't blame—" She paused, as if she just caught herself from saying the name. In fact, she was buying time as she scrambled for what direction to take. "I hope you don't blame the person who gave me a peek at that catalog. He was a good friend of Spencer's and mine, and he understood how our recent troubles have curtailed my activities." She sighed. "He was trying to do me a favor."

"And is that why you came to the gallery?" Whitcombe asked.

This time she merely nodded, as if the answer was too obvious to state.

"Amelia is only interested in the Mathers," Hank said. "But I wouldn't mind taking another look at the rest," he added, extending his hand to Whitcombe.

After only a slight hesitation, Whitcombe passed the catalog to Hank. "I trust that Spencer also shared our usual policy concerning the payment for our special items?"

"Are the arrangements the same as in previous years?" Amelia asked.

"They are. In the event you bid successfully, my assistant will issue a tax receipt for the cash, and will provide the account details to enable you to transfer the balance of the funds electronically."

The *balance?* She disguised her wince as a smile. "Excellent."

Whitcombe pulled back his sleeve and glanced at his wrist. Unlike her, he did wear a watch, and it was indeed a Rolex. "I'm sorry, but I can't neglect my other guests any longer," he said as he pushed to his feet. "I'm glad we had this chance to chat. You're welcome to relax here until the auction."

"I appreciate that, Rupert," Hank said, idly leafing through the catalog.

"Yes, thank you," Amelia added. "I look forward to doing business with you."

"And I wish you good luck." Whitcombe tipped his head toward the entrance of the suite. "I'll tell Juri to remain outside and escort you safely back to the lounge when you're ready."

"That's not necessary," Hank said.

"Oh, but I insist." Whitcombe smiled. "We wouldn't want anyone taking a wrong turn this time, would we?"

Amelia waited until the door closed behind him, then twisted to face Hank. "What—"

He tapped her lips with his index finger and cut his gaze toward the door. "Would you like a glass of water, sweetheart?"

"Stop doing that," she whispered, jerking her head back. "No, thanks," she said aloud. "It's refreshing enough just to be off my feet."

"We'll start downstairs in a few minutes, then. Are you still up for the auction?"

"I wouldn't miss it for the world, darling. You sure know how to show a girl a good time."

He watched the door for another half minute or so, then brought his head close to hers and spoke quietly. "I think it's safe to say that Whitcombe didn't find the ticket."

"I agree with you there. He figured I wanted the Mathers because I'd already seen it in the catalog, but I'm still not clear why."

"Could have fooled me. You navigated that conversation like a pro."

"It must be due to all the experience I've had dancing around the truth."

"Let's not get into that now, okay? We've got bigger problems."

"You mean that business about the electronic funds transfer?"

"For starters, yeah. Doesn't seem to be a

strictly cash auction after all. Whitcombe expects to be paid extra."

"But if the ticket's still in the painting, there's no problem. Once we get it, we'll have all the funds we need, regardless of what kind of commission or fee he wants."

"I suspect there's more to it than a simple commission." He put the catalog that he'd been leafing through in her hands. "Take a look at your painting."

She did. The jolt she usually got from seeing it was muted. Unlike the photos in the regular catalog, the colors in this one weren't as vivid, and the resolution wasn't as sharp. There was another more glaring difference: rather than only one painting on the page for item fifteen, there were two. The familiar landscape with the hill and the barns was accompanied by an entirely different landscape, one of foaming water and rugged rocks. Gnarled pine trees, bent from the wind, were silhouetted against a bold, orange-streaked sky. The composition was outstanding, and even the poor reproduction couldn't hide the masterful use of color. It was compelling and passionate. It also seemed familiar.

Hank pointed to the printed description. "Read this."

The second painting had three things in common with the Mathers. It was an Ontario landscape, it was done in oil on canvas, and it was exactly the same size, ninety-two centimeters by sixty. But the artist wasn't a rural doctor who painted for a hobby. "This painting is by A. Y. Jackson!"

"Yup. I don't know much about art, but even I've heard of him."

She frowned at the picture. She didn't recognize it specifically. It was the artist's unique style and subject matter that had made the painting seem familiar. A. Y. Jackson had been one of the artists known as the Group of Seven. They'd risen to fame in the last century for breaking away from the European Impressionists and depicting the beauty in the harsh Canadian wilderness. Along with the other members of the group, Jackson was a legend, a national icon. His work was featured in art books and displayed in museums. Prints of his distinctive Georgian Bay landscapes hung in schools and government buildings throughout the country, so it was no surprise that Hank had heard of him. She doubted there was anyone in Canada who hadn't.

And because Jackson's work was so highly treasured in Canada, as well as throughout the art world, it didn't often come on the market. Just one of his pieces would fetch a price well beyond the total value of everything at the Whitcombe Gallery.

"Why…" Her voice came out hoarse. She tried again. "Why would this painting be in the catalog?"

"The *special* catalog," he amended. "The one that's only given to elite clients. It's obvious why Whitcombe would want to keep it confidential." He paused. "How did you know about it, anyway? Or was that just a good guess?"

"I overheard Morticia." She ran her fingertips from one picture to the other. "I must be missing something. Unless this is a misprint, why stick an extra photo in an auction catalog? Maybe it's obvious to you, but—"

"Look," he said, flipping back a few pages. "I noticed there are duplicate paintings beneath other items, too. They couldn't all be misprints."

"This is crazy," she murmured.

"No, it's brilliant." He thumbed through the catalog from the beginning. "Counting the Mathers, there are six paintings with duplicates. Those are the six we noticed before because they were so bad. They're also comparatively worthless next to the other fourteen. Which pretty well guarantees that no one who wasn't in the know would want to bid on them."

She studied the extra entries he pointed out. She recognized the artists both by name and by their style. Every one of these paintings was outstanding, and would be snapped up by any serious collector, though none would be quite as valuable as a canvas by A. Y. Jackson.

Hank returned to the page with the Mathers. And the Jackson. "The auction's a public event. Whitcombe's hiding this in plain sight."

"Hiding what?"

"He's selling stolen art."

"What?"

"Shh. Juri's still out there. And that's another thing. This explains the level of security Whitcombe brought to the hotel. The cash bidding was just an angle so no one would question all the hired muscle. The stolen artwork must be worth a fortune."

The scope of what Hank was suggesting stunned her. "No. This is impossible. It's too far-fetched."

"Not when you think about it. My instincts told me the guy was shady."

She pushed the catalog back into his

hands, wishing she could push away his ideas as easily. Tipping back her head, she stared numbly at the ceiling, then slowly slid down on the couch until her head rested on the cushioned back.

No. Please, no. Her luck couldn't be this bad, could it? First a yard sale, then a car collector, then a flea market, now a fraudulent art auction. All she wanted was one small piece of paper that she'd bought at the corner Min-A-Mart. "This can't be happening. You're only assuming those extra six paintings are stolen."

"If they weren't, then why the secrecy?"

"There must be some other explanation."

"Nothing that fits. I'll bet the additional funds Whitcombe wants transferred into his account weren't for a commission. They're the balance of the purchase price for the hot paintings. The bid's probably only a fraction of it." Hank snapped his fingers. "Remember I learned that Whitcombe was involved in a case of stolen art when he worked for the AGO? The case was dropped when he claimed the painting was a forgery, but what if it was genuine? What if he made a deal with the thieves? He could have lied to get them off the hook in exchange for a cut. He could have opened his own art gallery to help them move the merchandise."

"Remind me never again to accuse you of having no imagination."

"I'm just putting together the pieces. This is making more sense all the time." He rapped the backs of his fingers against the catalog. "The bulk of these paintings are legitimate, and the cash does go to a real charity, so what better camouflage for fencing stolen goods? With the bids for the special items representing a set percentage of the actual price that's being offered, it can all be done in public. He even gives tax receipts for the cash. And this has been going on for years." He whistled softly. "It's so brazen, no one would suspect a thing. This is mind-boggling."

Oh, it boggled the mind, all right, because hers was reeling. She continued to contemplate the ceiling, seeking in vain for something that would disprove what Hank was saying. It was no use. She must be too upset to think straight, because his wild suppositions were actually sounding reasonable.

"But one thing bothers me," he said.

"You're kidding. Only one?"

"Whitcombe must be smart to pull off a

scheme like this. Why would he risk letting you in on it at the last minute?"

She rolled her head along the cushion to look at him. "That's easy. Spencer."

"Sure, it sounded as if your ex was in on the scam. That was quick thinking, the way you picked up on the implication, but it still doesn't explain why Whitcombe trusted you."

"Spencer was a crook, Hank. A lot of people believe that I was a bigger and better crook than he was, since I beat the charges. Why wouldn't our pal Rupert expect I would pick up where my ex-hubby left off, especially since I raised his suspicions at the gallery by my interest in the Mathers, and then showed up here? Since he doesn't know about the ticket, what else would he assume?"

"But you're divorced. And he thinks you're carrying my child."

"It's not personal, Hank. It's only business. Whitcombe sees me as a potential customer."

"Then he's about to find out he's made a big mistake." He folded the catalog carefully, slipped it into his jacket and pulled out his phone.

"Who are you calling?"

"The police."

"No!" She jerked upright and snatched the phone from his grasp before he could dial. "Don't even think about it!"

"Amelia, we have to tell the authorities what we've discovered."

"If we do, they might stop the auction. Wait until it's over."

"Those stolen paintings are probably in the hotel right now. This could be the only opportunity to catch Whitcombe red-handed."

"I don't care. This could be our only opportunity to recover the ticket. Or have you forgotten why we're here?"

"Things have changed."

"You said we were partners. We're supposed to be working together. That means we make the decisions together, too."

He held out his hand. "Give me the phone, Amelia."

"No. Besides, you have absolutely no proof there's anything criminal about this auction."

"I have the special catalog."

"That doesn't prove anything. There could be a perfectly innocent explanation for it, as well as for the whole cryptic conversation we just had with Whitcombe. We could have misinterpreted everything. You keep reminding me we shouldn't jump to conclusions unless we have all the facts, and we sure don't have much now. All you have is a convoluted theory you've concocted out of your tendency to overanalyze a situation and out of your dislike of anyone who makes more money than you."

He closed his hand into a fist. "So we're back to the money."

"That's the purpose of our partnership, isn't it?"

"What about doing what's right?"

"I *am* trying to do what's right. I care more about helping my family and paying back the people that Spencer fleeced than I care about some art collector's stolen Jackson. If it is stolen. You can't be sure of any of this. Your suspicions are pure speculation. What if you're wrong?"

"I'd rather err on the side of caution and let the police figure it out."

"Sure. They did a bang-up job figuring out Spencer's crimes in a timely manner. It worked out marvelously for me, didn't it? Losing my home and my business and paring down my possessions to what would fit in a plastic tub naturally gave me complete confidence in the capabilities of the police and in the competence of the justice system."

"What happened to you wasn't fair, but the law got it right eventually. Sooner or later you need to let the past go."

"I'll let it go when I get that ticket."

He exhaled hard, as if straining for patience, then stood and walked to the window. The vertical blinds clattered as he pulled two panels aside, braced his palm on the glass to hold them back and looked outside.

In the black tux, against the backdrop of the city lights, he seemed like a stranger. A determined, devastatingly handsome stranger, in spite of her ongoing efforts throughout the evening to ignore his appearance. This excursion—and their relationship—was supposed to be strictly business. They'd been perfectly straight about that. Yet who would have thought there would be so many occasions to touch each other? And to enjoy his company? The anxiety that currently had her pulse racing made her awareness of him more acute than ever.

As she watched him, the tall, broad-shouldered man in front of her merged with her memory of the boy who had taken her to the prom. How different he'd been then, his lanky frame not quite filling out his rented jacket, his blond-streaked hair brushing the collar of his white shirt. His hands had trembled as he'd pinned the corsage he'd brought her on her dress, and when he'd gallantly helped her into his old car, he'd caught her hem in the door. But then he'd smiled and she'd thought he was the handsomest boy in the world. And she'd believed their love would never end.

"What do you want to do, Amelia?"

She rubbed her thumb along the edge of his phone and forced herself to think. What she really wanted to do was to get off the couch and run to the window, slip her arms around his waist and press her cheek to his back. She wanted to apologize for her impatience. She wanted to apologize for the past, for her mistakes, for the obstacles that Fate kept throwing across their path. "I want to finish what we came here for," she said finally. "Buy my painting and get the ticket."

"You heard what Whitcombe said about the extra funds. The ten thousand I brought with me might have been enough to buy a Mathers, but it won't buy a Jackson."

"I don't want the Jackson. All I need is to get close enough to the Mathers to pry my ticket out of the frame."

"Even if we win the bidding, there's no guarantee you'll get that chance."

"Well, if we don't bid, there's no chance of it happening at all."

"Amelia…"

"Isn't it better to try than to decide ahead of time something won't work and just give up?"

Her words hung between them. They both knew she wasn't referring only to the ticket. His palm squeaked on the glass. He dropped his arm and the blinds swayed shut.

"Don't cut out on me this time, Hank. Please."

He turned to face her. "I won't."

"Then you'll see this through to the end?"

"Define *end*."

"We keep trying until we recover the ticket."

"Or until we both agree that recovering it is impossible."

"Fine."

"Good."

"Then what are we waiting for?" She got to her feet, retrieved her purse and hitched the chain over her shoulder.

Once again, he held out his hand for the phone.

Amelia wanted to trust him, she really

did, but the stakes were too high, and the past was a long way from being laid to rest. She slipped his phone into her purse.

"AND NOW WE move to the thirteenth item of this evening's program. I trust it will prove lucky for someone." Whitcombe smiled at his own joke. A few laughs rippled through the audience. Amelia watched two of his more moderately sized hulks, wearing white cloth gloves, carry an abstract painting from the doorway that was to the left of the raised platform at the front of the room. Under Evangeline's supervision, they placed it on the easel beside Whitcombe's podium, then retreated to resume their surveillance of the crowd. Someone who sat a few rows from the front opened the bidding at two hundred dollars. It quickly rose to four. When it lagged, Whitcombe extolled the merits of the painting, which was actually quite good, and reminded everyone of the worthy boys and girls of the inner city who were counting on these good people to provide the tots with a healthy, horizon-broadening experience in the great outdoors.

Amelia tuned out his spiel and looked at the catalog she held. It was one of the glossy, professionally printed ones that had been freely available in the lounge. The other one was still in Hank's jacket. There had been no need to refer to it once the auction had started. It had been clear to both of them when one of the "special" items came up. The bidding pattern was different. Of the hundreds of people in attendance, only a core of about a dozen showed any interest in the painting displayed on the easel, and it was the same group each time. They stood out from the rest of the crowd because of the intensity of their bidding. They weren't treating the auction as a good-natured competition to give a charitable donation but as a deadly serious battle.

They also stood out because of who they were. She recognized many of them from the pictures she'd seen in the financial papers or on the news. There were political figures from various levels of government, as well as a prominent author who wrote controversial exposés of politicians. There were bank executives, professional athletes, a judge and an aging folksinger. They didn't seem like the kind of people who would knowingly try to purchase stolen art, yet the special group of bidders held more notorious individuals as well, including the president of a brewery who had served time for tax evasion, and a trucking company executive who was rumored to have connections to organized crime. It wasn't surprising that Whitcombe assumed a notorious former financial advisor, who had let her husband take the blame for the fortune it was rumored they both stole, would fit right in with this company.

Whitcombe tapped his gavel on the podium to signal a sale. The elderly man who won the bidding waved jauntily to acknowledge the crowd's applause, then leaned over to kiss the cheek of the blue-haired woman beside him. He'd bought the abstract for sixty-five hundred dollars. Amelia's hopes rose. Until now, what she thought of as the regular paintings had sold for between five and ten thousand, which was in line with the going rate for work by those artists. The ones with the duplicates had gone for prices in the same range. She and Hank were still in this. Regardless of the extra funds needed to be transferred to Whitcombe afterward for the stolen paintings, the actual cash bid was still within their reach.

The two guards removed painting number thirteen from the easel and carried it out the way they'd come in. They returned with a pleasant watercolor of a sailboat scudding before a gathering storm. It was a relatively small painting that could have easily been carried by one person, but they didn't deviate from their routine. Whitcombe went into action. The bidding progressed leisurely. Amelia bounced her heel against the floor.

Hank nudged her leg with his.

She gritted her teeth at the sudden warmth she felt from the contact. It was only nerves. Waiting for her last shot at fifty-two…correction, almost forty-two million dollars would sharpen anyone's senses.

He dipped his head. His breath puffed teasingly across her ear. "I just thought of something."

She kept her gaze on the sailboat. "What?"

"The sizes of the paintings were listed in the catalog."

"So? They usually are."

"The dimensions of the duplicates were identical to the paintings they were paired with. That explains the crates."

"What crates?"

"In the gallery storeroom. They seemed bulky. They could have two compartments. Both paintings are probably brought here in the same crate so they can be shipped together to the buyer. It explains the heavy steel door with all the locks, too."

She wasn't sure when her denial of Hank's

theories had switched to acceptance. Everything she'd seen so far bore them out. His logic was relentless, and she hadn't yet found a hole in it, no matter how hard she'd tried.

But that was Hank, wasn't it? He had an outstanding ability to think things through. It was one of his greatest strengths. At times it was also one of his greatest flaws.

Whitcombe banged his gavel. The crowd applauded. Item number fourteen, the watercolor sailboat, was carried out. Amelia held her breath, not daring to blink, her gaze riveted on the doorway to the left of the platform.

And suddenly, there it was. The painting of the farm. The weathered barns, the sloping fields, the overly blue sky, all surrounded by the carved and warped wooden frame. The guards placed it on the easel and stepped back. Amelia dried her palms on her dress and leaned forward.

The painting didn't look any better on the fancy easel than it had when it had hung on the wall of Will and Jenny's back room. The composition was poor, the perspective was off, the execution was clumsy, but to Amelia, it was such a wonderful sight, it brought tears to her eyes.

"Item fifteen," Whitcombe said. "A work

by Dr. Jonathan Mathers, aptly titled *Farm on the Hill*. It is an excellent example of rural Ontario Romanticism from the mid-twentieth century."

A buzzing sensation went through Amelia's leg. She jerked.

Hank covered one of her hands with his and pressed it to her thigh to stop her from bouncing her heel.

"For this rustic gem, we'll open the bidding at three hundred dollars. Do I hear three hundred?"

A hand went up to their right. It was the political exposé author.

"Thank you," Whitcombe said. "And the children thank you. Now, will someone offer four?"

The man from the trucking company nodded his bald head.

"The bid is four. Do I hear five? Five hundred?"

"Five," Hank said.

The author's hand shot up again. "One thousand."

"Fifteen hundred," Hank returned.

"Two thousand." It was the former Leafs goalie.

The buzzing resumed. Vibrations tingled through her thighs. This time she realized the sensation originated from her purse, which rested on her lap. It must be Hank's phone, set to silent mode. She ignored it until the vibrations stopped—whoever was calling him would have to wait. Nothing could take precedence over this.

"Twenty-five hundred," Hank said.

"Come, my friends," Whitcombe coaxed. "We can do better than that. This is a true Canadian gem, a once-in-a-lifetime opportunity to go home with a piece of history."

"Ten thousand," the author called.

Ten? That was Hank's limit.

"Ten thousand, three hundred," Hank said.

"Fifteen," called the goalie.

It couldn't be over this fast, could it? A murmur went through the crowd. The bid had already surpassed the cost of any of the previous paintings by almost fifty percent. Several people who weren't among the special bidders shared puzzled looks.

Whitcombe beamed. "We thank you for your generosity, sir. You're an inspiration to us all, not only for your talent on the ice but for your true munificence." He lifted his gavel. "We have fifteen thousand going once. Going twice…"

"Wait!"

At the gravelly voice from the back of

the room, heads turned. A man was moving slowly down the central aisle. Unlike the other guests, he wasn't clad in a tuxedo. He was wearing a doctor's white coat and white trousers. As odd as his appearance was, few people focused on him. Everyone's attention was on the occupant of the wheelchair he pushed.

Amelia recognized him instantly, despite the ravages of age on his once burly frame. She had studied his biography as part of a business course. Wolf Hennerfind had literally struck gold in his youth, and had parlayed his share of the find into a worldwide gold mining empire. He had been a flamboyant figure several decades ago, but he rarely appeared in public anymore. His once-thick black hair had been reduced to scattered strands of white, and his fleshy features had shrunk close to the bone, yet his face still projected the aura of a vigorous man. And why not? Money was power, and his personal wealth was rated in the billions.

Whitcombe addressed the new arrival directly. "Mr. Hennerfind! We're honored you have decided to join us."

Hennerfind lifted one hand from the red plaid blanket covering his legs. He pointed at the easel that held the Mathers. "What's the bid for that painting?"

"Fifteen thousand," Whitcombe replied.

"I'll make it a hundred."

There was a collective gasp from the crowd. Even Evangeline was smiling now. Whitcombe went through the motions of asking for more bids, but none were offered. No one would be able to compete with what Wolf Hennerfind carried in his wallet.

She returned her gaze to the painting. Okay. It wasn't gone yet. As long as she could see it, there was still hope. If she could rig a distraction, find a fire alarm to pull or maybe just yell "fire" to get the guards and everyone else out of the room, she would be able to run to the dais and pull the ticket out of the painting....

Hank draped his arm loosely around her shoulders. She couldn't tell whether he was offering sympathy, or whether he was readying himself to prevent her from doing something stupid. It was probably both.

The end came more quickly than she could have imagined. The gavel clacked against the podium. The room erupted into cheers and congratulations because of the countless children who would be going to camp the following year. Rather than bringing the crowd to order, Whitcombe announced an intermission, reminding his guests of the open bar. As people rose, eager to partake in more free booze and the chance to gossip, Whitcombe went to speak with Hennerfind.

Amelia leaped to her feet before Hank could stop her and squeezed her way along the row of chairs to the aisle at the side of the room. The tide of people heading the other way blocked her path to the front. She stood her ground as they brushed past her, keeping her gaze locked on the painting, preparing to sprint the instant a gap opened up.

"Amelia, no." Hank moved behind her and looped his arm around her waist. He spoke against her ear. "The guards won't let you near it."

She threw her weight to the side, trying to break his hold but this time he had a firm grip. "Let go of me. It's still there."

As if on cue, the white-gloved hulks lifted the painting from the easel and carried it out of sight.

She jammed her fist to her mouth, fighting to hold back the sob. No. Please, not again. It had been so close.

Hank turned her the other way to join the retreating crowd. Unless she wanted to topple off her heels or create an even bigger scene, she had no choice but to go along. He maintained his grip on her waist as they crossed the lounge. He didn't speak again until they reached the comparatively vacant lobby. "There's nothing more we can do here, Amelia."

"There must be. We just need to think."

"I'll take you home."

"Wait! It's not over yet. I have an idea." She grabbed his hand as they neared the front entrance and tried to pry his fingers loose. "The back door!"

"What about it?"

"The hotel must have a loading bay or a delivery entrance. We could sneak in there and try to get to the painting before Hennerfind takes it away. That's probably where they were brought in."

Rather than loosening his hold, he tucked her closer to his side. One of the guards who was posted at the front door turned his head to regard them. Hank put on a smile and spoke to Amelia through his teeth. "You're right. The paintings probably were brought in through the back, which means Whitcombe would have tighter security there than he does here. I don't want you getting hurt."

Vibrations shot through her body where she pressed against him. "I already thought of that. We could do something to distract the guards first."

"Amelia…" He frowned and glanced at her hip. "Is that my phone?"

Of course, with her purse wedged between them, he would feel the vibrations, too. "Let it ring," she said. "We don't know how long we have before Hennerfind decides to leave."

He grabbed her purse with his free hand. The chain slipped from her shoulder before she could react. He thumbed open the clasp.

"Hank, let it go. This could be our last chance."

"It's after midnight," he muttered, releasing her so he could pull out the phone. "This call must be important."

"And what we're doing here isn't?"

He put the phone to his ear and answered anyway. An instant later, he held it out for her. "It's for you."

"Come on. No one would—"

"It's your brother."

It took a heartbeat for her brain to switch gears. All thoughts of the ticket drained from her mind to be replaced by a wave of dread.

Will must have been the one who had called before, too. She'd ignored it. She'd been too wrapped up in her own problems to consider what else might be happening….

Jenny!

Amelia grabbed the phone.

And she discovered that just when she'd thought things couldn't get worse, they did.

CHAPTER THIRTEEN

THE HOSPITAL CORRIDORS had been darkened for the night. Although visiting hours had ended long ago, Will had arranged with security to let them through. Hank's tux and Amelia's evening dress had raised few eyebrows at the nurses' station—the maternity ward was well accustomed to come-as-you-are arrivals. Amelia eased open the door to her sister-in-law's room.

A shaded light burned above the bed where Jenny lay. She looked as if she'd been through a storm. Her hair pooled on the pillow in tangles. Shadows deepened the hollows of her cheeks and beneath her eyes, and the rest of her face was as pale as the sheet that covered her body. Her much flatter body. Apart from the shallow rise and fall of her chest, she was completely motionless. An oxygen tube ran to her nostrils and an IV line was taped to the back of her hand. Wires trailed from beneath her hospital gown to a heart monitor. The steady beeps were reassuring, yet at the same time ominous. They sounded too feeble to represent a woman's life.

The baby was gone, but Jenny wasn't alone. On the room's other bed, Owen and Eric lay sound asleep beneath a blanket, cuddled together like puppies between the raised safety rails. Will was slumped in an armchair beneath the window, snoring softly. Timothy, clad in SpongeBob pajamas, was sprawled across his chest.

Hank squeezed her shoulder. "I can wait outside," he whispered.

She shook her head, covering his hand with hers. "I'll need help getting them to the car."

Will must have sensed their presence. He blinked and lifted his head. He looked as if he'd gone through the same storm that Jenny had. He was a wreck. Every line on his face seemed to have deepened since she'd last seen him. His cheeks bristled with unshaved whiskers. Though apparently he'd taken the time to pull on a pair of jeans before he left the house, he wore a striped pajama top and had no socks in his sneakers.

Amelia moved forward, intending to take Timmy, but before she could, Will shifted the sleeping toddler against his shoulder and rocked to his feet with him. He paused to look at Jenny, made sure that the safety rails of the bed where his two oldest slept were locked in place, then tipped his head toward the doorway and followed them out of the room. They went as far as a cluster of purple vinyl benches that were arranged near the end of the darkened hall.

Amelia put one arm around her brother, giving him a hug that wouldn't wake her nephew. All she managed to say was his name before her throat closed with emotion. She kissed his bristly cheek and pulled back.

"Thanks for coming, kid," Will said. He glanced at Hank. "And thanks for bringing her."

"Sorry for the delay," Hank said. "Phone trouble. How's your wife doing?"

"They stopped the hemorrhaging. All we can do now is wait."

Will filled in the details he hadn't given over the phone. He and Jenny had been about to go to bed when her water broke. Her contractions had come on hard and escalated quickly, and since the length of time she'd been in labor had gotten shorter with each of her three previous deliveries, they'd guessed the birth was imminent.

He hadn't wanted to bring the boys along,

but the neighbors who could have come over to stay with them were either on vacation or had already gone to their cottages for the weekend, and there hadn't been time to call in any of their regular babysitters. Even if Will had managed to find someone who had been free and had been willing to come over, he hadn't wanted to risk waiting for a sitter to arrive. He'd had no choice but to help Jenny to the van while Owen and Eric grabbed Timmy, and he'd brought the whole crew to the hospital.

"We were excited, not worried," Will said. "After all, this was our fourth time around. We thought we were old hands at this. We had the routine down pat. We never expected trouble."

"No one would," Amelia said. "Jenny told me all her checkups had gone fine."

"There was no sign of a problem until we were in the delivery room," Will said. "And all of a sudden her blood pressure just dropped. She passed out. They said something tore internally. She was losing so much blood." He clenched his jaw briefly. "One of the hospital volunteers had been keeping an eye on the boys out here, so they didn't see it."

Amelia shuddered, picturing the nightmares her nephews might have had if they'd witnessed their mother in that condition. And to think that for a while Will and Jenny had actually considered arranging to have the boys present for their new sibling's birth. "I'm so sorry, Will."

"I probably should have taken them home already, but I had to stay with Jenny. I don't want her to wake up alone, not after what she's been through."

"Of course, you should stay," Amelia said. "I never should have gone out of town tonight. I was supposed to watch the kids when Jenny went into labor."

"You couldn't have known this would happen now. None of us did. Jenny wasn't due for almost two weeks."

"I'm sorry I wasn't here earlier."

"The trouble would have happened whether you were here or not."

His reassurance did little to ease her guilt. "How's the baby?" she asked.

Will pressed his cheek against Timmy's head, then led them to the end of the hall and around the corner to the nursery where tiny, red-faced newborns were bundled in their bassinettes. He stepped close to the window. "She's in the second row, third from the left."

Amelia's eyes filled as she looked at her

tiny, perfect, brand-new niece. The baby's heart-shaped face came from her mother. The wisps of hair that showed at the edges of her pink cap unquestionably came from her father. She slept peacefully, mere hours old, unaware of the turmoil that surrounded her birth. "She's beautiful, Will."

"She's feisty, too. She came out wailing."

"She's a Goodfellow, all right," Hank murmured. "Just look at that red hair."

"Auburn," Amelia corrected automatically.

Hank peered at the card on the foot of the bassinette. "What's her name?"

"Right now, she's Baby Girl Goodfellow," Will said. "The name'll have to wait until her mother and I can decide together." He spoke briskly, but the light coming through the window was brighter than in the hall. It revealed his eyes were as moist as his sister's. "Jenny doesn't…" He swallowed. "She doesn't know we have a daughter. She said it didn't matter, but she couldn't fool me. I knew she wanted a girl this time."

Amelia rubbed his back. "Jenny will pull through this. She's a strong woman."

"Sure. She's had to be tough to put up with me and the boys. She's the best. One in a million."

"She feels the same way about you."

He started back toward Jenny's room. "She'd have my hide for keeping the boys out so long past their bedtime, but I can't leave until I know she's okay."

"Absolutely," Amelia said. "You stay as long as you need to. We'll take the munchkins home."

"I don't have a car seat for the little guy, or a booster for Eric," Hank said. He pulled his key ring from his pocket, detached the one for his car and extended it to Will. "Would you mind if I take your van and leave my car with you?"

Will turned to look at him. It was the first time he'd regarded Hank directly since they'd arrived. There was no trace of the animosity he'd carried for fifteen years. There was merely gratitude. He nodded once, then adjusted his grasp on his son so he could free one hand. "I hadn't thought of that," he said, fishing his own keys from his jeans. He exchanged them for Hank's. "That's decent of you."

"No problem." Hank peeled off his tuxedo jacket and reached for Timmy.

Amelia had believed Hank looked fantastic in his tux at their prom. A few hours ago, she'd thought the fully grown version was even more handsome. But there was nothing that could compare to the rush of warmth in her heart as she watched him wrap his jacket around the sleeping child.

OTHER THAN THE faint aroma of fresh paint that hung in the air, and the patches of white that the black mop dog now sported, the Goodfellows' house seemed the same as it had on that Tuesday evening almost three weeks ago when Hank had interviewed their neighbors. That had been the only other time he'd been invited inside. Since then, he hadn't gone past the front door when he'd come to pick up Amelia or drop her off. They had met in his office when they'd had business to discuss. He'd believed it would help him maintain his distance, and limit him from getting any further involved in her life. Yeah, right.

He stepped into the hallway to listen. Judging by the total silence upstairs, Timmy was finally asleep for the night. He had woken up as soon as Hank had stopped the family's van in the driveway, and it had taken two stories and a lullaby for Amelia to settle him again. In contrast, the older boys had roused instantly from their nap on the hospital bed and had been wide awake throughout the drive, yet had gone straight to their bedroom within minutes of arriving home. There hadn't been a sound from the basement since then.

"Lemon Soother or Sleepy Time Chamomile?" Amelia asked.

Hank moved to the kitchen. "Care to elaborate?"

"Herbal tea." She took two mugs out of the drying rack beside the sink and set them on the counter. "I'm too wired for anything with caffeine, but I can make you some coffee if you want."

He leaned one shoulder against the doorframe. She was still wearing the misty-waterfall dress, but most of her hair had escaped her braid and she'd gotten rid of her shoes. He'd left his own shoes at the door, too. He'd also ditched his tie and opened the top few buttons of his shirt. It was the kind of thing a real couple would do when they came home. Kick off their shoes and loosen buttons and belts, put the kids to bed and share some private time together while they talked about the evening.

Yet they weren't a real couple. And this evening had been anything but normal. If he were smart, he would just go home. Now that her nephews were safely tucked in for the night, there was no practical reason for him to stay. He could leave her brother's van with her and walk to his house. It would likely take him less than an hour. The exercise would help him unwind.

But his lack of smarts with Amelia was a well-established fact. Why change it now? "Herbal tea sounds great."

"So, lemon or chamomile?"

"Since I don't know what chamomile is, I'll choose lemon."

"Wise decision." She took two bags from a small, colorful box and dropped one into each mug. "I don't know what chamomile is, either, but it tastes like hay. Or what I imagine hay would taste like. Do you want some cookies?" she asked, opening another cupboard.

"No, thanks."

"That's good," she said, closing the cupboard. "It looks as if the boys finished them, anyway. Will and I are the ones who smuggle the bags into the house. Jenny's always trying to make them eat healthy snacks like apples or raisins. There are plenty of those. Want some raisins?"

"I'm fine."

The kettle whistled. She snatched it off the stove quickly, then held her breath and tilted her head toward the doorway, as if listening for one of the boys.

"I suspect it would take more than that to wake them up," Hank said.

"I hope they don't get nightmares."

"You and your brother did a good job downplaying the situation."

Her hand shook as she poured water into the mugs. She set the kettle down and used a towel to sop up the spilled water. "I hope we didn't downplay it. I hope it really will turn out to be nothing serious and Jenny will be back to her old self before we know it."

He hoped so, too. He'd been seven, only a year older than Eric, when he'd lost his own mother. He wouldn't want any child to go through that kind of pain. He pulled out his phone and handed it to her, even though there was a phone on the wall beside the doorway. "I programmed the extension of the maternity floor before we left," he said. "The nurses said you can call anytime for an update, so you don't need to worry about waking your brother if he dozes off again."

She smiled. It was the first one in hours, and it had more effect on his heart rate than a pot of coffee could have. He waited as she made the call. Though there was no improvement, Jenny's vital signs were stable, so at least she was no worse. That alone was a relief.

He carried the mugs to the table that had been built into the corner of the kitchen. The benches that were fastened to the walls on two sides would easily accommodate at least four kids. That, and the high quality of the furniture made him suspect it was Will's handiwork. He pulled out one of the chairs for Amelia.

"I need to thank you," she said. She put his phone on the table as she sat. "You've been terrific."

He slid aside a high chair that was built of the same maple as the rest of the set, then sat in the remaining adult chair. "All I did was drive."

"No, you did more than that. Our partnership agreement didn't extend to rescuing stranded kids."

"It's no big deal."

"It is to me. And thank you for covering for me with Will."

"Covering?"

"When you said you had phone trouble. That's kinder than saying I was too selfish and too absorbed in my own problems to think there could be an emergency."

"You're being too harsh."

"Hardly. You once believed I needed an intervention. You might have been right." She tapped her nails against the handle of her mug. Her gaze was still on the phone. "Aren't you going to call the cops?"

"What?"

"The auction's over. You wanted to tell the police about Whitcombe."

"I'll call them on Saturday."

"It already is Saturday."

"I mean later in the morning. Everyone would have left the hotel by now. The paintings would have been taken away, too."

She made a noise halfway between a laugh and a hiccup. "At least we know where my painting went. We won't need to hunt it down this time."

This time? Did she truly believe there was any hope left of recovering her ticket?

"Not that knowing who has it does much good," she went on. "I don't think we could afford to buy it back."

"We wouldn't be able to match Hennerfind's bid, that's for sure." Not unless Hank sold his house. He'd already cashed in his savings bonds to make up the ten thousand for the auction.

"I studied his rise to success in one of my economics classes. He was ruthless when it came to acquiring mining claims and gold refining operations, and he seldom let anything go once he had it. He's not what anyone would call a soft touch, so I doubt if he'd be moved into giving my painting back to me if I told him a sob story about how I lost it at a yard sale."

Hank grunted. Her sob story about losing her painting had done the trick when she'd tried it on him, but Hennerfind was no fool. "I doubt if you'd be allowed past his security to talk to him in the first place."

"And speaking of security," she began.

"I hope you're not suggesting anything illegal."

"Don't worry. I'm not crazy enough to try breaking into his house to steal it back."

"I'm relieved to hear that. My personal scruples aside, I definitely don't have the necessary skill set to burglarize a billionaire's place."

She braced her elbows on the table and dropped her head in her hands. "You know what the worst of it is? Hennerfind doesn't even know what he has. He's probably gloating over buying a stolen masterpiece. He has no idea the dummy painting is worth at least ten times more."

"I wonder what he really paid."

"A hundred thousand…"

"That was the cash bid, the amount on record. I'm talking about the extra funds he had to transfer to Whitcombe for the Jackson."

"I'll bet you were right about the bid representing only a fraction of the actual price. Multiply a hundred thousand by ten and you get a million, which still would be a bargain for a painting of that class." She lifted her head so she could look at him through her fingers. "Here's a thought. If you hold off phoning the police for a while, we could tell Hennerfind we'll inform the cops about his stolen Jackson unless he gives us the Mathers."

"I hope you're not serious, Amelia. Attempting to blackmail a man that rich and powerful would be extremely dangerous. You'd have to worry about Whitcombe and his goons, too. Plus whoever stole those paintings in the first place. They wouldn't tolerate threats to their scheme."

"Then why were you so eager to go to the police in the first place?"

"That's different. They can protect the identity of an informer. I don't even have to give them my identity. I can call in a tip anonymously." He stretched his arms across the table to grasp her wrists and tug her hands away from her face. "You said your-self that Hennerfind was ruthless. I won't allow you—"

"Hold on there. You won't *allow* me?"

"Poor choice of words."

She tugged against his grip. "You bet it was."

"Okay, then how's this?" Rather than re-leasing her, he enclosed both of her hands in his. "I don't want you to get hurt over some-thing as meaningless as money."

"If money is so meaningless, why did you insist I had to give you twenty percent of my ticket?"

"Because I was angry and wanted to make a point."

"Ten million dollars is certainly an effec-tive way of making a point."

"And because I didn't want to quit on you this time."

His honesty appeared to startle her. It sur-prised him, too. But now that there was no longer any prospect of retrieving the ticket, he couldn't keep up the pretense—to her or to himself—that the reason for their part-nership had been solely business. "I didn't want to quit," he repeated. "That's what you accused me of doing before, right?"

"I was angry, too. We'd been arguing about the past."

"Sure, because there was a lot that needed saying. I didn't want to do something else that would make me wonder years from now what might have happened if only I'd chosen differently."

"I've had a few of those 'might-have-beens' and 'if-onlys' myself."

"Do you remember what I told you at the coffee shop? It was just before you told me the truth about the ticket."

"I remember everything we said that day, Hank."

"I told you I wanted the chance to get to know you again. I think I have, in spite of all the baggage from our past that we keep tripping over."

She dropped her gaze to their joined hands. "I agree with you about the tripping-over-baggage part."

"We're a good team, Amelia."

"When we're not arguing."

"If you're expecting me to argue about how much we argue, forget it. That would make my brain hurt."

"Mine, too. My head's still swimming from what happened tonight."

"At the auction or the hospital?"

"Both." She chewed her lip for a while. "I've tried hard to concentrate on business and ignore everything else, but I can't. Look what happened when I ignored Will's phone call. I thought I could put my life on hold until I cashed that ticket, but life's been going on anyway. You were right. Jenny was right. I need to deal with reality."

There was no need to respond to that, so he didn't.

She withdrew her hands from his grasp and glanced around the kitchen. "She's got to be okay. I wish I'd been here for them, or at least answered the phone the first time Will called. I realize I couldn't have changed what happened to her, but I could have made things easier on everyone else. The whole thing feels like a bad dream."

"Yeah. Doesn't seem that long ago we danced at their wedding."

"They were so happy then."

"So were we."

She picked up her mug and blew on the tea. "Little did we know, huh?"

"Amelia, why did you marry Spencer?"

Her breath sputtered. She returned the mug to the table with a thump. "Where did that question come from?"

"Will and Jenny's wedding. Our past. One of the bigger pieces of baggage. Pick one."

"Marrying Spencer was a gigantic mistake. There's not much more to tell you."

"I think there's lots more. Did you marry him to prove I was wrong to turn you down? Or did you really love him?"

She resumed flicking her nails against the mug.

"For years I had assumed you married Spencer because he was rich," Hank continued. "But I'm pretty sure now that I was wrong."

It was a while before she responded. When she did, her tone was quiet. Thoughtful. "You weren't entirely wrong," she said. "His wealth did dazzle me initially. All my friends were talking about how he arrived on campus in a Jaguar and wore a three-thousand-dollar suit to his guest lectures. He was a rock star in the financial world, a boy-wonder phenomenon. I was flattered by his attention when he approached me. Any woman would have been. He made me feel special and sexy and important. He'd claimed later he'd fallen in love at first sight. It wasn't until years afterward that I found out he'd asked the professor which students were the most promising and had singled me out."

"He used you."

"Hoo boy, did he ever. All the time we were dating, I believed he really cared about me, but he was recruiting a business partner more than he was seeking a wife. And I admit I was seduced by the promise of running his company with him. Financial planning was exactly what I wanted to do when I graduated, and he already had an established client base and a thriving business. I could jump right in. I wouldn't need to wait to build a business of my own."

Yes, that sounded like Amelia. "You told me you made him a lot of money."

"That's for sure. I believed in him and in our ability to help people grow their wealth. I was young and impressionable. Because our clients recognized my sincerity, they trusted me with their life savings."

"They let you manage their money because you were good at it," he put in. "Not only because you came across as sincere."

"Whatever the reason, I'm the one who brought in most of the clients during my time at the company, not Spencer."

"Is that why you wanted to pay them back from the lottery winnings?"

She gulped her tea. "Did I say that?"

"Yes, you did. Tonight. You mentioned helping your family, too."

"Well, you can see for yourself that Will and Jenny need money. And even with forty-two million instead of fifty-two, there would still be enough to repair some of the damage Spencer did."

The millions would repair the financial damage, but it wouldn't heal what Spencer had done to Amelia's heart. "You wouldn't have given him the time of day if I hadn't broken up with you."

"I confess that played a part in it. I probably did go out with him initially to get back at you. It was the shock of losing my parents that really strengthened my feelings for him."

"Then you did love him."

"I thought I did. I wouldn't have married him otherwise, no matter how big a company he owned or how much his suits cost or how many Jags he drove." She shoved her fingers into her hair and dragged loose what was left of her braid. It sprang out in crooked chunks. "But I was in love with an illusion. I saw what I wanted to see and closed my eyes to the rest. I was an idiot."

"No more than I was for hurting you the way I did."

She sighed. "I can't blame you for that anymore, Hank. Just look at what Will and Jenny have had to cope with. Marriage isn't something for two kids to enter into on a whim. It takes maturity and wholehearted commitment to build a life together. I was wrong to rush you. It's good that you thought everything through."

"But I hadn't, Amelia."

"You realized we had no place to live or means to support ourselves. And you didn't want me to blow my scholarship. You were thinking of me."

"Not entirely. It wasn't only the practical aspects that scared me off—it was the commitment."

She jerked up her head. "But you said you'd *wanted* to marry me, only not right away."

"I know what I said. I've done a good job convincing myself it was true, too, but if I'd really wanted to get married, we could have worked through our problems together. Instead of breaking up with you, I should have told you that I wanted to wait. When I heard you were dating Spencer, I should have found a way to make you listen to me instead of running off to Alberta."

"I didn't give you much of a chance."

"You didn't marry him until you graduated, so I had four years to tell you how I felt. Four years! It's not like you were on the moon. At the very least I could have told you why I'd moved out west, and that I was saving what I earned for us, but I didn't. It's as if I set things up so I would fail. That's not the behavior of someone who's serious about a permanent relationship, but I didn't want to admit it. Not even to myself."

Silence fell as they both digested what he'd said. "So what changed?" Amelia asked finally. "Why the sudden realization now?"

It was a good question. He pondered it for another minute, then nodded toward the shadowed hall past the doorway. "Your nephews."

"The boys? Why?"

"Don't get me wrong, I'm confident Jenny will be fine, but seeing them in this situation reminds me of what happened after my mother died. My family wasn't like yours. My father closed himself off from me when the going got tough. I guess I got used to doing the same. It made me unwilling to take risks. Then you came along and knocked me out of my comfort zone because you were so different. I thought I had opened up my heart with you, but as soon as you got serious, I found reasons to back off. You were right. Our breakup was my fault. I used my caution like a kid with a security blanket."

It was an indication of how far they'd come that they could discuss the past without losing their tempers. In a way, Hank would have preferred to see Amelia get angry. It would have been easier to take than the sadness he saw on her face now. "We were both at fault, Hank," she said. "I should have been patient. I should have tried to see things from your point of view."

"Isn't that what we're doing now?"

She pushed to her feet, carried her mug to the sink and dumped the rest of her tea. Keeping her back to him, she braced her hands on the edge of the counter. "It doesn't matter anymore. What happened when we were teenagers is over. It was only another illusion."

"What was?"

"Our love. Our plans. Our dreams. They were as much a fantasy as my farce of a marriage. It was as much of a lost cause as chasing after my ticket, and believing the money would fix everything that was broken, and heal everything that hurt."

"Amelia…"

"None of it was real. I've just been deluding myself." She dipped her head. "But that's my pattern, isn't it?"

He shoved back his chair, closed the distance between them and then turned her to face him. "We all have our own ways to deal with pain. I'm sorry I've made you feel worse. I should have left the past alone."

"No, it's good we talked tonight, because it proved we were even more of a disaster as a couple than I'd realized. We were just too different. We still are."

This was going all wrong. He was making a mess of things. Again. He slid his arms around her back and pulled her closer. "There was one aspect of our relationship we got right, even as teenagers."

She placed her palms on his chest. "You're not listening to me."

He was listening well enough to guess what she was building up to say. He used his nose to nudge her hair aside and kissed her neck. "You still smell the same, you know that?"

"Hank…"

He kissed his way across her cheek to the

corner of her mouth. "I never forgot how you tasted, either."

Her nails curled into his shirt. Her breath hitched.

He fitted his lips over hers before she could say more.

The contact jolted him. He knew she was upset, and he'd meant to be gentle, but the feel of her breath on his cheek and her body pressed to his sent his pulse soaring. This wasn't like the angry kiss in the stairwell. It wasn't like the eager explorations of their youth, either. It was deep and rich and trembling with promise. He plowed one hand into her hair to hold her head steady and for a few precious moments there was only pleasure. Simple. Basic. Man to woman. Passion untainted by words or memories or regrets.

But then he felt the drop of moisture hit his jaw and he came back to reality with a thud. He lifted his head.

Tears sheened her eyes. There was more than sadness in her gaze now—there was determination. She pulled away from his embrace. "That kiss didn't prove anything, Hank, except to show we're still confusing chemistry for…something else."

He wiped her cheek with his thumb. "Chemistry's a good start, isn't it?"

"I don't want to start anything."

"I know things look bad now, but that's because it's late. We're both tired. And it's been a long night." He dug in his pocket for his handkerchief. "I should know better than to push you. My timing sucks, which is nothing new. I have a knack for finding the most unromantic moments possible to kiss you."

She lifted her palms and took another step back. "Don't."

"Don't what?"

"Don't be sweet or funny or give me your stupid handkerchief. Don't start up some corny pep talk about how everything's going to look better in the morning. It's not. Without the ticket, I'm right back where I was when I moved in here, and things won't get better unless I face that." She blotted her eyes with her sleeve. "Thank you for your help with the boys, but I think it would be best if you leave."

"Amelia—"

"I'll need some time to reimburse you for my share of your expenses to date. Once I get another job, we could work out a payment schedule for what I owe."

"Stop. You don't owe me anything. And this isn't over."

"Do you agree that recovering the lottery ticket is impossible?"

He wanted to lie, because he knew what she was leading up to now, too. "There might be something we haven't considered yet."

"Tell the truth, Hank. Do you agree it's impossible?"

He clamped his jaw and gave her a curt nod.

"Then it's time to dissolve our partnership and get on with our lives."

CHAPTER FOURTEEN

IT WASN'T THE first sleepless night that Amelia had spent since she'd moved into her brother's house. It was the first one she'd spent in the living room, though. She watched as the dawn lightened the clouds beyond the front window. They were tinted red, and the air was already thick with humidity. A storm was building somewhere. Wasn't there a rhyme about a red sky in the morning? A bad omen? A warning for sailors?

Well, she didn't need any help from the weather to mess up her life. She'd done a terrific job of that on her own. In fact, she'd been all set to hold herself one super-duper pity party after she'd sent Hank home, but her nephews had crashed it before it could get started.

Timmy stirred against her left side, his hand groping for his stuffed rabbit. She slid it against his fingers and waited until his eyelids stopped twitching, then picked a piece of popcorn out of his hair and lobbed it toward the bowl on the coffee table. It bounced off her feet, which were propped on the table alongside Owen's. His head lolled against her right shoulder. Eric was sprawled sideways in the chair across from the couch, his legs over one arm and Toto snoring on his lap.

No matter how much the adults had tried to reassure them, her nephews had sensed the seriousness of their mother's condition after all. One by one they had woken up, demanding their aunt's attention, but there had been nothing more she could say that would help. They'd just needed to know they were loved. They were no different from grown-ups in that respect. Maybe adult troubles couldn't be soothed by gorging on popcorn at 3:00 a.m., or by cuddling with a stuffed rabbit, but that basic need to be loved never went away.

Kids had a knack for knocking problems into perspective, didn't they?

Amelia touched her fingertips to Timmy's hair. She'd always wanted children. Spencer had wanted to wait, so she had channeled her yearning for a family into her devotion to her nephews. Hank had once said he wanted lots of children because he'd been an only child. With his patience and his sense of fairness he would have made a great father. Not like Basil. She'd known they hadn't gotten along. It had been one of those background facts she'd noticed but had never bothered to analyze. Same with the fact that Hank was still single. She'd never bothered to wonder why. It was perfectly clear to her now that losing his mother and growing up with a distant, critical father had profoundly influenced his outlook on life. She wished she'd figured it out years ago, but that was her, wasn't it? Skimming right past anything that hurt. By pushing him to prove his love, she'd driven him away.

And maybe she'd driven Spencer away, too. Granted, he'd been dishonest and manipulative, but he would have had the same need to be loved as everyone else. He'd probably sensed she hadn't really loved him. That could be why in the end he'd turned to his blonde bimbo. He'd been unfaithful to his wife, but hadn't she broken their wedding vows first? She'd promised to love him, but deep down inside she must have realized that her heart belonged to someone else.

Does he know you still love him?

How many times now had she remembered Jenny's words? There was a reason she hadn't been able to shake them off. Sending Hank away might have been her biggest mistake of all.

But it had been the only sensible choice. She was in no position to consider jumping into a relationship. If she was ever going to trust her judgment again, she needed to put her life in order first. No more wallowing in what-might-have-beens. No more moaning about her fate or waiting for magic solutions to drop into her lap. As Hank had once told her, there were no shortcuts to the future. The only way to get there was to work at it one day at a time.

And maybe, once she had paid her debts and was back on her feet, she could risk dreaming again....

Her eyes burned. Now who was giving pep talks?

Moving carefully so as not to wake the boys, she extricated herself from the couch. She used the phone in the kitchen to call the hospital for an update, but the nurse she spoke to reported there had been no change in Jenny's condition. Amelia returned to the living room and tiptoed to the computer desk in the corner. The click of the keyboard didn't disturb her nephews, so she spent almost an hour cruising the job listing sites.

The results weren't encouraging. She was composing a résumé when the phone rang.

She made a dash for the kitchen, but the sound of the phone woke the dog. Toto jumped from Owen's lap and scrabbled behind her, barking at her heels. She skidded to a stop at the kitchen threshold, keeping her gaze on the living room as she reached around the doorway for the receiver.

"Amelia?"

It was her brother's voice. She ignored the teeny part of her that had thought it might have been Hank calling. She'd cut their ties and sent him away. He was only doing what she'd asked. She cupped her hand around the mouthpiece. "Will, I called earlier. The nurse said there was no change."

Timmy's head appeared above the back of the couch. Owen rubbed his eyes as he shifted to his knees to face her. Eric slid to his feet.

"The nurse was wrong," Will said.

"What happened?"

"Are the boys okay?"

"They're fine."

"I heard the dog bark. Are they still asleep?"

Owen came over to stand in front of her, his expression solemn as he studied her face. Eric joined them next and slipped his fingers into her free hand. Timmy hugged her leg. He didn't appear to notice when Toto trotted off with his rabbit.

"They're all standing right here with me, Will," Amelia said. "Sorry that I couldn't keep them in bed."

"No, that's great. I'm glad they're up. Their mom'll want to talk to them."

"Jenny's awake? Is she okay?"

"She woke up ten minutes ago, more gorgeous than ever and hungrier than our daughter."

For what felt like the hundredth time in the past day, her eyes filled, but this time it was with happy tears. She knelt on the floor, taking the phone away from her ear momentarily so she could put her arms around her nephews. "Oh, Will. That's wonderful!"

"The doctor wants to keep her here for a while, but she—" He paused. Jenny's voice sounded in the background. He laughed. "She told me to stop yakking and give her the phone, but I want to be the one to tell you."

"What?"

"We're naming the baby Hope."

HANK SHOVED HIS hands in his pockets and turned to regard his father's car lot. The rising sun glinted red on the streams of soapy water snaking over the pavement toward the sidewalk. Although it would be another three hours before the place opened for business, the student Basil had hired for the summer was hard at work, washing the inventory. Hank had held the same job for a few weeks when he was sixteen. He'd liked working outside, and he'd never minded the early mornings or how wet he'd get from the spray of the high-pressure hose. He'd done his best to polish each vehicle to a mirror shine, but as usual, his performance hadn't met his father's standards. And as usual, rather than finding a solution to a difficult situation, Hank had quit.

He had the urge to turn around now, too. After he'd walked home from the Goodfellows' place, he'd been up most of the night, wrestling with his thoughts. He was tired. He wasn't in the best of moods. Acknowledging his own responsibility for his breakup with Amelia all those years ago had been tough, so this likely wasn't the ideal time to address another topic that he'd left simmering for decades. Yes, if he tried, he could come up with dozens of logical reasons to delay this confrontation. Before he could, though, he walked to the door at the side of the showroom that he knew would be unlocked and headed for his father's glassed-in office.

Despite the early hour, Basil was already at his desk. His head was bent toward his computer screen as he clicked two-fingered at the keyboard. A pale gray suit jacket hung from a padded hanger that was hooked on the coat tree behind him. His shirtsleeves were rolled to his elbows, and wire-framed glasses perched on the end of his nose, sure signs that he hadn't expected company. He looked up, startled, when Hank rapped on the open door.

"Hello, Dad."

"Hank! What are you doing here?"

"I'd like to talk to you."

Basil glanced back at the computer screen. "As you can see, I'm rather busy at the moment."

Hank stepped into the office and closed the door firmly behind him. "You don't open for three hours. Aside from the kid out on the lot, there's no one else here. You can spare me a few minutes."

Basil hit several more keys, then took off his glasses and smoothed his sleeves to his wrists to fasten the cuffs. He rocked back in his chair, a new, ergonomically designed, imported leather one that had probably cost more than all of Hank's office furniture combined. He studied his son. "You look terrible."

"I suppose I do."

"What's wrong?"

"That's a very good question. It's exactly why I'm here, to figure out what's wrong."

"Do you need a loan? You told me you had a promising new case. Didn't it work out?"

"This isn't about my business, Dad. This is about the two of us."

"I don't understand."

Hank dragged one of the extra chairs around the desk to Basil's side and sat so that they were face-to-face. He studied his father's wary expression, searching for the best way to begin…. No, it would be better simply to jump in rather than overanalyzing this, too. "It wasn't all right when you pulled out of that father-son golf tournament the other weekend. I made out like I didn't care, but I did."

"All right then, if it was that important, we can play a few rounds next month once I get some free time."

"I don't want to play golf, Dad. That's not the point. The truth is, I hate golf. I'd rather go fishing."

"Fishing?"

"We used to go all the time, remember? Getting up early, drifting around on the lake, talking about whatever crossed our minds. That was great. It was fun. But it all changed after Mom died. Why?"

"I don't know what you're talking about."

"It wasn't just the fishing trips, it was everything. You didn't have time for me anymore. We didn't take vacations, we didn't talk, we hardly ever saw each other."

"It isn't like you to whine, Hank. You're grown up enough now to realize I was trying to make a living, aren't you? A car dealership doesn't run itself. I had to concentrate on my business to be successful."

"Yes, I understand now, but I was seven years old when she died. I missed her."

"We both did."

"And that was why you were always here, wasn't it?" Hank asked, although he didn't really need an answer. He'd already figured out this part. He gestured toward the glass wall that separated the office from the showroom. "You closed yourself off from the hurt and threw yourself into your work."

"It was difficult to be a single parent."

"I get that, but try seeing the situation from my point of view. When Mom died and you buried yourself in your work, I felt as if I had lost *both* my parents."

Basil flinched. "I did the best I could. You never complained before."

"That's true. And that's my fault. Things could have been different if I'd told you how I'd felt, but I learned not to. I didn't want to give you something else to criticize about me."

"Criticize?"

"You've made it perfectly clear that I've been a disappointment to you because I don't share your interest in making money, and I don't devote myself to my career. I realize it must be hard for you to accept the fact I'll never be as successful as you or your friends or the sons of your friends, but it might be nice if now and then you could swallow your aggravation with me long enough to have a conversation that doesn't have to be scheduled into our day planners."

It was only when Hank heard his voice echoing from the glass that he realized he'd been shouting.

Basil stared at him, his expression stunned. He pressed back in his chair.

Hank shoved his own chair backward and stood. He got as far as the door, then turned. "You know what the worst of it is, Dad? I saw how empty your life was. I tried my best not to be like you, but I am, anyway. I realized that I've closed myself off from love just like you did."

"You're not a disappointment."

Hank snorted. "Yeah, right."

"And if I criticized you—"

"If? *If*? Every time you see me you point out something I'm doing wrong."

"That's because I'm trying to help you. Believe it or not, I only wanted the best for you, son. That's why I've pushed you to succeed."

Hank reined in his temper, trying to process his father's words. "Whatever your intentions were, I've always felt that you view me as a failure."

"Well, I don't, but if I came on too strong sometimes, it was because you wouldn't listen. The more I tried to guide you, the more you seemed to ignore me. I got the impression you preferred not to even see me."

"Maybe I *would* want to see you if you didn't nag me every time you opened your mouth."

"And maybe I wouldn't have to nag you if I felt you actually valued what I said."

Hank wasn't the only one shouting now. Strangely enough, though, seeing his father's anger somehow helped dissolve his own. "We've got a real problem when it comes to communication."

"Looks like we do."

"But it wasn't always like that, Dad."

Basil rose to his feet and came to stand in front of Hank. Their gazes locked. "Your mother found it easy to talk about her feelings, but I don't. I've always been better at making money. That's what I'm comfortable with. She was the one who made our house a home, and did all the things that made the three of us into a family. When she died I was lost. The best part of me was gone. I didn't know how I was going to get through the next day, let alone the rest of my life...." His voice roughened. "You were right. Everything changed."

Hank nodded.

"And I'm sorry if you feel I let you down," Basil continued. "But you're wrong about one thing. You're a lot more like your mother than you are like me."

"How?"

"You got her soft heart and her talent for reading people. You got her patience, too. Those are qualities I've always admired in you."

"I didn't know that."

"Well, you do now. She used to—" Basil broke off as the phone on his desk rang. He glanced over his shoulder. For an instant he wavered, as if he were debating whether or not to answer, but then he gave his head a brief shake and placed his hand on Hank's arm. "There's a pot of coffee in the lunchroom. Can I pour you a cup?"

It was only coffee. A few more minutes together. Not much when stacked up against years of antagonism.

Yet this was the first time in his life that Hank had seen Basil ignore a ringing phone. And it was the first time in years that his father had actually touched him.

And even though they stood on a tiled floor in a glass-enclosed office, Hank felt the ground shift, like a boat rocking in the breeze. He swallowed hard and clasped his father's shoulder. "Thanks, Dad. I'd like that."

AMELIA GLIDED TO a stop beside the bike rack. The bicycle was Jenny's, a sturdy five-speed with a wire mesh carrier on the back. The bike had several advantages over Will's old Chevy. There was never a problem getting it started, it was easy to find a parking spot and it cost nothing to run. And as a bonus, riding it gave her a free workout. It wouldn't be that great a mode of transportation in the rain, though. She eyed the haze of clouds to the west. The sky had been red again this morning, and the air felt charged, as if a storm was coming.

On the other hand, the feeling could be due to her nerves.

She leaned over the handlebars for a while until she caught her breath, then threaded the lock through the wheel. As she reached into the carrier for her canvas shopping bag, she thought longingly of the butter-colored leather briefcase she used to own. When she'd done this in the past, she'd worn one of her power suits rather than a jersey top and a pair of capri pants, and she'd arrived in her Beemer rather than on a Raleigh. Her hair would have been freshly trimmed and straightened, not frizzed out from the humidity and held back by a scrunchie.

But a job was a job, and she badly needed to talk herself into one. Preferably before Will and the boys got back from visiting Jenny and Hope. Finding a place of her own was Amelia's next priority. She likely wouldn't be able to accomplish that before they brought the baby home next week, which was just as well since Jenny would be needing help anyway, possibly for a few months. Amelia had been alarmed by how weak her sister-in-law had seemed when she'd visited her yesterday. She'd been pale, and her arms had trembled from strain as she'd lifted them from the bed to give her a hug, yet the doctors were optimistic that eventually she would make a full recovery.

And that's what mattered, not a lottery ticket. Their house was still too small, and Will still had to scrounge for a paycheck, yet they'd named their baby Hope. They'd seen nothing ironic about the name. They'd meant it, in spite of their financial situation. The love that kept their family strong was already stretching to include the newest member. Their joy over her birth wasn't something that money could buy.

Amelia blinked to clear her vision. The tears were coming as easily as ever, which was probably a good thing. She'd saved them up for too long.

The Sunday lunch rush at Mae B's was over. Aside from a trio of teenage girls who were nursing weeping glasses of soft drinks at the table beside the front window, there were no other customers. Brittany of the purple-streaked ponytail was wiping off a table toward the back. She smiled automatically, but the welcome froze when she recognized Amelia. She straightened her frilly apron and hurried over. "I'm sorry," she said. "I didn't know."

"Know what?"

"That Uncle Ronnie gave me your job. I mean, I'm not sorry that I have it, but I didn't know it was yours. And you were so nice to me on my first day, helping me with the bow and all."

"It's okay." Amelia walked past her toward the kitchen. "Are the Bartons in today?"

Brittany pivoted and started after her. "Why? Did they call you? I didn't mean to break those plates. It was an accident. Some kid dropped ice cream on the floor and I slipped."

"It happens to all of us. Don't worry about it. I'm not here to get my old job back, I just want to talk to Mae and Ronnie."

"Oh. I guess that's okay then."

Amelia laid her palm against the swinging door. Doubts over what she was about to do crept into her mind, but before they could take hold, she pushed the door open.

Mae was sitting at her desk in the corner. Amelia couldn't see Ronnie, but she could hear the rattle of metal-on-metal from behind his work counter. A moment later he straightened up, holding a ladle in his hand like a club. He shook it in the direction of the freezer. "Can't we put it off until next month, Mae?"

"We could," Mae replied. "But if the motor goes out in this heat, we'll lose everything in there."

Ronnie muttered something inaudible and dropped the ladle into the stockpot.

Amelia cleared her throat. "Hello, Ronnie. Mae."

They both swiveled to look at her. Mae spoke first. "Amelia. I mailed your final check more than two weeks ago. It's not here."

"Yes, I know. Thanks. How's Brittany working out?"

"Good," Ronnie said. "She's learning fast."

"I'm glad to hear that."

"I hate to be rude, but why are you here?"

"I'd like to help you with your restaurant."

"We don't need another waitress."

"Maybe you don't need one now, but I'm willing to guarantee that within six months, you will."

"What are you talking about?"

Amelia smiled and reached into her canvas bag. "I worked here for nearly half a year," she said, withdrawing the report she'd prepared that morning. "During that time

I learned a lot about your business. You're both experts when it comes to dealing with food, but I'm an expert in dealing with finances. Here are my suggestions."

Mae looked at the stapled pages as if they'd come from the exterminator. "My cousin does our books."

"Has she ever waited tables? Is she aware of how your air conditioner drips over one of them? Has she observed the trends in how customers order, and how you could reduce your operating costs by altering your menu with the seasons?"

Ronnie crossed his arms. "No one's complained about my menus."

"They wouldn't complain. You're a talented cook. But haven't you noticed how few people want hot soup in August? That's just one example that I've listed. I've also worked out a strategy for reducing your taxes by investing in new equipment. In addition, there are local initiatives available through the municipality for small businesses that you could be taking advantage of."

Mae exchanged a glance with her husband. "I don't know...."

Amelia decided to be blunt. "I understand how you would be reluctant to trust me with your finances, since the media rushed to convict me of my ex-husband's crimes. Please remember that the police and the courts had plenty of time and resources to uncover the truth, and they ruled me innocent. I probably should have fought harder to repair the damage to my reputation, but after the trial I wanted nothing more to do with the media. I just wanted to lick my wounds. I was living one day at a time and didn't want to face my future." She halted. This was far more information than a prospective client needed to know, but it was hard to stop the flood of words now that they'd started. That was probably because she'd been saving them up for a long time, just like the tears that cropped up so easily lately. Amelia cleared her throat and returned to the topic. "I respect you both for taking a chance by hiring me last winter, and I hope I proved my trustworthiness to you during the time I worked here."

"You did," Mae said. "Your receipts always added up to the penny."

"And you never shortchanged us on your time," Ronnie added. "You always did a full shift."

"It's not your reputation that's the problem," Mae said. "We realized that was a load of nonsense after the first month. We just can't afford to pay a second accountant."

Grinning wouldn't be professional, nor would pumping her fist in the air, so she managed to suppress both. "This would be completely no-risk on your part. If you agree to hire me, I'll charge you a percentage of the extra income that my advice will bring in. If your profits don't increase, then I don't get paid. That's how confident I am in my skills."

They traded more glances. Amelia did her best not to fidget. Finally, Mae picked up the report and nodded to the extra chair. "Let's talk."

Half an hour later, Amelia left the restaurant. She still had no more money in her pocket than when she'd arrived, but the fact she hadn't been thrown out was encouraging. In truth, the visit had gone better than she'd expected. Although working on spec would be risky, she'd decided it was her best bet. She needed to establish a successful track record in order to attract more business, and Mae B's was a good place to start. It was a modest operation that was familiar to her. In a small town, word would spread fast if she couldn't deliver on her promises.

She was counting on word spreading just as fast if she did deliver.

To her surprise, she spotted Hank leaning against the bike rack when she returned to her bicycle. A pair of sunglasses hid his eyes. The muggy breeze that ruffled his hair had knocked the typical stray lock over his forehead and flipped up one side of his shirt collar. One hand was wedged into the pocket of his knee-length shorts while the other held a cell phone to his ear. He ended the call when he saw her approach.

Oh, he looked good. It had been less than two days since they'd parted, yet she already missed him. She had to consciously maintain a steady pace to keep herself from jogging the rest of the distance to him. What had happened to being sensible?

He waited until she neared before he spoke. "How did it go?"

Horrible. I've missed you. "I'm not sure what you mean."

"The job interview. Will told me why you were at Mae B's."

She held the canvas shopping bag to her chest. "He did?"

"Uh-huh. It surprised me, too. That he told me, I mean, not that you had a job interview."

"Will's feeling good these days. He's grateful for your help."

"He told me Jenny's on the mend. I'm glad she'll be okay."

"Me, too. We all are."

"So, did you get your old job back?"

She shook her head. "I didn't bother asking. Mae already made it clear she didn't want me waiting tables for her anymore."

"That's too bad. If you like, I could ask around, see if anyone else is hiring."

"Thanks, but I'm not going back to waitressing. I figured I'd offer my services to local businesses, sort of a combination financial advisor and efficiency consultant. I'll need a lot of clients if I'm going to make a living at this, but I think it's a niche I could fill. If your offer to ask around extends to that, I'd welcome any recommendation."

He smiled. "Sure, I'd be happy to help. Anything you need."

She wished he wouldn't smile. Even with his sunglasses, she could see those endearing crinkles at the corners of his eyes. Her fingers itched with the urge to brush his hair off his forehead. "Hank, why are you here?"

He fiddled with his phone. "I needed to talk to you."

"I thought you understood. I don't want

to start a relationship. I need to put my life back together first."

"Yeah, I heard what you said, and I do understand. I'm not trying to pressure you. This is about your painting."

Her gaze went to the phone. Of course. He would have called the police by now to tell them what he suspected about Whitcombe's auction. "I hope they don't want to question me. I don't have much I can add. How did they react when you told them?"

"Who?"

"The cops. Are they going to investigate Whitcombe?"

"I haven't contacted them yet."

"But you said you were going to call them yesterday morning."

"That can wait." He shoved the phone in his pocket. "I got to thinking about what you said, that we know where the painting went."

"Hank, we both agreed there's no chance of retrieving it now."

"Not necessarily."

She hated the spurt of excitement that followed his words. It was three weeks to the day since she'd found her numbers in the paper, but she was over it, wasn't she? No more useless dreams, no more fantasies. She'd already taken the first step toward her future. She wasn't counting on that ticket to solve anything.

Yet she once again thought of the leather briefcase she used to own, and the Beemer she used to drive, and the house she'd wanted to buy for Will and Jenny....

She shoved her canvas bag in the bike carrier and bent down to open the lock. "Forget it, Hank. There's no way. That ticket's gone."

"I have an idea how we can get it."

"Short of breaking in to Hennerfind's house, I don't see how."

"I did some research on him. Collecting art is one of his hobbies. He has a particular interest in the Group of Seven."

"He can afford to buy the best."

"So, do you think an art connoisseur like him would put the Mathers on his wall next to all those masterpieces he owns?"

"Are you kidding? He'd probably throw..." She straightened up fast. "He'd throw it away!"

"Uh-huh. I also did some research on where he lives. Tomorrow is garbage day."

ON THE PREVIOUS occasions when a case had required Hank to do a stakeout, he'd been happy to have a low-end, nondescript car. It didn't usually attract much attention. Unfortunately, it did attract attention in Forest Hill. Most of the vehicles driven by residents of this posh Toronto neighborhood were either sleek, imported sedans or hulking, luxury SUVs. Only the gardeners or the household help would drive cars like Hank's, and they wouldn't be parked on the side of the road at 5:00 a.m.

He watched in his rearview mirror as a car approached slowly. It pulled to a stop when it was alongside his. It had a light bar on the top, but it wasn't a police vehicle. According to the crest-shaped sign on the door, it belonged to a private property protection company. A spotlight blinked on.

Hank shielded his eyes from the glare. "Morning, guys," he said pleasantly. "What can I do for you?"

A man spoke from behind the light. "What's your business here?"

"I'm working. I'm a private investigator."

"Prove it."

Hank took a card from his wallet and held it up.

The spotlight clicked off as someone got out of the passenger side. Hank had parked beside a towering oak tree that stretched its limbs over the sidewalk, as far from a streetlight as possible, so he could see only a vague silhouette of a man in a peaked cap and a short uniform-like jacket. He shone a flashlight on Hank's ID, then lifted the beam to study Hank's face. "Mr. Jones, people around here value their privacy."

Hank was well aware of the laws that applied to someone doing surveillance. He also knew he wasn't obligated by law to tell this man anything, but if he didn't want to get into a spitting contest, it would be best to cooperate. "Sure. I understand. I'm not intruding on anyone, I'm parked legally on a public street."

"Who are you watching?"

"Sorry, I'd like to tell you, but that's privileged information. You wouldn't want me to lose my job, would you?"

The man leaned down to shine his flashlight through the interior of the car. The light paused on Amelia's face. "Who's that?"

"My assistant," Hank replied.

"You need to move along."

"No problem. We'll be gone by breakfast." He returned his card to his wallet. "Say, is there a Tim Hortons around here?"

The man snickered at the mention of the donut shop chain. "You're in the wrong neighborhood for that, buddy." He clicked off his flashlight and returned to his car, apparently deciding Hank posed no threat to the local residents if he was dumb enough to expect to find a Tim's nearby. His retreat also might have been helped along by the raindrops that had begun to spatter the pavement.

Hank raised his window as the security men drove away. "I was hoping this would hold off another few hours."

"What?" Amelia asked. "The rain or getting hassled by the rent-a-cops?"

"Those guys won't be a problem, they're only doing their jobs. I meant the rain. It could get bad."

"It'll be a relief if it washes away this humidity. I've felt as if a storm's been building for days."

As if to reinforce her words, a rumble of what could have been thunder, or could have been a plane, vibrated through the car. Hank grimaced. "Digging through garbage is bad enough when it's dry."

"We'll manage." She patted the storage nook beneath her door handle. "I see you still have your umbrella."

"I brought some work gloves, too. They're in the bag in the backseat. You can stay in the car if you want, since trash hunting was my bright idea. It could get icky."

She leaned forward, bringing her face close to the windshield, which was becoming blurred with water as the spatters thickened. "I'm the one who thought it was a brilliant idea to put a lottery ticket in that painting. If anyone should get icky, it's me." She crossed her arms on the dashboard. "Assuming, of course, that we get something to dig through."

Hank returned his gaze to the wrought-iron gates at the end of Wolf Hennerfind's driveway. So far, the space was empty. He'd once heard that in certain Toronto neighborhoods, the residents weren't expected to bring their trash to the curb—the garbage men walked up to the back door of the house to fetch it. He didn't know if that was still the case in some areas, but he'd made sure to verify that was no longer the practice on this particular street.

A thick yew hedge blocked the view of Hennerfind's house from here. Only the peak of the roof was visible. From what Hank had been able to see as he'd driven past, the place was a large, Tudor-style two-story set well back from the road and covered with ivy. It was stately and imposing, and the grounds encompassed at least two acres. The land alone would be worth a fortune in this section of the city.

"We're just early," he said. "They haven't put it out yet."

"He might not throw out the painting today, anyway. He might not decide to get rid of it for weeks."

"Then we can come back every Monday until he does."

"How long would you keep it up?"

He would keep it up as long as Amelia was willing to accompany him. He couldn't tell her that, though. She was already skittish enough about the relationship thing. And he sure wasn't going to tell her that whether or not they ever found her lottery ticket, he planned to keep finding excuses to be around her, no matter what she claimed about how ill-suited they were. He had the patience to wait her out. She was still talking to him, which was encouraging. He had to believe she'd come around eventually.

It might help his cause if the next excuse he found to be with her didn't involve picking her up before dawn to hunt through a rich man's garbage. "I'm not sure," he said. "By the way, do you remember Ian Taylor? He was a few years behind us at school."

"I think so."

"I heard he's expanding his uncle's real estate company. My dad said he's a real go-getter, which in Basil-speak means he's dealing with big money. He could make a good prospective client for your new business."

"Thanks. I might give him a call."

"Great."

"Provided Wolf doesn't toss the painting today." She wiped some condensation from the windshield. "On the other hand, I might call Ian even if we do find the ticket. It felt good to draw up that financial plan for Mae and Ronnie. I'd forgotten how much I enjoy helping people realize their potential."

"You were good at it."

"Yes, I was."

"Mae and Ronnie don't blame you for Spencer's crimes, do they?"

"They said they don't. Otherwise, they wouldn't have become my clients."

"Then maybe it's time you stopped blaming yourself. You weren't responsible for your ex-husband's actions. You didn't steal anything. In fact, because of his crimes you lost more than any of your clients did."

"Why are you bringing this up now?"

He gestured across the road to Henner-find's house. "You told me that you wanted to use the lottery winnings to replace the funds that Spencer stole."

"Among other things."

"But what he did wasn't your fault. The guilt isn't your burden to bear. You're not obligated to pay anyone back."

"You make it sound easy."

Hank thought of the tentative peace he'd made with his father. It was a good first step, yet there was still a long way to go. "Changing your attitude is never easy, Amelia. Just promise me you'll think about it, okay?"

He'd expected her to argue. Instead she nodded. "I've got no shortage of things to think about, Hank, but I'll be sure to add it to the list."

Light flashed through the car. He glanced at the rearview mirror, wondering if the security people had decided to return, but the street was dark. Thunder rumbled a few moments later. Within minutes the rain intensified. It slashed past the branches of the oak tree overhead to drum on the roof. The noise reminded Hank of the last time he and Amelia had sat through a storm in his car, when they'd been waiting at Kemp Forsythe's place. Then he remembered the first time, when they'd parked by the lakeshore.

He settled his back against his door so he could look at her.

Even in the shadows, he could discern the stiff set of her shoulders. Was she remembering the same thing that he was? Or was she impatient to search for her ticket?

And it was *her* ticket. If they did manage to find it, he had no intention of taking the twenty percent he'd demanded. He wasn't sure when he'd decided that. Sometime during the past few days, anyway. For one thing, Amelia had more use for the money than he did. For another, all he'd ever really wanted to do was to make her happy. And to love her. Which he did. Still.

He wasn't sure when he'd decided that, either. That was one of the problems with love. It couldn't be analyzed or reasoned out logically. It was one of those things you simply had to feel, to trust, to take a leap of faith on without worrying about where you'd land. Amelia had had it right even when they'd been teenagers.

Yet what he felt for her now wasn't the same as before. Sure, he'd loved the girl she used to be, but he loved the woman she'd become much more. He loved her stubbornness and her courage and her wit and her warmth and her fierce devotion to her family. He loved her melted cinnamon freckles. And her syrup voice, her oil-rainbow-on-water eyes, her grass-in-the-spring scent and it's-auburn-not-red hair. He loved how doing something as ordinary as sitting in a car, in the dark, listening to the rain, seemed right because they were together.

She reached out suddenly and grasped his knee. "Hank, something's happening."

He returned his gaze to the driveway. The wind had come up. It was difficult to see past the rain that now pelted the side window, but he did glimpse movement across the road. One side of the wrought-iron gates swung inward. A figure in a bright yellow hooded raincoat pushed a large, wheeled plastic garbage can to the curb, then turned back up the driveway.

Amelia reached for her door handle.

Hank extended his arm in front of her. "Wait. The gate's still open. There could be more."

She took her hand away from the door and thumped her head back against the headrest.

A minute later, the yellow-coated figure returned with a second large can, wheeled it beside the first and went back through the open gate. The third time the figure appeared, he was dragging something behind him. He propped it against one of the cans. A flash of lightning lit the scene momentarily, revealing a large, flat, rectangular shape.

Amelia gasped. "Hank, it's a packing crate! You were right!"

Even though he'd guessed this might happen, he hadn't entirely believed it. "How about that."

The figure in the yellow raincoat disappeared up the driveway again. This time, he swung the gate closed behind him.

Hank twisted to get the gloves from the backseat. "Okay, we might as well—" His words were drowned out by a roll of thunder. And by the slam of the passenger door. He turned to see Amelia already dashing across the street. He followed at a jog.

She was leaning over the packing crate when he reached her. She hadn't bothered to take the umbrella. The rain was darkening her blouse and glistening from her hair. "It's empty!" she shouted.

He angled his back to the wind to help keep the rain off the crate while he regarded it himself. It was made of wood, just like the ones he'd seen in the Whitcombe Gallery storeroom. And just as he'd surmised, the lid opened to reveal two separate compartments, each one large enough to hold a painting. If he'd had more time, he might have enjoyed having this guess confirmed, too, but the rain was getting worse, and the crate was indeed empty.

He tossed Amelia a pair of gloves and pulled on his own, then turned to the garbage cans. They were larger than they'd appeared from the other side of the road, but they weren't big enough to hold a three-foot by two-foot painting. Not unless it had been taken apart.

Amelia must have been struck by the same thought. She opened the lid of the can closest to her and tipped it on its side. Plastic garbage bags tumbled onto the sidewalk and rolled to the base of the yew hedge. Hank upended the can and gave it a shake to dislodge the rest of the bags. They both recoiled. The pounding rain couldn't mask the smell. This was kitchen garbage. He motioned her back, intending to go through it on his own, but she grabbed the nearest bag and opened it. Once they'd searched through every bag in the pile, he tipped over the second can and shook it out.

Lightning flashed again, brighter and closer than before. Thunder followed within seconds. He dropped the can and caught Amelia's arm. "The storm's getting too close." He had to shout to be heard over the wind. "We should go back to the car for a while. This won't last long."

"Not yet!" She spun from his grasp and fell to her knees on the pile of bags. "Look!"

A gust rolled one of the discarded cans into his legs. He pushed it aside and saw what Amelia had spotted. A jagged piece of wood had pierced the plastic of one of the larger bags and protruded from the side.

"It's the frame!" she cried, clawing the other bags aside. "See the carving?"

"Amelia…"

"The ticket must be in here." She tugged the bag with the wooden fragment loose from the heap. She shrieked as the bag suddenly split open. Pieces of carved wood tumbled to the sidewalk. Remnants of painted canvas still clung to some of them. Amelia crawled after one that trailed a strip of painted meadow. "Hank!"

He scooped it up before the wind could catch it.

She peeled off her gloves and took the fragment from him, her fingers shaking, then sat back on her heels and curled her body to shelter it as she peered at the wood.

He squatted beside her for a closer look at what she held. Something small, pale and square, like the corner of a folded piece of paper, was wedged between the carved frame and what was left of the narrow wood slat that the painting would have been stretched on.

Amelia grasped the edge of the paper and plucked it out. Lightning flared as she unfolded it, enabling Hank a glimpse of the triangular OLG logo and Lotto 6/49 in bold print, plus a series of numbers that were instantly seared across his brain: 1, 3, 4, 17, 23, 29. This was it. There was no doubt. They'd actually found it. They'd beaten the odds.

Thunder crashed, leaving his ears ringing. In spite of the wind that whipped Amelia's hair and the rain that streamed down her face, she smiled. Then grinned. Then whooped. She refolded the ticket, secured it between her palms and curled her hands protectively to her chest. "We did it, Hank!"

The look on her face was worth at least ten million. He discarded his own gloves, grasped her shoulders and kissed her. It was quick and sloppy and tinged by the garbage they knelt on, but she didn't seem to mind any more than he did. He helped her to her feet and turned toward the car.

And the world exploded in a blast of blinding white....

CHAPTER FIFTEEN

AMELIA FOUND HERSELF on her back, rain filling her mouth and needles from Hennerfind's yew bushes poking her face. She coughed, gasping for breath, and rolled away from the hedge. Plastic slid beneath her hands. The stink of garbage was overpowered by the smells of ozone and charred wood. "Hank!"

She could hear nothing over the ringing in her ears, other than the continued drumming of the rain and a strange hissing. She got to her knees, blinking hard to clear the spots from her vision. Flames danced up the trunk of the oak tree across the street. Chunks of bark and splinters of wood smoldered on the roof of Hank's car and littered the pavement where he was sprawled facedown and motionless....

"No!" Amelia screamed, scrambling to her feet. She ran to his side. A broken tree limb at least two feet thick lay near his head. She flung it aside. "Hank!"

He moaned.

Yes, oh yes. If he could moan, he wasn't… She fell to her knees, not wanting to complete the thought. "Are you okay? Are you hurt?"

He braced his palms against the road and pushed himself up. He glanced around dazedly. "What the…"

"It was lightning," Amelia said. "It struck the oak tree." She touched her fingers to his forehead. Blood oozed from a scrape near his hairline. "I think you got hit by a branch."

His gaze steadied on her. "Are you all right?"

"I'm fine." She grasped his arms. "You need to see a doctor. You could have a concussion."

"No problem. My head's harder than oak, or so I've been told."

She suppressed the urge to shake him. How could he joke? She took another look around. Steam hissed from the tree as the rain began to douse the flames. The smell of smoke stung the back of her throat. "Your forehead's scraped raw. It needs to be cleaned."

"The rain's doing that." He caught her wrists and drew her hands in front of her. "Amelia, where's your ticket?"

For a moment, his words didn't make sense. Nothing mattered except making sure Hank was really okay, because she didn't want to lose him, she couldn't conceive of life without him, and this wasn't the time to think about any of that because they were sitting in the middle of the road with a burning tree on one side and a heap of garbage on the other and her hands were empty....

Her hands. Empty.

She heaved herself to her feet. "Oh, no."

Hank braced his knuckles on the pavement and shoved himself to stand. He staggered sideways a few steps until she grabbed his arm to hook it over her shoulder. She slipped her arm around his waist as they both surveyed the debris.

"We'll walk a grid pattern," he said. "Do this methodically. Back and forth, so we don't miss anything. It's got to be here someplace."

She didn't need to search. She spotted a pale speck against a blackened piece of bark less than three feet away. She pointed, then went to pick it up.

The paper was wet now, but it must have been dry enough to ignite when it had blown against the burning bark. Fire had consumed most of it. All that remained of Amelia's fifty-two million, four hundred and eighty-five thousand, seven hundred and twenty dollar ticket was a sodden smudge of ash and one small corner of paper with the Lottery Commission logo.

It was gone. Truly, irrevocably gone.

She let go of the scrap. She watched it drift into the puddle at the edge of the road and from there to the gutter. She didn't look away until it disappeared through the grill of a storm drain.

The rain thinned. Thunder still rumbled but it was farther away. The sky beyond the smoldering oak seemed lighter than just a few minutes ago. A dog barked somewhere in the distance. A car honked. A siren blared. Life went on. A new day was dawning. She shivered, suddenly aware of her dripping hair and wet clothes.

Hank moved behind her and crossed his arms over her midriff. He rested his chin on her shoulder. "I'm sorry, Amelia."

"You couldn't have done anything."

"I hate to see you sad."

Out of the jumble of emotions that roiled through her as she stood in the shelter of his embrace, sadness wasn't the strongest. She hiccupped. "Do you know the odds of winning the lottery?"

"Not exactly, but they're pretty slim."

"That's right. It's more likely for a person to get hit by lightning." She waved her hand toward the tree. "Do you think Fate's trying to tell me something?"

"Like what?"

"When I first lost that ticket, I thought I could fight what Fate had dished out."

"I remember that's what you said."

"I was looking at it all wrong. I only saw what I'd lost. Now I see what I've already won."

"I don't understand."

"It was never about the money, it was about the search. It was about trying. It was learning what really mattered." She turned to look at him. "It was about finding you again. That's what the ticket brought me."

"Finding me?"

Does he know you still love him? She lifted her hand to his face. She couldn't fight this anymore, either, and there was no reason to. "I can live without the money, but I don't want to live without you. I love you, Hank."

He blinked. His eyes gleamed. It wasn't from the rain. "You love me?"

"Of course, I love you. I never stopped. I know it was only a few days ago that I told you I didn't want to start a relationship, but I was trying to be sensible. I thought I had to fix my life first, but without you, my life will never be right. And I'm sorry if I'm rushing you again, and I realize I must look horrible and smell worse, and this is hardly the most romantic time and place for a confession, but love is too precious to risk and I don't want to take the chance that—"

The rest of her words were lost in his kiss. That was fine with her, because the kiss said it better.

EPILOGUE

AMELIA FLEXED HER fingers on the steering wheel of her new car so she could admire the glint of her diamond in the sunshine. Strictly speaking, the car wasn't really new. It was a three-year-old, economical subcompact that had just come off a lease. The engagement ring wasn't that new anymore, either. She'd been wearing it for more than two months. Unlike the car, though, the ring would only get better with age.

"Hey!" Hank rapped his knuckles on the window. He held a rake in his other hand. "Are you going to sit there all day?"

She shut off the ignition and got out of the car.

Hank tossed the rake on a leaf pile and swept her into a hug and an enthusiastic hello kiss. His lips were cool but quickly warmed. So did hers. He smiled against her mouth. "Do you like the car?"

It was a far cry from the Beemer she'd had to give up last year, but with winter approaching, it was better than a bicycle. "What's not to like? It starts when I turn the key, and it's got a roof and a radio."

"Dad better have given you a good deal."

"He did. He gave me the special family discount."

"The what?"

"It's new. I suspect he just made it up." She picked a leaf off Hank's sweater as they walked to his house. "I think he's mellowing."

"You're a good influence."

"I can relate to him, because there was a period when my life revolved around my business, too. By the way, he liked the investment plan I worked out for him. I told him I'd give him the family discount on my fee. He seemed to like that, as well. He's coming here for dinner on Saturday."

"Wow. That'll be the second time this month. How'd you manage that?"

"I said we're counting on his help to organize our wedding. I'll get some takeout from Mae B's since I took the liberty of inviting myself over for dinner, too."

"Since when do you need an invitation? In another two months, you'll be living here."

"But I'll still need to pick up dinner, unless you want to live on popcorn and herbal tea."

He laughed as he led her to the porch swing. "Whatever, I'm glad you'll be here to act as mediator with Dad."

"Don't give me that. You two are coming along fine on your own."

"Slowly."

"That's to be expected, since he spent a lot of years behind his walls. The Jones men can be stubborn, you know."

"Nah. Not us."

"But I believe they're worth the effort." She settled on the swing beside Hank. Luckily, she happened to love his stubbornness. And his analytical nature. She loved the way he carried a clean hankie, and drove slowly, and stopped at amber lights. She loved the tenderness that tempered his strength, and the caring, generous heart that powered his choices. And she adored the little-boy lock of hair that always managed to fall across his forehead. She lifted her hand to smooth it back.

The grown-up lines beside his mouth and at the corners of his eyes deepened. He turned his head to kiss her wrist, then pushed his boot against the floor to set the swing in motion. The chains creaked lazily overhead.

This was one of her favorite spots in his house, although it wasn't really inside the house. There wouldn't be many weeks before the weather turned too cold to sit here for long. Right now, though, the sky was a perfect, crisp October blue, and the maples in the yard were a spectacular red.

There were a lot of trees in Hank's yard. The veranda where they sat wrapped around the front and two sides of his house. The large, homey kitchen faced south, and had a huge bay window to let in the sun. The second story held four bedrooms, far more than a bachelor would need. Hank had bought the place after she'd married Spencer. He'd used the money he'd earned in Alberta to make the down payment. He might have believed he'd given up on her, but with her first visit to this house, it was clear that he hadn't. This was exactly like the home they'd envisioned when they'd talked about their future all those many years ago.

Hank stretched his arm along the back of the swing and tucked her closer to his side. "I missed you today."

"You saw me at lunch."

"That was only for an hour." He kissed her nose. "I think we should elope."

"If we do, Jenny will probably strangle me with her measuring tape. She's been exercising like mad to fit into the dress she made for the wedding."

"I would have thought that running around after your nephews would give her all the exercise she needs."

"Oh, that reminds me. I meant to show you the pictures I took of Hope this morning." She reached into her jacket to take out her new phone. Well, her month-old phone. She'd bought it to keep in touch with her expanding list of clients. Mae and Ronnie had been so impressed with her ideas for their restaurant that they'd kindly spread the word, and her business was growing more quickly than she could have dreamed. Besides gaining a steady income, getting back to work had turned out to be the best way to atone for her error in judgment. She didn't need any lottery winnings in order to prove to everyone, especially herself, that she hadn't been to blame for Spencer's crimes.

Just like her family didn't need any lottery winnings to be happy. She thumbed the button to access the latest photos. "Here's Eric pushing the baby carriage. Timmy put his rabbit in there to keep her company. Isn't that sweet?"

"Another Goodfellow woman, well on her way to wrapping men around her little freckled finger."

Amelia laughed as she scrolled through the pictures. Her nephew had let the baby "borrow" his rabbit because Hope had begun to get fussy whenever Will had left for work. Lancaster Cabinets had recalled their entire workforce and had needed to add an extra shift, thanks in large part to a new contract to supply custom kitchens for a luxury condominium project in Toronto. Will himself had been responsible for landing that deal. The condo developer kept his forty-foot cabin cruiser at the Port Hope Yacht Club for the summer, and they'd met when Will had been skimming algae there. They'd started talking about their work, as men do, and to hear Will tell it, the Toronto man had been thrilled to learn there was a company so close to the city that was capable of high-quality work at noncity prices.

Fate certainly did work in strange ways.

Hank kissed her ear. "You like kids."

"Of course, I like kids."

"That's another reason to elope. December's a long way off."

She elbowed him in the ribs. "I thought you wanted a real wedding."

"All I want is you, Amelia." He nibbled her earlobe. "But I suppose it would be nice to throw a party and show off what I caught."

"You caught? What am I, a fish?"

"I could never confuse you with a fish. You taste way better, and you were a lot harder to reel in." He waited until she put her phone away, then took her left hand in his. He rubbed his thumb over the diamond. "Sometimes I can't believe how lucky I am."

"I feel the same way. Maybe we need to go through bad times to appreciate the good."

"Like how good the sunshine feels after a storm."

She leaned her head on his shoulder and turned her face toward the sky, thinking about how Jenny had once described love. If it truly was a living thing, then hers and Hank's had come out of its dormancy to grow by leaps and bounds. It wasn't only the big events that tested and strengthened their love. It was as much the little, ordinary moments of everyday life, like having dinner with their families, or talking about their days, or just sitting on his porch swing— soon to be *their* porch swing—and watching the world go by. Each day deepened the trust between them. She and Hank would always make a great team.

"By the way. I have a present for you."

"Hank, I have everything I need. Really."

"It sort of matches this," he said, tapping her ring. He straightened one leg and lifted up his sweater to reach his jeans. An oblong shape stretched the denim over his pocket. He withdrew it and handed it to her.

She sat up, studying the box in her hand. It bore the imprint of a jeweler. Wasn't that just like a man, to keep something expensive in his jeans while he was out in the yard raking leaves? "Seriously, Hank. You shouldn't be buying me things. Our budget's going to be badly stretched by the wedding."

"This was already yours. I'm just returning it."

"I don't understand."

"Open it."

Something in his tone told her he wasn't as casual as he was trying to seem. This was important to him. She lifted the lid, then folded back the layers of tissue paper. When she saw what was inside, the air whooshed out of her lungs.

It was a watch. A gold one. With a diamond at twelve o'clock. And a tiny scratch on the crystal where she'd caught it against a shelf once. And a strap that was worn at the edges from fifteen years of daily wear.

"Hey, it was supposed to make you happy."

She shook her head, unable to speak past the lump in her throat. She lifted the watch from the box and slipped it on her wrist. It felt just as priceless as the day her parents had given it to her.

"Sorry I took so long to track it down. I've been looking for it since you told me how you had to sell it to pay for Will's furnace." He took his handkerchief from another pocket and dabbed beneath her eyes. "It had changed hands five times. I found it in Oshawa."

She pressed her fingers to his lips. "Just when I think I couldn't possibly love you any more than I do, you go ahead and do something like this."

He smiled. "Oh, yeah? Wait until you hear my news."

"What could possibly top this watch?"

"The cops have arrested Rupert Whitcombe."

The sudden change of topic startled her. Hank had gone to the police the day after the ticket had burned up. He'd backed up his theories with the special auction program as well as the double packing crate he'd taken from Hennerfind's garbage, but the authorities had been understandably skeptical. Once they knew where to look, though, they uncovered solid evidence of a conspiracy that proved every one of Hank's assertions. He'd been one hundred percent correct. The scheme had been operating successfully for several years, but Whitcombe's success with his annual auctions had made him greedy. Because of his arrogance, he'd expanded his operation past the point of discretion. As soon as the police turned their attention to the list of special bidders that Hank had provided, which was verified by the surveillance video from the Dalton Hotel's security cameras, they found no shortage of witnesses who were eager to testify against the gallery owner in exchange for immunity. The witnesses included his accomplice Evangeline, aka Gillian Edwards.

Still, the speed with which the case developed was unexpected. "That was fast," Amelia said.

"It seems Interpol's been tracking the art theft ring for years. They'd already amassed reams of evidence. They just hadn't been able to figure out the last link in the chain."

"I'm glad Whitcombe and the thieves are being brought to justice."

"The insurance companies are glad, too. A lot of those canvases were worth millions, just like the Jackson."

"It would be hard to recover them, wouldn't it?"

"You'd be surprised. Some of the people on Whitcombe's special clients list were more worried about their reputations than holding on to their stolen art. I heard a few of them caved after nothing but a phone call."

"I hope that means we won't need to testify."

"Chances are we won't."

"That is good news. I've had my fill of courtrooms."

"Understandable, but that's not the good news I meant."

She crossed her arms. "Okay, I can tell you've got something else you're bursting to say, so you'd better spit it out before I need to get rough with you, because I wouldn't want to risk damaging my new-old watch."

He grinned. "We don't need to worry about our budget, Amelia. You can have the biggest, fanciest wedding you want."

"Why?"

"The companies who insured those stolen paintings have been offering rewards to anyone contributing information that leads to their return."

"Which in this case is you?"

"Yup. I got the official confirmation this afternoon. We're going to be rich."

Talk about Fate working in strange ways. She glanced at the sky to check for thunderclouds.

"Not lottery-ticket rich," Hank said, "but once you put your financial genius to work on what we're paid, you'll be a millionaire again before you know it."

Amelia laughed. "Hank, I already am rich. What we feel for each other is worth more than a million lottery tickets."

"Then do you want me to turn down the money?"

"Don't you dare!" She grasped his cheeks and pulled his face close to hers. She spoke against his lips. "I'm not crazy, Hank, I'm just in love."

* * * * *

ReaderService.com

Manage your account online!

- Review your order history
- Manage your payments
- Update your address

*We've designed
the Harlequin® Reader Service
website just for you.*

Enjoy all the features!

- Reader excerpts from any series
- Respond to mailings and
  special monthly offers
- Discover new series available to you
- Browse the Bonus Bucks catalog
- Share your feedback

Visit us at:

ReaderService.com